Most gay men wouldn't expect to see their dreams come true in a small town in the Deep South. But the road to true love can lead to the unlikeliest places . . .

Disowned by his conservative Peruvian parents, Lito Apaza headed for gay-friendly Atlanta. Resilient, charismatic, and successful, he's built a life on his terms—with a new family of friends and the unconditional love of his dog, Spot. Then his job forces him to relocate to tiny Black Lake, Alabama. Here, being fabulous isn't exactly the town motto. However, Lito can't help who he is any more than he can curb his feelings for a certain sexy ex-soldier.

A former dog handler in Afghanistan, Dave Schmidt now runs a volunteer K9 search-and-rescue team. Until he met Lito, his nights were free. As their hook-ups grow hotter, Dave and Lito have to admit this could be something nearer to romance. It's not what Lito expected. And Dave isn't used to the scrutiny of being visibly gay. Yet everything they've been secretly searching for could be right here in Black Lake. If Dave and Lito want a future together, one of them will have to make the first move . . .

Visit us at www.kensingtonbooks.com

Books by Wendy Qualls

The Heart of the South Series
Worth Waiting For
Worth Searching For

Published by Kensington Publishing Corporation

Worth Searching For

Heart of the South

Wendy Qualls

LYRICAL PRESS
Kensington Publishing Corp.
www.kensingtonbooks.com

First Electronic Edition: February 2018
eISBN-13: 978-1-5161-0186-3
eISBN-10: 1-5161-0186-3

First Print Edition: February 2018
ISBN-13: 978-1-5161-0187-0
ISBN-10: 1-5161-0187-1

Printed in the United States of America

Dedicated to the SARTEC K-9 Unit in Huntsville, Alabama.
You and your dogs do the impossible and you do it well.
And also to my Sheltie, Haiku, who once did it all with me.

Chapter 1

The local pet store was painted an eye-searing yellow, the "Pawse Awhile" logo a vivid orange above it. It was tucked away on a side street behind the Publix and *completely* not what Lito expected, which was why it had taken him forty-five minutes to find. One of the frustrating things about moving to a small town (considered "almost a city" if you asked the other residents, who clearly had never seen a real city to compare it to) was having to find replacements for all the chain stores that seemingly didn't exist outside Atlanta. PetSmart included. Lito's old neighborhood had been quirky, more "poor hipster" than urban chic, but he'd relied on corporate mega-marts more than he'd realized.

Case in point: Black Lake had exactly one Starbucks. It also had a farmers' market, a six-screen movie theater, approximately eight thousand different flavors of Baptist church, and no nightclubs for at least an hour in any direction. Spot had finished the last of her hard-to-find brand of kibble, though, so "Pawse Awhile" it was. Lito clipped her on her leash and headed inside.

The painfully bright color scheme extended to the interior as well. The building was bigger than it looked from the front—not quite on a PetSmart scale, but still promising. It was busy too. A surprising number of people wandered the aisles with various-sized dogs, although nobody looked like they were actually shopping for anything. Spot whined and sniffed the air but stayed at Lito's side. He gave her a proud scratch behind the ears for being on good behavior.

"Take another minute and then bring them back in," a perky blonde in a Pawse Awhile polo shirt called out from a little partitioned-off area in the middle of the store. "Remember your 'heel' command if your pup starts pulling—they need to know you're there on the other end of the leash and you're paying attention. Use your clicker when they look at you."

Obedience class. That explained how busy the store was. Lito skirted around a woman with two toy poodles and an older man with a wrinkly bulldog puppy and headed for where the dog food section seemed likely to be. Spot kept craning her neck up at him, tail wagging at half-mast, but she trotted alongside like she was trying to show those upstart mutts how it was done. She probably was, honestly—Lito had never done the formal obedience training thing with her, but even when he first took her in, Spot had been determined to prove she was better-behaved than all those other, more *boring* dogs out there. Maybe he spoiled her a bit, but it was nice to not be making this move to a new place all by himself. Even if the only "person" he knew here outside of work wasn't actually a person at all.

"Heel! No—*heel*, Sherman!"

Lito didn't have any more warning than that before some sort of hound mix was suddenly right behind him, nipping at Spot's hip. Spot whirled with a growl, warning the dog to back off, but Sherman merely growled back. Within seconds the two dogs were clinched together on their hind legs, mouthing and gnawing and generally making aggressive noises at each other. The hound's owner, a tiny brunette with giant earrings and way too much makeup, stood frozen in place. Which was completely useless, damn it. She didn't look like she'd be able to overpower her dog anyway, meaning Lito was going to have to break up the fight. All hundred and thirty pounds of him. *Yay*. Because wading into a literal dogfight was exactly what he'd wanted to do today.

On the bright side, neither Spot nor Sherman looked like they were trying to cause any real damage. Spot was annoyed, definitely, but the growling and batting at each other's necks didn't have any malice to it. Lito grumbled right back at them and lunged for Sherman's trailing leash.

"Hold up," a male voice interjected. "Lumpy, Woozy, *down*." A sturdy shoulder brushed past Lito's, then Lito found himself at eye level with the man's collarbone as the guy deftly inserted himself into the fight.

And *damn*. There were probably better times to notice some seriously impressive biceps, but since the dude was a good head taller than Lito was and the biceps in question were right there for the ogling, Lito couldn't help but ogle. He smelled nice too, from the quick impression Lito got when his nose was near the guy's shirt. More importantly, though, the dude seemed to know what he was doing around dogs. His two huge Rottweilers (he named his dogs Lumpy and Woozy? Really?) were now lying across the entrance to the aisle, panting happily. Neither looked like they were planning to move anytime soon.

Lito sidestepped as best he could within the confines of the shelves and tried to find a way to be useful. Seriously Built Dude had Spot's collar in one hand and the hound's in the other and was hoisting them both back and up, onto their hind legs. It couldn't have been easy—Spot was seventy pounds on a good day and the hound was a bit shorter but much fatter. Lito ended up having to twist under the man's arm to reach Spot and get a hand on her collar. Seriously Built Dude let go and focused on the poorly trained hound, keeping it off balance but without choking it. When he turned the dog so his body was between it and Spot, Lito did the same. Spot settled immediately.

"Easy, Sherman," the man crooned. "There you go. Down—good boy. You can come get him, ma'am. He knows he wasn't supposed to do that— see how he won't make eye contact and keeps looking at your feet? Just be firm with him and keep him at heel while you walk him back to class and he'll get the idea." The guy surrendered the dog's leash to the apologetic woman, then turned his attention to Lito and Spot. "Yours okay?" he asked.

"Fine, I think." Lito ran a hand over Spot's shoulder and hip where the other dog had been mouthing her. Her tan fur was dark with dog drool, but she seemed both uninjured and unbothered. Now that the fun had ended, she was much more interested in the new guy's own dogs, who were still lying flat on the floor like they'd been glued there. Lito cleared his throat. "Yours are really well-trained," he ventured. "Spot doesn't usually have an issue with other animals, but that doesn't mean she's happy about being jumped from behind."

The guy laughed. A nice, full laugh, his whole frame relaxed now that the woman had reclaimed her dog and was a safe distance away. "I wouldn't be too keen on it either," he said, and extended his hand. "I'm assuming we haven't met before—I'm Dave Schmidt. You're welcome to let your pup introduce herself to my two, if you want. They both love attention and they're not picky about who it's from."

Dave didn't seem to be in any particular hurry to go, so he probably wasn't involved with the puppy class. Scratch that—the two Rottweilers blocking the end of the aisle were *still* lying quietly on their stomachs, panting happily. No way they needed obedience classes. Lito let Spot have a bit more slack in the leash and took a few steps toward the dogs. Spot looked up hopefully, her brown eyes searching for permission.

"Good girls," Dave said in a clear command voice. "Up. Go on; greet."

Both dogs heaved to their feet. Within seconds, they and Spot were circling and sniffing each other in little huffs. The Rottweilers met with Spot's approval, clearly, because she was back to her normal, friendly self almost immediately. It was a bit awkward to stand there next to a total stranger while their dogs made instant friends, but Dave was watching them with a faint smile on his face that totally had Lito scrambling for something to say that wouldn't make him sound like an idiot. "How old are they?" he finally asked.

That faint smile turned on him. "Got 'em as puppies, almost eleven years ago. Time flies. Yours?"

"Around two, as far as I know. Friend of a friend found her last year."

"Ah."

Damn it. Really not going so great with the "don't make yourself sound like an idiot" thing. "It's a bit of a long story," Lito explained, "but the short version is that she was wandering around downtown Atlanta by herself. My friend's ex passed her on his way to work for three days in a row and finally decided screw it, might as well see if she's friendly. She was, obviously. The vet said she'd be fine once she had her shots and a few good meals. The ex couldn't keep her, so he asked my friend, who brought her to me."

"She's lucky to have landed with you, then," Dave said. "Were you looking for a dog at the time?"

"Vaguely." Telling Ian *yes* had been a totally impulsive thing, but Lito would have been lying if he'd said he hadn't already been considering getting a pet. Plus Spot had good timing. Lito had earned a promotion—with the accompanying raise—the month before, and as of three days earlier he was suddenly down two apartment-mates. Todd and Trixie had been shit apartment-mates, but without them his crappy little two-bedroom was already feeling empty. "I think it's more that he knew I couldn't say no," Lito added. "She was all ribs and wagging tail back then."

That faint smile morphed into a grin. "I've been there a few times. Obviously you're taking good care of her." Dave folded his arms and shifted his weight to his rear foot, all but leaning back against the shelf. He looked totally up for a nice long chat with a complete stranger in the middle of a pet store.

Lito didn't mind the chat either, truth be told. Two weeks in Alabama and this was the first semi-decent conversation he'd had with anyone outside work. If the guy was packing some serious eye candy under that t-shirt, all the better. His posture and the tone of his voice suggested he might have been flirting a bit, even. Maybe. It was hard to tell whether that was observation or wishful thinking. Dave didn't *sound* gay, at least not the way guys back home tended to talk when they were plugged into the whole Big Gay Scene thing, but there was a reason Atlanta barely counted as "the South." That smile, though, and the approving eye-check when he looked Lito up and down right before they shook hands…

"You said Atlanta." Dave was nominally watching the dogs, now snuffling at each other and waggling their entire butts with excitement, but his body stayed angled toward Lito. "Are you in Black Lake for a visit, or . . ."

"Been in town a few weeks," Lito admitted. "The company owners wanted me on a project here instead of back in Atlanta and the chance was too good to refuse. It's been an adjustment." *Bit of an understatement.* "I assumed you could tell I was new because I was the one person in town you didn't already recognize—isn't that how it's supposed to work in places like this?" He realized how much the question made him sound like an asshole a moment too late, but it really had been bouncing around in his head for the past two weeks. Backpedaling would have made it even worse, though. Christ, everyone in earshot was going to think he was some douchebag city boy.

"Black Lake isn't *that* small," Dave said. He snorted. "I'm sure there's five or six people I haven't met yet, at *least*. Maybe even as many as a dozen." His eyes sparkled and he shot Lito another tiny smile. "I'm pretty sure I know all the dogs, though. The big ones, anyway. I tend to keep an eye out."

"Oh?"

"You ever heard of K-9 search and rescue?"

"Like the guys who go through the wreckage after a hurricane and try to find survivors? I've seen it on the news, I guess."

"Not as much for hurricanes around here, this far from the coast. We mostly get lost hikers and kids who wander away from home." Dave jerked his thumb toward his dogs. "These two have been doing it with me since they were pups. My buddy Rick and I started a team—hell, guess it's been ten years ago now. North Alabama Search and Rescue, or NALSAR for short. We respond to call-outs all over Alabama, plus a few up in eastern Tennessee and some parts of north Georgia." He cocked his head slightly to one side. "Don't suppose Spot likes running around outdoors and getting lots of exercise, does she? Two's a good age to start, and she's the right size for it."

The question felt a bit out of the blue, but it was nice to *finally* get a social invitation after being cooped up in the new rental house for so long. Well, a semi-social invitation. And from someone who hadn't side-eyed

Lito's hot pink shirt or his earring like he was going to spread gay cooties.
"She never got to run as much as she wanted to in Atlanta," Lito answered,
"but I can't imagine she'd object. She usually gets along well with new
people and with other dogs. Has so far, at least."

"How about you?"

"Get along with other dogs?"

Dave huffed. "You know what I meant." He fished in his jeans pocket
and procured a slightly worn business card. "If you're new in town, it might
be fun to come out to a practice or two and see how you like it. The team
are all friendly and it's good exercise. Plus, you know—it's great volunteer
work. Make a difference and all that. Anyway, Spot seems to have made
new best friends with Lumpy and Woozy, which is a good sign. We're
always on the lookout for new recruits."

"Which of us is the recruit?"

Dave grinned. "The pair of you, if I have anything to say about it.
There's no pressure if you try a few times and don't like it, obviously, but
I promise it really is fun. For you and your dog both. We practice twice a
week up on the mountain at the state park, weather permitting. The website
with directions and all the details is on the card." He pressed it into Lito's
hand. "I'd love to see you there on Tuesday, if you can make it."

"I…yeah, I think I'd like to." Lito's palm tingled where Dave's
fingertips had brushed against it. "I've never been an outdoorsy type, but
it sounds interesting."

"Oh, it is." Dave snapped his fingers twice, and both his dogs jumped
to attention. "I've got to get going, but when you come on Tuesday you
can tell me all about why you named a solid-yellow dog 'Spot.'"

"It's not nearly as interesting a story as you're probably imagining."

"I look forward to hearing it anyway." Dave patted his thigh, which
brought his dogs over to sit on either side of his legs with an almost military
precision. He didn't even need to bend down to pick up their leashes—they
each leaned in so he could dispense a good ear-scratch before tracing the
leash back from where it clipped onto their collars. Spot whined and looked
up at Lito's face, clearly disappointed that playtime was done, but she let
her new friends go without any further protest.

Lito got in one last gawk as the man walked away. He looked just as
good from the back as he did from the front.

Damn.

Chapter 2

Dave got to the parking lot his usual half hour or so before everyone else. The team had a standing agreement with the state park system to use this little corner of the hiking trails for their twice-weekly practices, but arriving early meant he could make a point of being obvious about it. Two excited ninety-pound dogs off-leash and the giant "NORTH ALABAMA K-9 SEARCH AND RESCUE UNIT" sign on Dave's Grand Cherokee tended to make other dog-walkers think twice before wandering through the middle of the search exercises. No hikers were around today, though, despite the comfortable September temperatures. Lumpy and Woozy got in a good long lope through the tall grass before the rest of the team arrived. Neither of them was fast as they used to be—Lumpy was developing cataracts and Woozy's arthritis slowed her down more often than not—but they knew the field well. It meant Dave was able to sit on the lone picnic table and enjoy the quiet without having to worry about either of them disappearing past the treeline. Eventually Lumpy brought him a stick and they spent a while playing fetch while Woozy chased butterflies.

Dave knew that the chances of the cute guy from the pet store showing up were slim to none, but that didn't stop him from hoping. The team could sure use him. Even though their core members had remained relatively stable over the years, fresh blood was always welcome. Especially fresh blood with a well-behaved dog. Spot—Dave had stopped being surprised years ago at how well he remembered dog names and how terrible he was with their human counterparts—had tolerated the hound mix pouncing on her fairly well, which was a promising sign. Her owner hadn't freaked either. Dave took the stick from Lumpy and threw it again, causing the two dogs to bump hip-to-hip as they raced each other to retrieve it. The crunch of tires on gravel behind him heralded Rick and Sharon's massive van.

"Gorgeous weather tonight, isn't it?" Sharon called out. "Heya, Dave." She hopped out of the passenger seat and went to get Rick's wheelchair from the trunk. Dave followed and helped reassemble the parts without even having to think about it anymore. "Looks like your two got started on the frolicking early," she added.

Dave turned around to see Lumpy rolling on her back in the grass, making totally undignified snuffling noises and ignoring him entirely. Woozy was flopped on her stomach, back legs out to the side, panting and grinning at the van. She had the stick trapped under her front paw like she expected it to get away. Playing before practice always made them act a decade younger…and then sleep for fourteen hours afterward. Dave shrugged. "I think they miss their pack when they're home by themselves."

"Don't really blame 'em," Rick said from his post in the driver's seat. "I miss us too."

"You've got your own pack," Sharon countered. "Human and canine both." Rick and Sharon's boarding kennel wasn't huge, but it was usually more than half full. Many of the dogs were regulars. No way in hell Dave would be able to deal with the constant noise, but Sharon always insisted it was the best burglar alarm ever. Running the kennel also let both of them be around animals—theirs and other people's—for as much of their day as they could stand. The two of them were a damn good match for each other.

Sharon and Dave helped Rick transfer down to the chair, then Dave let their dogs out from the back seat while Rick got himself settled. Scratch, the terrier, and Sniff, the bloodhound, both bounded from the van and immediately started mock-fighting with Lumpy and Woozy. It really was a beautiful evening to be outside—the day's heat was slowly dissipating but it still smelled like summer. Dave retrieved the binder of NALSAR paperwork from his Jeep and went to join Rick and Sharon at the picnic table. Sharon chatted happily about her nephew's soccer team while Rick and Dave half-listened and scratched out a bare-bones meeting agenda. Nothing like waiting until the last minute.

Speaking of which… "I invited a new guy this weekend, by the way," Dave interjected. The total non sequitur was enough to surprise Sharon into silence. Which was just as well, since the rest of the team would probably get there before Sharon finished her story otherwise. "No idea if he's going to come," he added, "but his dog was really sweet."

Rick raised one eyebrow. "Let me guess—the two of you chatted for a few minutes, mostly about dogs, then you pounced on him and invited him to practice without actually learning his name yet."

That was…embarrassingly accurate. *Crap.* "Well, his *dog*'s name is Spot…"

"You," Rick said, wagging a finger in Dave's direction, "are wonderfully predictable. And always an optimist. Let's hold off on mentioning this mystery man to everyone else until we see if he actually shows up though, okay? It'd be nice to have someone new now that you're not running Lumpy and Woozy anymore, but there's a long road between you extending the invitation and him actually getting his dog certified."

He had a point, much as Dave hated to admit it. Most new recruits didn't stick around for more than a month or two, but that didn't mean Dave's invitations *never* bore fruit. Witness the fact that NALSAR was now six people (and seven dogs) instead of just him and Rick. The gradual growth of the team meant having actual team meetings and filing for non-profit status and a shit-ton of paperwork, but it also meant having enough scent-trained dogs that Lumpy and Woozy could enjoy their retirement. They still loved playing with the pack and got hopeful whenever Dave geared up for a call-out, but anything more than the gentle lope through the fields like tonight was beyond them now. It hurt to see them slowing down.

The rest of the team straggled in over the course of the next twenty minutes, followed by the arrival of a little orange Saturn Dave didn't recognize. He was all set to dissuade incoming hikers until he saw the driver. Well, passenger—Spot was sitting proudly in the front seat and taking it all in. Alert, curious, but not freaking out at the sight of the team or the other dogs.

"Hey." The guy from the pet shop got out of the car and gave a sheepish little wave. "I guess I'm in the right place. Should I let Spot out? I wasn't sure whether you wanted me to bring her or not."

God, he was just as cute as Dave remembered—short and earnest, with his black hair slicked into a meticulous swoop over his forehead and wearing a peach polo shirt which had probably never in its life been accidentally thrown in with the wrong load of laundry. Dave had enough fashion sense to know he'd never be able to pull off the look himself. It definitely worked on the pet shop guy, though.

The dude also had a tiny, sparkly diamond stud in his right ear, which Dave had somehow managed to miss earlier. Chances of him being straight plunged distinctly southward in Dave's mind. *Hell yes.* He'd been hoping, after their previous meeting—the dude set Dave's gaydar pinging like crazy—but Black Lake wasn't the kind of place where you just blurted out things like *"hey, nice to meet you, would it freak you out if I hit on you for a while?"*

Not that Dave intended to do that. Sex was for the occasional hookup in places that weren't Black Lake. At the very least, though, the guy being probably-gay was making Dave feel like less of a perv for appreciating the finer points of his ass in those tight-cut jeans. Dude had a bubble butt well worth appreciating.

"Let's see how social she is," Rick said, after Dave had been standing there silently for what was probably a bit too long. "Dogs leashed and everyone get in a circle, please—we can do human introductions while the pups sort themselves out." He motioned for the guy to have a seat on the edge of the picnic table. "Usually we put 'em on long leads and let them romp together a bit while we have our team meeting, but we try to be a bit more controlled when we've got a newcomer. Oh, and don't be embarrassed if you forget all our names." He jerked his head toward Dave. "This twit is terrible with them, but we still let him keep coming back."

"Dave, right?" the guy said instantly, looking up at him with an innocent openness on his face. It made Dave wish they were already good enough friends that he could earn that smile a lot more often. "I'm not gonna forget someone who names his dogs Lumpy and Woozy."

Of course *he* would remember names. For both Dave and the dogs. "They're short for Heffalump and Woozle," Dave explained. "Like from *Winnie the Pooh*? The nicknames were just too good to pass up." He whistled, the two short tones that meant *get your asses over here*, and Lumpy and Woozy both came tearing over to plonk their butts down as close to his legs as possible. "I'm not going to forget a yellow lab named Spot, either. Lab mix?"

"He did blank out on yours," Rick interjected with a grin, "but don't take it personally—it's because you're not a dog. I'm Rick Sulzer, and my wife Sharon's over there with our own pups. Scratch is the terrier/Pitt mix and Sniff is the bloodhound."

"Lito Apaza. Nice to meet you."

Lito. Got it. Dave repeated the name a dozen different ways in his head so he wouldn't embarrass himself like that again. Rick already had enough ammo. Now all Dave needed was to screw up and call the dude *Lisa* or something by mistake.

"Go ahead and put Spot on her leash and bring her around to the dogs one at a time, okay?" Rick said.

Soon they had a reasonably well-behaved circle of dogs and handlers, spaced far enough apart the dogs couldn't reach each other but close enough the humans didn't have to shout to be heard. There were some playful growls and a lot of whining and snuffling, but Spot seemed genuinely enthusiastic about meeting so many potential new playmates. Even Scratch didn't lose her shit when Spot came to investigate her—that was probably a first. Lumpy and Woozy both snuffled Spot politely and then flopped back down to lie on the grass.

The people introductions went well too, although Dave had a sneaking suspicion Lito was more than a bit overwhelmed by it all. Everyone was polite and friendly, but there was definitely an undercurrent of "fresh meat, must impress" which would have put off anyone. Probably best to get to the actual training and save the business meeting for the end. Rick offered no objection to the sotto voce suggestion, so Dave called an end to the meet-and-greet and started dividing everyone up for practice runs.

"Sharon, Scooter, Steve, the three of you take the north trail and run Nikita on a nice and easy single-person find to start with." This part, the logistics of training, was a piece of cake. It was also something he could still help with even with Lumpy and Woozy out of the game. "Scooter, I want you behind a tree about fifty yards off the path somewhere to the left. Steve, pay extra attention to Nikita's ears—last time she picked up on the scent but you rushed her past it, so she'll probably need a find or two to trust her nose again. Janet, give Zeus's toy to Lito and get Zeus ready for a ground search. Lito, you okay with being 'lost' and then found? I'll walk you in on the south trail—I want to watch Zeus run this one."

Lito nodded. "As long as you're telling me what to do, preferably using small words, I'm up for anything."

The team broke quickly into the two groups. Rick gathered the other dogs' leads and looped them through the industrial-strength carabiner he'd clipped around the base of the picnic table. His job was usually to hold down the fort for the pups who weren't practicing a search yet and to act as a buffer against any wayward hikers who pulled into the parking lot after practice was underway. The wheelchair made it impractical for him to do much off-trail work, but he was a genius at sorting through dog behavior issues and he usually took the time at base camp to work on making sure all the pack members played well with others. Adding Spot to the mix would be fun for the dogs and probably a nice challenge for Rick as well. Lito passed Spot's leash off and obediently followed Dave to the trail entrance. It was more of a wide gap in the underbrush than a true trail, really, but Dave could probably have navigated the entire park blindfolded by now and had no problem picking it out from halfway across the field. Judging from the awkward rhythm of Lito's steps as they worked their way past the treeline, the guy had a ways to go before he could say the same.

"You're not violently allergic to poison ivy, are you?" Dave asked, the question suddenly popping into his mind. "We can work around it if you are, but there's a non-zero chance we're gonna see some today." The woods in Alabama were full of it, so "non-zero" was perhaps understating it a bit. At the very least, Rick could use some help setting up the incident command station when they got called out on a search. And dammit, Lito hadn't even made it through one full practice yet, so Dave really ought to stop putting that cart before the horse.

Lito just shrugged, though, and gingerly sidestepped the branch Dave was holding out of the way for him. "Never had the chance to find out if I'm allergic or not," he answered. "I hope it comes down on the side of 'not.'"

"No poison ivy in Atlanta?"

"No woods."

Dave tried to wrap his head around the idea of voluntarily living somewhere without trees nearby. It sounded like hell, to be honest—and far too much like the endless scrub he spent so long patrolling on the Pakistan/Afghanistan border. "No wilderness camping trips when you were a kid?"

That won him an amused snort and another one of those addictive smiles. "I've never particularly been Boy Scout material," Lito said. "And I grew up in the middle of Miami, also not known for its vast forests, so... yeah, this is all new to me."

Okay, so Dave couldn't exactly picture Lito as a Boy Scout. He was doing a decent job of keeping up, though, which was promising. Dave drew them to a halt behind a fat hawthorn bush and checked the sight lines.

"So do I just stand here?" Lito asked. "Or try to hide, or what?"

"Right where we are is fine." It was a warm-up run for Zeus and Janet, but the hawthorn was a good hundred yards into the woods and well off the trail. Zeus would have to use his nose no matter how visible Lito was from the sides or back. "You've got the toy?"

Lito held up the chew rope and nodded.

"Then all you need to do is to hang out and let Zeus come to you. He'll come close enough to verify that you're here, may sniff you a bit, then he's—hopefully—going to run back to Janet. She'll give him a 'show me!' command, he'll acknowledge, and then he's going to lead her back to you. When he finds you the second time, wait until she praises him and then give him the rope. It's okay if he sees that you have it the first time, but don't give it to him until he's successfully completed the find."

"Got it."

"You got cell signal out here, just in case?"

Lito dug a phone out of his pocket and swiped across the screen with his thumb to unlock it. "One bar."

"Let me get your number, then. In case of a sudden tornado or, I don't know. Biblical plague, maybe." *Christ.* Dave started berating himself the moment the request passed his lips. That had definitely not been his smoothest pick-up ever, but it felt like his one plausible shot at getting Lito's digits and somehow, the idea of going home alone at the end of practice without a way to get back in touch was totally unthinkable.

"Oh, are we expecting one of those?" Lito looked pointedly at the clear sky. It looked like he was attempting to keep a straight face, but his lips were twitching. Maybe Dave hadn't put his foot in his mouth too badly after all. "Hmmm…I don't give out my number to every strange man who asks, Dave-Schmidt-who-likes-Winnie-the-Pooh, but I think I might make an exception for you."

* * * *

He got that I was teasing, right? I didn't just totally embarrass myself? The little flirtatious comment had popped out all on its own with no input from Lito's brain, probably because he'd been busy admiring Dave's shoulders—and backside—during their short hike. Attempting to pretend "no really, I wasn't checking you out just now" was doing a number on his ability to focus. Lito rattled off his number and tried not to watch too keenly as Dave keyed it into his own phone.

"Got it," Dave said. "I'll text you in a minute so you'll have mine too. The official one on the NALSAR card I gave you is actually Rick's."

His tone held absolutely no hint as to whether he'd been offended by Lito's instinctive 'hell yes' response. Or had even caught the teasing subtext. It meant that when Dave headed back for Janet and Zeus, Lito was left standing in the woods alone and wondering whether Dave was questioning the wisdom of having invited him along to practice at all.

The woods were beautiful aside from what was going on in Lito's head, so he tried to make himself relax and appreciate the quiet. The heat of the day had already dissipated and a breeze was picking up, making the leaves around him rustle gently. Somewhere off to the left a bird was hopping around in the underbrush, popping in and out of view as it searched for worms or berries or whatever it was little brownish songbirds ate. Lito had never really taken the time to be out in nature like this, alone and with no agenda, but it was incredibly peaceful. The beep of a text alert a few minutes later actually made him jump.

> *Janet is taking Zeus off-leash now. It may take a*
> *minute if he wants to run around and burn off steam*
> *first, but I promise I'll come find you even if he doesn't.*

> *Can't promise you won't find me strange, but I appreciate*
> *being the exception to your usual rule ;-)*

That answered that. Lito saved Dave's number in his contacts list, the plain letter "D" where a photo should be reminding him that he hadn't recalled Dave's last name—the business card Dave had given him just said "NALSAR." And had Rick's number, apparently. The generic "Dave ???" was also an unwelcome reminder that almost every other person in Lito's contacts list was either back in Atlanta or had to do with work. He hadn't expected to make new friends in Black Lake immediately, of course, but he hadn't put much thought into how much he appreciated his social life until he didn't have it anymore. How long would it take to rebuild one? Months? Years?

Lito stuck his phone back in his pocket and sat down to wait. Then pulled it back out to look up images of poison ivy, just in case. *Good to be prepared, right?* He was halfway through an informative—and slightly terrifying—"how to not die in the woods" web tutorial when he heard the unmistakable sound of a body crashing through the underbrush. Zeus homed in on him with eerie accuracy: the collie was trotting along happily, then froze and stood stock-still with his nose in the air. The moment he got a good solid sniff downwind, he was crashing through the brush again, straight for Lito. It really was impressive how Zeus narrowed in so easily—the time between that long pause and Zeus practically bowling Lito over was maybe twenty seconds tops.

Lito held perfectly still like Dave had told him. Zeus came close enough to snuffle his neck a few times, nuzzle the bright orange chew toy, then dash back off with an excited bark. He could hear Dave and Janet picking their way through the woods a ways off. Zeus barked twice more, sounding thoroughly proud of himself, then commenced doing laps between Lito and Janet until she and Dave had covered the rest of the distance. At Dave's nod, Lito passed Janet the toy and she threw it a few times. Zeus wagged his tail so hard he looked one accidental thump away from spraining it.

"A solid find," Dave pronounced. "Watch his ears for his tell—that first time he looked up he was distracted by something else, but when he turned off the trail back there he was smack dab in the middle of the scent cone and his ears were what showed the difference. Good job on letting him work it out himself."

Janet nodded, still tugging on the rope end of the toy. Zeus wriggled his whole body in excitement trying to pull on the other. "Your name's Lito, did I remember that right?" she asked. "Did Zeus come all the way in, or just stare at you and run off? We're still working on that."

Lito cleared his throat. "Came and sniffed me, nosed at the toy, then took off." Mind-blowing, really, when he really thought about the physics that accuracy must have involved. "I've got to say," he added, "Y'all and your dogs may do this all the time, but it was pretty impressive to see it up close."

Dave and Janet both preened a bit at that. "Want to see how Spot does?" Dave asked. "Let's head back and see how she's getting on with the other pups, then swap her out with Zeus and see if we can't get her to show off."

Zeus settled down immediately once Janet clipped his leash on. Lito was glad Dave knew his way around the woods, because after sitting out there for so long he wasn't a hundred percent sure he'd have found the parking lot on his own. Not without having to look up a map of the park, anyway, and even then the map probably wouldn't have been much help unless he stumbled back over the trail.

"How'd it go?" Rick asked once they got back in speaking range. He'd transferred from his wheelchair to the picnic table and was half-reclined on the bench. Lito noticed with a little jolt of surprise that Rick had left his shoes on the footrest of his chair—and that the shoes had apparently just been for show, because his new position made it apparent the man was missing his feet. *Crap. Don't stare.* Lito quickly refocused his attention on Spot. The six dogs not already training had all been put on long lead lines so they could play while still being nominally under control. Lito guessed it meant Rick probably spent half his time untangling them.

"Our fluffy boy done good," Dave proclaimed. "Janet too." He motioned for her to clip Zeus's leash to one of the spare lines. Spot looked up at Lito from where she was lying between a chocolate lab and a German Shepherd, totally at ease, and wagged her tail. "I see Spot's settling in, at least. Lito, go ahead and put her back on her regular leash for this. We'll use the other side of the picnic area so she's not distracted by her new friends."

Spot certainly did look like she'd been enjoying herself. "Stands to reason she'd make friends sooner than I did," Lito joked. Half-joked. "It's amazing how the dogs all get along so well, though. Do you ever have to deal with them fighting?"

"Eh." Rick waggled his hand in a 'little of this, little of that' gesture. "It's not automatic, if that's what you mean. It took my Scratch—he's the mangy-looking mutt over there—a good six months before he quit trying to challenge Dave's two. Woozy's the matriarch of the pack, though, and she's pretty laid back about enforcing the pecking order as long as everyone's behaving. She seems to have taken to Spot well."

"Spot likes her too." Lito gave his pup a good scratch behind the ears, which got her panting up at him in adoration. "Then again, Spot gets along with everyone. She'd make a terrible burglar alarm."

"Does she like hot dogs?" Dave asked. He pulled a plastic baggie of hot dog chunks out of his jacket pocket. "If she's not food-motivated we can work our way through some other options, but these are usually a good starting point."

All the dogs immediately stopped what they were doing and sat at attention, looking hopeful.

Dave gave them each a treat and a pat on the head, then led Lito and Spot across the parking lot so their view of Rick and the other dogs was blocked by the team's cars. He pulled out a handful of hot dog pieces and handed the rest of the bag to Lito.

"You ready?" he asked. "This is just a first step, so don't expect too much from her yet. We're going to do a nice and easy back-and-forth. I'll take her collar, you crouch down, and I'll give her a 'find' command. You call her name and give her a piece of hot dog when she gets to you. Soon as she eats it, you tell her 'go find!' and I'll take over calling her. The idea is to help her associate the command with the reward. High energy, lots of excitement, lots of encouragement. Don't be afraid to make an idiot of yourself. The more enthusiastic you are, the more she'll feel she pleased you."

Oh, wonderful. Lito knew he should have figured that Spot's training would start like this, but looking like an idiot in front of Dave hadn't exactly been on his agenda. Smelling like an idiot too—the bag of hot dog chunks was slightly warm from having been in Dave's pocket and if Lito could identify the smell already, they had to be the olfactory equivalent of a flashlight in the face to Spot. Hopefully there was somewhere with running water in the park so he could wash his hands before having to drive home.

Aloud, though, Lito just said, "got it." He'd spent a ridiculous amount of time training Spot to come when called when he first got her—a necessary thing, when Atlanta's sparse dog parks were the only place she'd been able to really stretch her legs—so it wasn't entirely surprising that Spot figured out the drill by the second lap. Getting to gorge herself on hot dogs every thirty seconds probably didn't hurt, either. Eventually Dave started taking careful steps backward in between Spot's back-and-forth trips, increasing the distance and moving off to one side or the other so she had to actually go to *him* and not just the place she last got a treat. Lito was reminded of an old math problem he'd hated: two cars moving at X speed Y distance apart have a dog going back and forth between them, so how far did the dog run?

"Step behind that bush there," Dave called out. "Don't say her name this time but don't try to hide all that well either. See if she can extrapolate. Spot, go find!"

Either she extrapolated brilliantly or she really could smell Lito's hot dog hands, because the bag was almost empty. By the time they were done, Spot had sprinted full-out for twenty minutes straight and had eaten the equivalent of what was probably two whole hot dogs. She was still prancing around Dave's feet when he beckoned Lito over and clipped her back into her leash.

"That's what I'd call a good first day," Dave pronounced. Hearing such blunt praise from Dave (for his *dog,* even, not actually for him!) might have made Lito walk a bit taller. When they got back to Rick, the rest of the team had already reassembled.

"Started without you," Rick declared without looking up. "You already know the old business part since you did half of it and I'm assuming Lito doesn't care yet."

Lito didn't, really, but if he was going to give the whole search and rescue thing a shot—and going by how much fun Spot had been having, he'd be an idiot not to—it was worth paying attention to even the boring parts. He took a seat on the bench next to Rick and folded his hands together neatly on the table. "I'm listening."

"Excellent." Rick passed a clipboard to Dave. "On to the treasurer's report?"

"Yeah, thanks." Dave took the clipboard and put it down without even glancing at the papers on it. "Long story short, that boat Janet's friend offered to sell us for cheap ended up having some major mechanical issues. Getting them fixed would have bumped the price up well above what the boat was worth. Sharon's sourcing out some more possibilities, trying to see if anyone will give us a discount for being a non-profit, but we're still talking several thousand bucks. We've got fourteen hundred thirty-two dollars and seventy-six cents in the account, with"—he did look down at the papers now—"last month bringing in a fifty-dollar donation and expenses of seventy-two dollars even. So if y'all know of a business that might like to sponsor us a boat, a trailer, or anything like that, let me now. Thus endeth the treasurer's portion of the evening, unless there are any questions."

"That's it for the whole meeting, actually," Rick said. "We've got no new business, so it was a short one today. See y'all Thursday!"

"The K9 search team needs a boat?" Lito asked Dave quietly as the rest of the team started packing up.

"We need a flat-bottomed one with low sides for water searches," Dave answered, matching Lito's volume. "Once you and Spot have mastered air scent and cadaver search, we'll start you on those. It's a lot less work for you both—the dogs lean over the side of the boat and bite at the water and can tell by the taste and smell whether there's anything underneath. Then it's up to a lot of math with currents and temperatures and whatnot to figure out where the source of the scent is. Most non-K9 rescue groups we work with, if they have a boat at all, don't have one with a low enough bow. For a long time we used...someone else's...but now we need a replacement. Haven't been able to do water search training for almost two years now and it's starting to be a problem since nobody else around here can, either."

"Ah."

"We're all volunteers, we don't charge money for searches, and we don't charge for educational talks to schools or other organizations." Dave rattled it off like he was reciting something he'd repeated a million times before. "NALSAR subsists on donations from the community to cover as much of our equipment as we can and our team members self-fund their individual gear. Sometimes we do fundraisers, or groups give us a donation as a thank you for us coming to speak, but that's all strictly voluntary." He heaved a deep breath and blinked a few times. "Sorry; that whole speech has kind of melded together by now. Took a while to get it right so I didn't keep floundering every time I was asked something."

"What he's not saying," Rick cut in, "is that he tends to go on autopilot anytime he has to ask for money on behalf of the team because he really, really hates it. But the rest of us are worse and Dave knows practically everyone in Black Lake, so..."

"Gee, thanks." Dave turned his attention to Spot, pointedly ignoring Rick. "You have fun today, pup?" he asked in a goofy, sing-song-y voice. "Want to come back Thursday and do it again? Tire out Lumpy and Woozy a bit more? You do? You *do?* Yeah, I thought so." He scratched behind her ears in the exact spot she liked it—must have been able to read her mind somehow—and she thumped her tail furiously against the leg of the picnic table. "You can come too, of course," he directed toward Lito with a bit of a smirk.

Mooning around after Dave was the only thing in Black Lake that Lito had yet found he looked forward to. Spot enjoying practice was a bonus. "Yeah, if I'm invited," he drawled, teasing back. Was Dave flirting? It felt like flirting. "Seems Spot has a crew now. She might not even notice if I just dropped her off."

"Oh, she definitely would." Dave's eyes sparkled. "You're the bearer of the hot dogs."

Chapter 3

"You were right, you bastard." Rick downed the last of his beer and held the empty bottle up to Dave in a mock toast. "Lord knows where you keep finding them, but that new dog yesterday played beautifully with the rest of the pack. Friendly and not at all put off by Scratch being a little shit to her at first. She's got to have some Golden in her, you think? She looks mostly lab but it's mixed with something else."

Dave shrugged. "No clue. Lito said when we first met that he'd tell me why he named a plain yellow dog 'Spot,' but I never did get the story. You're probably right, though—too much fur for a lab. She's got the persistence, though."

The VFW was nearly empty, result of it being a Wednesday and still early yet, but Isaiah the bartender (and janitor, and event coordinator, and all-around decent guy) was glued to the tiny television at the other end of the room so Dave got Rick another bottle himself. Isaiah saw him stand, looked up, and waved.

"Guess we'll just have to hope Lito comes back so you can ask," Rick said, tossing a five on the counter. "You think he'll stick?"

God, Dave hoped so. There really was no way to tell, unfortunately. Not this early. "Maybe?"

Rick huffed. "That last girl you found wouldn't have been a good fit anyway. Her heart was never in it. I know we do need more bodies—"

"Going a bit beyond *need* at this point."

"Still."

He wasn't wrong, Dave had to admit. Debbie had been a sophomore at the community college and living with her parents, but her six-month-old puppy had been an absolute dream to work with. Energetic, focused, starved for attention, and ridiculously eager to please. The lady at the shelter where she'd adopted him had recommended NALSAR as a way she could encourage him to burn off some energy. The two of them had lasted for about six weeks before Debbie decided the dog team interfered too much with her social life and called it quits. Dave fervently hoped her pup was getting some alternate source of exercise, wherever they were now.

"One more pair would work. If they were able to do regular call-outs." That was the main issue. "We're treading water right now, but only having four available dogs means we can't afford for anyone to have a work conflict or be too sick to search when we get asked."

"Five dogs," Rick corrected. "Sharon can run both of ours, in a pinch."

Doesn't matter. "Five, then. Still four handlers. Lumpy and Woozy do fine for school visits, but they're not getting any younger and we've been hurting for two years now. Even one more team member would help a lot."

"It's not going to replace Jessica, you know." Rick drummed his fingertips on the bar, suddenly more interested in the scarred wood than in looking Dave's way. "Whoever we find to join us, whether it's Lito and Spot or someone else, it won't be the same. Jessica's gone and even though Steve is dealing with it okay, we've got to start being proactive in how we patch the team back up again."

Dave didn't want to talk about it. Didn't want to even think about Jessica, actually, but Rick was right. "Would be a hell of a lot easier to get back on our feet with more people on our side," he grumbled, exaggerating the petulance in his voice purely to hear Rick snort. "For all that Jessica and Steve pissed each other off at every possible opportunity, she and Copper were a good team. And I think it was the first decent father-daughter bonding time that those two ever really had."

"That's on Steve, though." Rick toyed with the label on his bottle, picking at one corner. It was a pretty strong indication he was trying to work himself up to broaching some topic he didn't really want to discuss. *That makes two of us.* "Look," he finally said. "I'm not saying I'm not enjoying what we do, but...maybe it's time to let the team become a little more casual? Cut back on the practices, keep running the dogs we have, but not kill ourselves trying to respond to every call-out in a three-state radius? It's just—it feels like we're spread too thin. We can't keep everything going like it was five or ten years ago. *You* can't keep everything going like it was. Eventually something's gotta give."

"I can start looking for a new dog," Dave blurted out. It was something he'd considered, and rejected, many times over. "I know I said I'm not ready for a third pup right now, but it would get me back out there on the ground—"

"Dave. Shut up." Rick pinned him with a *we both know you didn't mean that* look. "Not six months ago you were sitting in this exact spot and telling me you couldn't afford the time and the money to take on another puppy. You said you were more help to NALSAR in a non-handler capacity, and that hasn't changed. Lumpy and Woozy are tolerant as hell but that doesn't mean they need you splitting your attention."

Damn. "I hate when you're right." Between Woozy's arthritis and Lumpy's one-two punch of cataracts and canine diabetes, Dave's pet budget was already stretched beyond what most people would consider reasonable. Adding another dog would require all three mammals in the Schmidt household to approve, and—despite his pups' laissez faire personalities—the chances of finding the right new dog were fairly low even if he *could* justify it.

Rick chuckled half-heartedly. "I know you don't want to think about it," he said, "but sometimes you've already done all you can do. Someday when you're old and lonely, I'll help you find the smartest puppy ever and you can get back out there as a dog and handler team. For right now, though, we need to take things one step at a time." He glanced down at his wheelchair and grimaced. "So to speak."

Fifteen years of friendship had rendered Rick's missing feet—among other completely inappropriate topics—an old joke between them. The IED responsible had also taken Dave's explosives detection dog, who had really been the one doing the work anyway. Whom Dave was steadfastly *not* going to let himself think about.

"You don't like steps anymore," Dave teased.

"Jackass." Rick grinned and kicked Dave's shin with his own. "I'll have you know this chair goes *down* stairs just fine, as long as they're little ones. It's getting it up that's the problem."

"Hey, whatever problems you have with keeping it up, keep those between you and Sharon—"

"Screw you," Rick interjected. "Just for that, you get to run the business meeting next practice."

"Enjoy it while we still have a team to practice with."

Rick shook his head, the levity falling away. "Just…give it time, all right? We'll see if this Lito guy works out or not, but if not…NALSAR doesn't have to be your whole life, you know. You can do other things. It's allowed."

Dave knew. Of course he knew. But what else was there?

* * * *

Hope you had fun last night! See you
tomorrow? - Dave, Lumpy, and Woozy

The dude signed his texts as if they were from his dogs. That was really damn adorable. Lito unclipped Spot from her leash and topped off her water bowl so she could rehydrate after their run. There was no question she enjoyed being out and about with him as they covered what had now tentatively become their "usual" route, but she had obviously loved getting to play with the other dogs during search team practice even more. She'd also loved the frantic dash-back-and-forth-for-treats without having to slow her speed for her poor bipedal human. Lito's new rental house had a small backyard—a luxury they'd never had in Atlanta—but it wasn't fenced. Letting Spot charge around out there unsupervised probably wasn't a good idea, no matter how much she might have disagreed with him. Lito poured himself a cup of ice water and downed it in one go. Damn, it was muggy and miserable out there. *Autumn, my ass.* He refilled the glass, pulled out his phone again, and thumbed out a response.

Woof, woof! - Spot

Pretty sure that's "can't wait" in dog. - Lito

It was five minutes to seven, so Lito headed for his living room and turned on his PlayStation. He and some of the guys in Atlanta had a standing "date" for gaming on Wednesday nights, and he was extra-thankful for that fact now that he was two and a half hours away from everyone else. Or farther, for some—Brandon was now living out in the suburbs on the east side of Atlanta with his new boyfriend, Paul, and Jericho was on the home stretch of a three-year stint in Haiti. He had crap internet access most of the time but he joined them whenever he could. Black Lake felt like the middle of nowhere, Lito decided, but it definitely could have been worse.

Tonight the gang ended up being him, Brandon and Paul, and a handful of the usual crew. Lito slipped on his headset, got comfortable on his beat-up secondhand sofa with Spot lying on his feet, and signed in.

"—and look who's here," Chris said, his voice loud through the headphones. "Lito, my man! How's exile?"

"Oh, screw you."

"That good, huh?"

"He means he misses your twink ass," Ian chimed in. "Both your ass specifically and the rest of your hot bod attached to it."

"None of y'all have ever gotten *that* close to my ass," Lito countered. "Like I'd share it with you losers."

"As opposed to that dude with the rainbow squid tattoo last year? Yeah, real winner there."

Ian had a point, but Lito couldn't flip him off over audio chat so he settled for taking another gulp of his water instead. "We playing Overwatch again tonight, gentlemen?"

"And he changes the subject. Nice." Chris laughed, but they settled into the game with no more than the usual amount of bickering. Paul and Brandon were the best players in their little circle—by far—but Lito usually managed to not drag their group's team down *too* much. He snagged his favorite character, the one with the ice powers, and relaxed into the sofa cushions while everyone else worked out who got dibs on DPS and who got stuck playing the healer. As so often happened, Brandon finally ended up handing out assignments so they'd have a balanced squad. He was excellent at battle strategy, as evidenced by the fact that they won their first two games handily. The crew usually got their asses handed to them when Brandon and Paul weren't online.

"But seriously, Lito," Ian said during a lull between rounds, "I want to know how your new job is treating you. Or, you know. Not *new* necessarily— you said you're still doing a lot of the same stuff?—but new location. This is the first time you've lived in a small town, right?"

It was, and Lito was a bit surprised he'd remembered. Attention to detail wasn't usually Ian's strong suit. "Miami, Orlando, and Atlanta," Lito answered. "And Lima, technically, although we moved when I was still too little to remember it. So yeah, it's an adjustment."

"Is it terrible?"

"Believe it or not," Paul cut in, "most of Alabama got electricity way back in the eighties. Some of the towns even have *cars*."

"Fuck you." Ian said it with a laugh. "Just for that, *you* get to play Mercy this next round. I'm sick of having the big glowing 'healer' target on my back."

Now that Lito thought about it…Paul was from a town about the same size as Black Lake, wasn't he? He'd moved in with Brandon in Atlanta after some sort of messy fallout when an ex outed him to the conservative religious college he'd been teaching at, but the whole thing had finally been worked out a few months earlier and he and Brandon seemed perfectly happy together out in suburbia now. "It's not as terrible as I'd feared," Lito admitted, "but I still miss you guys like crazy. It's lonely here."

Adam, who'd been pretty typically quiet so far, made a sound of commiseration. "Hard to imagine you staying lonely for long, dude," he said. "You attract friends the way flowers attract bees."

"Only friends like you guys." Friends who *got* him. "I think it's safe to say there aren't a lot of people like y'all in Black Lake. I only accepted the move because I didn't have much of a choice if I wanted to keep my job. I like it, I'm good at it, and Dayspring practically built their purchasing and renovation procedures around me. If I have to get exiled to Bumfuck, Alabama to keep doing my thing, then that's what I've got to do."

"I thought it was because you hated telling your bosses no," Chris chimed in.

"You hate telling anyone no," Brandon teased. "Except Ian."

Ian mumbled something that sounded like "screw you."

They weren't entirely wrong. Ronald and Betty ran their hotel chain like a family business, and Lito had long ago been adopted into the fold. And yeah, so maybe he was "the gay designer." Might as well own it, right? Even if the new office was a bit…less welcoming than he'd hoped.

"It's different here." Painfully so. The *not-rightness* was hard to explain, but Lito tried anyway. "I'm the only man at work. Also the only non-white person, the only non-straight one, and the only one who's ever lived within reasonable shopping distance of an IKEA. Everyone's been nothing but nice, but it keeps feeling like the old 'bless his heart' kind of *Southern* nice, you know? Like they're not sure what to make of the strange gay decorator so they're just faking it. I still haven't met my new direct supervisor, either—she's been on a business trip all week. I'm really hoping she's not as weird-Southern-sweet as the rest of them."

"So find somewhere else to get your socializing in," Brandon suggested. "Join a rec league. Take up swing dancing. Whatever."

"Right, and dance with who?" Lito could just picture the looks he'd get if he showed up at whatever passed for the local watering hole and started grinding on random dudes. Probably not just evil looks—a full-on beatdown was more likely. "I don't think there's much of a local LGBT scene. Can't spit without hitting a church, though."

Ian made an amused noise. "Take Spot for lots of walks and hope you run into a cute guy with a compatible dog, maybe? Isn't that where you found that personal trainer dude way back when?"

"I, um." Prior experience suggested he really ought to tell them about NALSAR now so they could get the teasing out of their systems all at once. "I'm thinking of joining a search dog team, actually. The rescue-lost-hikers-in-the-woods kind. I mean, I've only been to one practice so far, but it was fun. Spot loved it."

"Damn, dude!" Adam exclaimed. "Go you, getting out of your comfort zone! Never would have taken you for a nature type. Not with that whole 'city boy' thing."

"Oh, me either." Hell, he'd never even *been* anywhere that could be termed "nature" until he was already an adult, Miami's beaches excepted. "It's kind of nice, though. There's about half a dozen people on the team and they all seem pretty easygoing. I bumped into the team trainer at the pet store this past weekend and he invited me out to see it for myself. I was curious, and bored, so…yeah."

"Ha!" Ian sang a few bars of "bow-chicka-wow-wow" cheesy-porn-style music. "Let me guess—the trainer dude is hot. And built."

Lito rolled his eyes at Ian's totally predictable guess. The guy made for a terrifically reliable friend, probably Lito's best friend in their little group, but he had sex on the brain 24/7 and rarely had much of a filter. Sometimes it was a wonder he managed to make time for things like eating or going to work. "He's…not bad looking," Lito admitted. "No reason to think he plays for our team, unfortunately."

"Like that's ever stopped you from appreciating when something good is in front of you."

No point arguing with that. "I try to be subtle, at least." Had it been only in his imagination that Dave was eyeing him with more than just professional interest? Or that Dave's texts were a touch flirty? "Afraid this one is wishful thinking, but if he ever lets me take a picture of him and his dogs I'll send it to y'all. I honestly can't tell whether he spends all his free time at the gym or whether he, like, chops his own firewood or something, but you'd appreciate the chance to ogle."

"Hot damn," Ian said, and whistled. "You know me so well. Although I guess chances are if he *is* gay, he's probably in the closet. Can't imagine otherwise living way out there."

Yeah, thanks. There was an awkward moment of silence while nobody wanted to point out that Lito *was* living "way out there," thankyouverymuch, but then Brandon put them in the queue for the next capture-the-flag battle and the game eventually resumed. Lito found himself paying significantly less attention than he had been before.

Was it possible Dave was in the closet? r anything other than one hundred percent straight? Unlikely, Lito had to give Ian that, but that didn't mean it couldn't happen. Both of them liking cock didn't mean Dave would be interested in Lito's cock (or any other part of him), of course, but Dave hadn't seemed to mind Lito flirting a bit. A very little bit. If nothing else, daydreaming about Dave was going to make a nice little fantasy until Lito got settled into his new, much-less-LGBT-friendly life.

However long that took.

Chapter 4

Lito Apaza. Lito Ah-PAH-sah. Dave had been repeating the name in his head off and on for the last forty-eight hours, hoping he could actually come up with it when practice rolled around, but he was pretty sure he still wasn't pronouncing the "z" correctly. Lito didn't have a discernible accent—at least not one Dave could place—but he made some words sound much more fluid than Dave ever could. It was sexy in a way Dave probably shouldn't have been thinking about. His own time in Afghanistan got him away from home long enough that he at least realized he *did* have an Alabama twang in his voice, but not long enough for him to lose any of it.

"Hey, boss, did you know you're muttering to yourself out loud?"

Dave turned and only barely restrained himself from flashing Mike a rude gesture. The two of them were repainting some of the playground equipment at the community center, so flipping off a coworker right in front of a Head Start classroom was probably not a good idea. Even if the playground itself was closed until the paint dried. "At least it's someone worth talking to," he slung back. "All that's been on your mind lately is football."

"Football and Rhonda." Mike grinned. "She found this new recipe for a cheese dip and it's *amazing.* Wanna come over for the game Saturday? Rhonda said you're welcome to hang."

"Sounds fun. Thanks." Dave wasn't anywhere near as rabid about college football as Mike was, but the three of them had gotten together for a few games in the past. It was always entertaining. Particularly because Mike was an Alabama fan and Rhonda rooted for Auburn even when the rival teams weren't playing each other. The result was usually some Army-worthy insults being traded back and forth. Dave played his fair share of ball in high school—never a star player, but solid nonetheless—so Mike ragged him about his apathy to the sport nonstop during football season. "Count me in unless something comes up," he said. "Did you do the inside part of the pirate ship yet, or just the hull?"

They were making pretty steady progress, all things considered. Dave's to-do list for his crew was never empty, but for once they were reasonably caught up on the normal mowing and picking up trash. The nice weather had seemed like a sign that he and Mike should get the playground done before winter set in. He had four other guys besides himself in the Parks & Rec maintenance department, but Mike was the only other one who was full-time. All four were more than happy that Dave, as their supervisor, was the one who had to deal with the paperwork.

Which...Dave checked his watch. He'd hoped to finish up a few more little things while they were here—oil the squeaky hinge on the gate, check the perimeter of the community center building for fire ant hills and wasps' nests, maybe pick up some of the debris that inevitably littered the edges of the ball field—but it was getting on toward four o'clock. If he attempted all that and still wanted to shower before NALSAR practice at six, he'd have to cut a lot of corners. There was the issue of leaving a freshly painted playground unguarded too, which was just *asking* for disaster. It couldn't be helped, though. At least if he and Mike came back in the morning, they'd see any vandalism before it had too much time to set in. If they finished up quickly and skipped the rest of the list, he'd have time to run back to his little broom closet of an office at city hall and finish next week's assignments for the guys. He tried to be fair about accommodating the part-timers' schedules—especially since he ditched work for a search often enough and they always adjusted for him—but there was no predicting the weather with any certainty for more than a few days out. Outdoor work would have to be subject to change.

Mike was fortunately a solid worker who could talk and paint at the same time. Dave let him chatter about Rhonda and football while they touched up the last few peeling boards on the play structures, but his mind was mostly focused on the team. And Lito Apaza. *Ah-PAH-sah.* Who was small and feisty and adorable and had a beautiful "amazed" expression which Dave was going to enjoy coaxing out of him as often as possible. Even if nothing happened between the two of them—Lito was either gay or the most gay-sounding straight man of all time, but that didn't mean he'd be interested—even if they merely became teammates, Dave could still appreciate those wide eyes and that slow smile. He resolved to earn another impressed look at practice if Lito and Spot showed.

"Think that was the last one," Mike announced. "You need to get going, right? Dog team tonight?"

"Yeah, but we still ought to—"

Mike shooed him toward the truck and started collecting their painting debris. "You take these back and I'll fix my time sheet in the morning. Grab me a bag and one of the litter sticks, would you? I'll keep myself busy."

"You sure?" It was technically against the rules to leave Mike behind when they had both ridden to the site in the work truck. Rhonda's house was less than two blocks away, though. No mystery to why Mike would rather finish his day at the community center than ride all the way back to city hall and then have to wait for his brother to come pick him up.

"If we both sit here babysitting the playground and literally watching paint dry, you'll be late for your practice," Mike said. "Dude, I recognize when you're thinking about your dogs." He handed Dave both buckets and helped him batten them down as best he could for the drive back. "You had me an hour and a half short this week anyway, with that fence thing finishing up so quickly on Monday. Hint, hint."

He had a point. Dave shook his head and sighed. "If you want to pick up trash for another hour and a half, go ahead. I can't count it as overtime, but as long as you remember to bring the litter stick back in the morning and you don't let someone who can fire me see you out here after five and still on the clock, I don't have a problem with it. I'll fix your schedule so you get credit for the time when I get back to my office."

"You're awesome, boss." Mike gave him a sloppy salute that would have probably earned him extra latrine duty if he'd actually been in the Army. "Go save some lives out there tonight!"

"If we find any surprise dead bodies, I'll let you know."

He left Mike cheerfully stabbing empty potato chip bags and daydreaming about Rhonda. The other guys were already done and gone for the day when Dave got back to his office, so he made up the next week's schedule and then half-assed the rest of his paperwork. Nobody would be around to complain until tomorrow anyway. He got home in time for a longer shower than he expected—which felt *so good* after being hunched over and painting all day—and a quick dinner of reheated leftovers before he called Lumpy and Woozy to the car and headed back out for practice. The sight of Lito's little orange Saturn when he got there made something in his gut do a little wriggle.

He'd said he couldn't wait until next time. Having the text sitting on his phone was one thing, but seeing Lito actually sitting at the picnic table chatting with Rick and Sharon was much nicer. Lumpy and Woozy both leapt out of the car the moment Dave opened the door and commenced burning off whatever energy they'd accumulated from lying around all day.

"Can't believe we actually beat you here," Sharon teased. "Steve called to say he wasn't going to make it tonight and Scooter had to cover an extra shift so he'll be late. Janet's on her way."

"You want to run your two?"

Sharon inclined her head toward Lito. "This one's been wriggling out of his skin to get Spot going again. I'll give you a hand with her, if you want."

Lito huffed. "I am not. I just said—"

"—that Spot has been looking forward to this for two days," Rick finished for him. "We can read between the lines, thank you."

Dave had to work hard to suppress his grin. *Guess I'm not the only one who's been eager to spend time together again.* "Spot's the excited one, is she?"

Lito rolled his eyes, but his cheeks looked a little pink. His skin was too dark to tell for sure. Dave found he really liked the thought of Lito blushing, though.

"Let's get her off-lead and into the woods a bit, shall we?"

Lito and Sharon tagged along behind him as he led them a little ways up the north path and then off the trail to a relatively flat area without too much undergrowth. Spot trotted along perfectly at Lito's side, even without the benefit of a leash. Obviously she thought the world of her owner. That was a good sign, both in terms of her trainability and about Lito's character. The treats or the toy were only minor rewards for the dogs. What mattered more was praise from their human—and really, who wouldn't want Lito's attention?

Dave offered Sharon the bag of hot dog pieces but she already had her own. He sent her about ten yards away and had Lito grab Spot's collar. "Ready?"

Spot remembered the previous practice well, it seemed. Either that or she really, *really* liked hot dogs. Dave and Sharon had done this countless times with new dogs and handlers, some who'd stuck with the team a while and some who didn't, so she already knew the right distance to move away each time without needing Dave to prompt her. Spot's tail was wagging madly as she pranced back and forth.

"Try standing behind this tree next," Dave told Lito. "Think of this as hide and seek—one treat each time she comes to you and then lots of praise. High, excited voice like last time."

Spot slowed in the center of the training field, head cocked in confusion, but she got a visual on Lito quickly enough and bounded over to him.

"She's so proud of herself," Lito said to Dave, ruffling Spot's ears and getting her even more wound up. "Send her back?"

Sharon had already ducked behind a rock. "Yep."

"Should I switch positions?"

Dave glanced around—and then couldn't help himself. "Both of us. Here." He tugged Lito over to stand behind a shortish pine a few yards away, then got out the rest of the hot dog bag and took Lito's place behind the original tree. "Gonna see if she notices I'm not you."

Lito laughed—quietly, but open and charming and just exactly like Dave had hoped to hear. "Don't think anyone's going to get us mixed up," he murmured. "You'd make a terrible Lito, but you do pretty damn well as a Dave."

Why that made something inside him twist, Dave didn't want to examine.

"Good girl!" Sharon cooed. "Ready? Ready? *Go find!*"

Spot took one short, disdainful look at Dave, then went straight for Lito and slobbered all over him.

* * * *

Lito spent the weekend getting the rest of his Atlanta stuff put away. There was something satisfying about condensing the stack of not-yet-unpacked boxes to one small corner of the living room instead of them covering every surface of the house. Even after he got to work on Monday morning, he still felt like he was glowing. Slightly dimmed for having to be at the office, but glowing nonetheless.

"You must be Lito."

The voice came out of nowhere, making him jump. *Christ.* Lito made a mental note to put up a mirror next to his monitor so he could see the doorway behind him, then stood and offered his new boss a polite handshake. "You're Ms. Bronton, I'm guessing. And yeah, that's me. You caught me by surprise—it's nice to finally meet." He'd been at this particular Dayspring Inn & Suites office for two weeks already, but his new supervisor had left for a two-week business trip literally the day before he started. Her absence hadn't made the transition any easier. The woman before him had the sharp business-suit-and-heels look the Dayspring owners tended to look for in their female managers; it wasn't hard to imagine her ruling this little office with an iron fist. That was fine with him as long as she was fair about it.

"Glad to finally meet you face-to-face too," she said. "And 'Vanessa' is fine. You're really not what I expected, but Ronald and Betty think the world of you and I have high hopes for you settling in here." She paused a moment and took in the scattered wall decor Lito had put up in his office so far. "You're the one behind the new mint-green theme I keep seeing, aren't you? I like it."

"Thanks." When Lito had first fallen into the night clerk job at the middle-of-nowhere Dayspring Inn on the I-4 south of Orlando, the chain had still been clinging to its kitschy Florida roots. Peach and teal pineapples, fake seashells embedded in the concrete, 1950s beach music, the whole shebang. By the time he worked his way up the ladder to the Atlanta corporate office and started getting to make actual design decisions instead of just rubber-stamping purchase orders, the owners were willing to potentially maybe *possibly* consider trying something a bit less tacky.

Lito took that sliver of a chance and ran with it. Two years ago, the entire chain underwent renovation for his new-and-improved design scheme and reviews went up practically overnight. Now the Alabama locations were supposed to be a test case for Dayspring going entirely local—local artists, local flavor, individual design accents. He'd done some networking with artists before, back in Atlanta, but Ronald and Betty hoped this could be a for-the-foreseeable-future thing.

"Anything you still need, please do let me know." Vanessa pulled a business card out of her purse and put it on the corner of Lito's desk. "I'm not in the office all that often but I try to check email at least a few times a day and if you send me a text, I'll call you back as soon as I can. You've met everyone else?"

"I think so. Carrie gave me the grand tour." Lito slid the business card into his pocket. The office was seven women plus him. Six who made up the chain's entire customer service department, booking corporate events and taking complaints, plus Vanessa. She was the regional manager for the state of Alabama and—the way Lito heard it—spent ninety percent of her time on the road.

"Anyone tell you about lunch today yet?" she asked.

Lito shook his head.

"Walk with me, then." She waited for him to log out of his computer, then walked him to the conference room at the end of the hall. "It's not really a meeting, necessarily, but I order lunch for the office whenever I've been away so everyone can catch me up. You can consider the ones after today optional."

The way she said it suggested that they weren't, really, but he nodded anyway.

"Do you like fried chicken? If you're new in town you might not have tried Mama Josie's yet, but it's pretty amazing Southern home-cooking. Or—sorry, I shouldn't assume. It may be a bit different than what you're used to."

What, because I look gay? Or because I'm brown? Lito tamped down the instinct to bristle. It wouldn't be the first time someone had made assumptions about him based on either demographic, but his first face-to-face meeting with his new supervisor—his supervisor on paper, at least; he hadn't really had a direct boss other than the chain's owners in ages—wasn't really the best time to fuss. And truth be told, he really didn't eat a lot of red meat, but that had nothing to do with anything she might have "assumed." He may not have made the rounds of the local restaurant scene, such as it was, but that didn't mean he only ate Mexican food. Although it wouldn't surprise him if at least one of his coworkers assumed that all Latinos eat tacos for breakfast, lunch, and dinner—they hadn't shown themselves to be the most culturally educated people so far.

He was being pissy, and some part of him knew it was probably not the best mood to be in at the moment. "Sounds good," he said instead, and held the door for her as they entered the conference room. Everyone else was already there, chatting and unloading the aluminum carry out trays onto the counter.

"Lito!" Carrie waved him over and pulled out a chair for him next to her own. "You and Vanessa finally met today, eh? I told you she'd love you."

She had. At length, and in a too-friendly way that made him wonder why she felt it was so important to reassure him that the office was *so welcoming* and everyone would just *die* of pride now that they had the Dayspring Inn & Suites decorator based out of their location. Lito wasn't a "decorator"—or rather, he was a "decorator" the same way the manager of an art gallery was a "painter"—but obviously everyone had received advance word of The Gay Designer and it was a difficult stereotype to shake. He knew he did look the part, and hell would freeze over before he went back to trying to pass for a boring straight dude, but Black Lake wasn't the easiest place to be The Gay Designer in either.

Luckily the fried chicken was good. So were the mac and cheese, the okra, and the collard greens. They all ended up filling their plates for seconds and thirds.

And gossiping. Christ. Lito got to hear *all* about someone's sister's engagement, someone else's infertility woes, and somebody's neighbor's loud cat. Vanessa occasionally asked a few work-related questions about various clients or phone calls they'd received, but the overall atmosphere was one of a sewing circle rather than a business meeting. Everyone was very white, very heterosexual, and very *female*.

"Liam wants a reptile-themed birthday," the corporate accounts lady was saying. "Not any specific reptile, necessarily, just reptiles in general. So now I've got two weeks to figure out how to entertain a dozen six-year-olds and I don't have the first idea what to do. What did Mason have for his, do you remember? I know it's been a few years."

Customer Complaints woman shrugged. "Chuck E. Cheese, I think. I was still in the sleep deprivation stage with the twins being two months old at the time."

"Lot of help you are. This one has to be at our house because, and I quote, 'I want my friends to see how stinky my dog's breath is.'"

No one else had small children, from what Lito had gathered. He cleared his throat. "Easiest would be to throw together a couple of reptile-themed activities and then just let them play," he said. "Pin the tail on the alligator, 'lizard races' where they all have to speed-crawl, that kind of thing. I could probably rustle up some kid-sized boxes so you can have them all decorate their own turtle shells, if you want—I've still got a ton of moving boxes I haven't gotten out to the recycling yet. And party food gives you lots of chances to include gummy worms, green grapes for 'turtle eggs,' lettuce and cut fruit, whatever."

Corporate accounts lady's surprised look slowly morphed into one of appreciation. "Thanks," she said, nodding. "Those all sound like things Liam would love, actually."

"You don't have children, do you, Lito?" Carrie asked. "Sorry, I just assumed you were on the young side for that. And because, well—yeah."

And gay. Thanks. She didn't have to say it; everyone else in the room must have been thinking the same thing. "I'm twenty-five," Lito said, "and no. I don't." It wasn't the first time he'd been mistaken for younger than his real age either. Hell, he still got carded every damn time he and his friends ordered drinks, which definitely got old after a while. Especially when the rest of them had all been accepted as twenty-one *ages* ago. "It's just me and my dog. Although I do like kids just fine when they're other people's responsibility."

Vanessa laughed. "Fair enough. Kindergartners can be an acquired taste sometimes."

"So since we're finally getting to know you better, I have a question," Carrie chimed in, dropping her fork on her now-empty plate. "This is totally random, but I saw some paperwork that said your real name is Carlos. Is 'Lito' a middle name, or a nickname for 'Carlos' somehow? I've heard it before, I think, but I've never been close enough friends with anyone Hispanic to ask."

Everyone's attention was definitely on him now. Like he was in a circus and being asked to perform for the visitors.

That's me, the exotic Latino wonder. Nothing like having to educate people about your ethnicity because they never bothered learning on their own. "It's like 'Billy' for 'William,'" he said, forcing a patient smile. "'Carlito' would be 'Little Carlos,' and everyone shortens it. 'Lito' is what I've always gone by, though."

"Huh. I never knew that."

Lito half-expected someone to ask him what part of Mexico he was from—or whether he truly was a real live homosexual and if so, could he teach them about that too?—but someone else brought up her grandson's unusual nickname and from there it descended into a "strange things people name their children" discussion. Vanessa let them chatter on for a few more minutes before pushing her empty plate away and leaning back in her chair. "All right," she announced. "I've got a backlog of emails to catch up on and I'm sure you all have work waiting for you too. Anything else I need to know about before I go bury myself in paperwork?"

One by one they all shook their heads. "Anything from you?" Carrie asked Lito. "Do you get, like, decorating emergencies or something?"

Or something. "On occasion," he answered, "but nothing at the moment. And it's not so often emergencies with the decor itself. Usually it's more like an artist flaking out and not actually getting us the paintings we paid for, or a contractor trying to substitute different materials than what we ordered. I do a lot less picking color swatches than you'd think."

The owners of the Dayspring chain had a "firm commitment to the community," as they usually worded it in their promotional material, which translated to each location having a slightly different local vibe. They all now had the same base color scheme, thanks to him, but the lobbies and individual rooms had widely varying layouts and that meant fewer chain-wide economies of scale. It also meant Lito spent half his time on the phone trying to get managers to send him usable—and white-balanced—pictures of the problem areas so he didn't have to drive all over the southeast to look at poorly lit corners and odd stained spots on the ceiling.

"That makes sense." She nodded politely at Lito, then at Vanessa. "Guess we'll get to chat more later, then?"

"Undoubtedly." *Whether I want to make friends with you all or not.*

Chapter 5

Dave got the call around noon on a Sunday in early November, just after the first real cold snap of the year. Thirteen-year-old Grayson White told his mother he was walking to a friend's house to work on a group homework assignment. When he didn't come home by the next morning, she called the friend's parents—only to learn that Grayson hadn't been by all weekend and the whole supposed homework assignment was news to them. The Cullman County Sheriff's Office spent the afternoon tracking down the boy's usual haunts and finally called in Dave and the NALSAR team when it became clear the kid was actually missing. He lived way out in the country, more than a mile from the nearest neighbors and a full three miles from the friend's place, and there were a hell of a lot of woods in between. Even better, Cullman County was an hour and a half away from Black Lake and they only had a few good hours of light left. *Sunset at 4:30 in the afternoon. Thanks, Daylight Savings Time.* Dave sent the group call-out text and went to go put his pack in the Jeep. His phone rang not a minute later.

"Hey," Lito said. The sound of the wind over the speaker in the background suggested he was outdoors somewhere. "Just saw the text— do you want me to come? I mean, Spot's obviously not ready to run a real search after only two months of practices, but I'm free if you want me."

"Definitely! This would be a good first call-out for you." A missing kid was usually big news, meaning a crowded staging area, but this particular search was pretty rural. Incident command was likely to be just them and the sheriff's office—probably a little less hectic and a lot easier for Lito to see how all the pieces fit together. "I'd like you to get a chance to see how it works," he added. "Leave Spot at home; I'll pair you up with one of the other handlers. Bring your gear. You want me to pick you up? There's really no reason to drive your own car all the way to Cullman if you don't have your dog along."

"Sure. Thanks." There was the sound of a door slamming. "Just got home from taking Spot for a run now, but I'll be ready by the time you get here. Oh, and I'll text you my address. I'm renting a house in that little neighborhood that butts up against the back of the high school."

"I know it." He had spent a fair amount of time skulking around just off school property when he'd been a student there—not smoking or getting into trouble, just hanging out with friends because there was nowhere else to go past nine o'clock at night when Walmart closed. "Be there in twenty."

Lumpy and Woozy were both on high alert the moment Dave opened the closet where he kept the rest of his search gear, but they were going to have to be disappointed. He disappointed them most of the time, nowadays. He still brought them along for practices, PR events, and talks to school groups, but that was about it—their tails wagged just fine even if the rest of them were slowing down. Dave dumped his coat and his first-aid pack on his bed, then sat on the edge of the mattress to change into his work boots. Lumpy immediately jumped up and settled with a huff of finality on the DayGlo NALSAR coat like she was just *daring* him to try to go without her.

"Twit." Dave gave her an extra-thorough ear scratch. "I know, I know. I'll be back later, you two. Try not to tear up the house too much while I'm gone."

Lumpy rolled over onto her side and tried to lick his leg without exerting the effort to actually raise her head.

He finished loading the SUV and let them both outside one last time, in case the search went all night, then ushered them back in through the garage and closed the door. They never caught on that he was actually leaving without them until about five seconds after he started the engine. When he got home there would probably be drool all over the sofa and possibly a disemboweled dog toy on the bed—Woozy took it personally when she wasn't invited along. It was a good thing she kept her destructive tendencies to her own toys…and didn't mind that all her chewables came from the dollar store.

Lito's house turned out to be a charming little white ranch, identifiable even at a distance by his distinctive orange Saturn in the carport. The houses in the neighborhood were all what a real estate agent might call "cozy." Lito came out to meet him in the driveway.

"Thanks," he said, climbing into the passenger seat. "Siri is great for helping me find my way around town most of the time, but I'm not sure

I'm up to the 'After three miles, turn left onto unnamed road' level of navigating quite yet. Especially if cell reception is spotty."

"It usually is." That was a main reason the team still kept two-way radios on hand—often they were well and truly in the middle of nowhere. "You have a preference on music? Feel free to pick a station."

"What do you usually listen to?"

"Whatever's not on commercial at the time."

"Gotcha." Lito found some inoffensive pop music and they made small talk for the rest of the drive. He was an unabashed fan of Taylor Swift, Dave learned, as well as having no shame whatsoever about singing along to the good parts when something came on that he liked. He had an amazing voice, something Dave had always envied. His own wasn't terrible but was nowhere near "amazing." Finally pulling into the White family's driveway and needing to get his brain into work mode created a fair bit of cognitive dissonance.

The farmhouse was set well back from the road, up a bit of a hill. Sharon, the county sheriff, and a dark-haired woman who was presumably the boy's mother were already waiting on the porch. Rick was organizing papers in the back of their van and gave a little wave as Dave pulled up. Two patrol cars were parked in the yard, lights on but no sirens, with officers leaning on them and chatting quietly with each other. *A perfect low-key first search for Lito.* The sheriff broke off to come greet them.

"Thanks for making the drive," he said, offering a solid handshake to Dave and Lito both. "Been a while since you've been out our way."

It had. Probably three or four years, at least. "Given the current circumstances," Dave answered, "I'm going to say that's a good thing." The last one had been, what? The schizophrenic transient guy, maybe? Dave had vague memories of searching for a man who'd supposedly been a regular at the local soup kitchen until suddenly he wasn't. The search was mostly memorable because people rarely bothered checking up on the homeless. He'd run Woozy on that one—*yes.* Winter, almost four years ago. No luck, but a police officer found the guy panhandling in Birmingham a few weeks later.

The routine of setting up the search quickly took priority over anything else. Dave headed over to join Rick, Sharon got Scratch and Sniff sorted, and Lito ended up chatting with the boy's mother on the porch while they waited for everyone else. Even with his brain on autopilot, though, Dave kept finding himself sneaking glances at Lito. The mother seemed to be opening up to him, occasionally smiling and once even letting out a surprised laugh. Lito talked with his hands as well as his words, graceful gestures as he described something to her, and Dave had to look away. *Really not the time.* The other three team members rolled in right as Dave, Rick, and the sheriff were finishing up the nitty-gritty of splitting the woods into single-unit quadrants. It was a fairly straightforward search—no water in the immediate area, neurotypical search target who was presumably capable of answering when called by name, the usual terrain. Dave sent Scooter to round up everyone for a pre-launch briefing while the sheriff did the same with his own team.

"What did the kid's mom say?" Scooter asked once they'd assembled, nodding subtly toward where the woman now stood alone on the porch.

Dave looked to Lito. "Anything new? Seemed like you two were having a good long conversation. We don't usually talk to the families much—"

"Shit, I didn't mean to—"

"—but what I was about to *say* was, it's really useful when someone does make a connection." Heaven knew Dave sucked at dealing with frightened or grieving families, but Lito seemed like a natural. "If you're good at looking approachable and you can help the family understand what we're doing, it can really be a help. Did she add anything new?"

Lito relaxed his stance a bit. "We were just chatting about Grayson," he said with a shrug. "Kid likes basketball, has a crush on a classmate named Beth that he thinks his mom doesn't know about, and gets decent grades in school. It sounded to me like he's a bit of a loner, though—he's on the basketball team but his mom said none of his teammates were particularly friends. I didn't ask about anything too specific about him going missing because I figured she'd already been over it with someone else."

"That's good. Perfect." Dave jotted the info down on the edge of his command sheet and handed it off to Rick. "On the off chance he's not somewhere else and we do find him, he may be non-ambulatory. Sometimes the ability to chat about something else—basketball, probably, in this case—makes the difference between a panicking search target or a calm one. Okay, assignments."

"Three teams," Rick said, smoothly taking over the lead. The two of them had done this a million times, it felt like. "Steve, you and Nikita take the wedge from the road south. You're bounded by the road on this side, the cotton fields on the west, and the two-lane road a mile south of here. It's paved, so you won't miss it. Work your way east and pay special attention to places a thirteen-year-old might have gotten hurt, particularly any gullies or steep rock faces. Take a couple of the sheriff's guys with you and make sure they've got appropriate gear for the terrain before you leave."

"Got it."

"Scooter, you and Cheerio have the east side, from the road north. Sharon, take Scratch and cover the west. Make sure you take two deputies apiece. Janet, I'm keeping you and Zeus here as the relief team, or for when one of the other three calls for a second opinion on a hotspot. Who's got cell reception?"

Nobody had more than one bar, which meant they'd all have zilch once they were out in the woods. *Te-fucking-riffic.* The radios made for one more thing to carry. Maybe someday the team would get the money to upgrade to a newer, lighter model. Steve, Scooter, and Sharon ran a quick radio check with the base station in Rick's truck, then they went to get their dogs ready. Lito hovered attentively next to Rick, silently taking it all in.

"You go with Scooter," Dave told him. It would have been nice to pair up together, but Scooter tended to get more frustrated the longer the search took. Lito had the people skills to counteract that. "He's a good kid with a good head on his shoulders. Cheerio likes to range out pretty far, though, so help keep an eye on her. She's going to be focused on the scent and Scooter will be focused on her, so your job is going to be keeping the rest of the group from making it harder for them."

Lito huffed quietly. "Dunno how effective I'll be at that, but I'll try."

"It's not bad." Dave glanced over to where the sheriff's deputies were milling around. "Law enforcement in areas like this are almost always good ol' local boys. Most of them are comfortable with being in the woods, but that doesn't necessarily mean they know about how an air scent search is run. Keep them back behind Scooter, follow the exact path he takes so you don't mess with the scent cone, and try to keep them from doing anything stupid."

"Define stupid?"

Dave took a moment to review his mental "most frustrating search moments ever" reel. "Had a guy light up a cigarette right next to me once. Killed Lumpy's sense of smell for a good forty-five minutes. Car exhaust does that too, for future reference. Um…sometimes you get guys who don't bother bringing their own water, or who don't have a flashlight because it was daylight when you started. Inappropriate footwear for the terrain, although that's more an issue with volunteer searchers. Just—be aware, be polite, and be helpful. And absorb what you can for next time. I'm going to shadow Steve doing the same thing."

"Got it."

"Also...don't tell him I said this, but help Scooter keep his head on straight, okay? When he get tired he gets sloppier and starts missing Cheerio's tells. Don't worry about that part, just stay positive for him."

Lito nodded solemnly. "I'm ready to give it my best shot."

* * * *

Lito had only shared the usual kinds of casual interactions with Scooter at practices before, so it was nice to get a chance to chat as their crew picked their way through the woods. Scooter had close-cropped blue hair, was twenty-one to Lito's twenty-five, and was going to school part-time to become an EMT. He worked evenings and weekends at his parents' restaurant.

The EMT thing prompted some chatter back and forth with one of the sheriff's deputies, a blunt-spoken blonde who apparently had been considering a similar career path before she went into law enforcement. Lito focused on not twisting an ankle, trying to watch Cheerio as she ranged back and forth in a wide arc in front of them, and interjecting occasional noises of agreement as the conversation called for them. Dave had made it sound like Scooter would be paying full attention to Cheerio and therefore shouldn't be distracted, but he didn't seem to be having any problems walking and talking at the same time—unlike Lito—so Lito gave up and settled for calling Grayson's name every few minutes.

"Think we're going to find him?" he asked the other deputy, who was walking next to him.

The man grunted something that sounded like a negative.

"I'm honestly not expecting to," Scooter called back over his shoulder. "Our task is to clear the area. If he's in our quadrant, Cheerio will pick up his scent, but chances are he won't be."

"Most runaway teens are found hiding out at a friend's house," the male deputy explained to Lito. "No reason for him to be out in the middle of nowhere by himself."

"Gotta check, though." Scooter held back a branch for the rest of them as they squeezed through an overgrown patch, Cheerio bounding along ahead. "Once you get to the point you can trust Spot to *not* find someone who's not there—and to tell you when she's sure—that's when you're ready for call-outs."

It was going to take *forever*, judging from Spot's performance in training over the past several weeks. She was all about getting extra treats but less enthusiastic about the "finding people" part. "She's excellent at 'not finding things' already," Lito admitted. "Should see her when I have to give her a pill."

Scooter snorted. "You know what I mean. But speaking of seeing things…" He unclipped a flashlight from his belt and thumbed it on. Lito hadn't noticed how dark it was getting, but the light made a big difference. Being able to see his feet, for one. "Y'all make sure not to break your necks out here, okay? It's harder at dusk. If it comes down to you either falling down a hole or blinding Cheerio by shining your flashlight right in her face, though, it's a good thing we've got two almost-EMTs right here with ya."

He got a huff from the male deputy and a giggle from the blonde. More than a hint of flirting there. She looked to be in her early twenties too, and Scooter was obviously trying to be charming. Lito had to wonder whether the whole "pick up women during a missing kid search" ever actually worked for him. It didn't seem like it should—but then again, he and Dave had been maybe-possibly flirting ever since that first meeting in the pet store. Mostly via little "that was good" texts back and forth the morning after practice, but also the occasional joke when Lito did something stupid or Spot did something particularly clever. Even if Dave wasn't into dudes, he was—at the very least—okay with being subtly flirted at. And *Christ,* Scooter and the deputy had left "subtle" behind several miles back. The male deputy caught Lito's eye and made a face. *Not just me, then.* The blonde's attention kept Scooter from grumbling, at least.

They slogged on for another two hours in the dark. Which was an hour less than it should have been, thanks to the time change. Normally an extra hour of sleep in exchange for an earlier sunset would have sounded like a decent trade, but then again he normally didn't spend his whole afternoon and evening traipsing around a rocky hillside with only a flashlight to see by. Eventually Scooter relegated him to map duty. Lito called out Grayson's name every few minutes—shushing everyone else when he had to so they could hear if there was a response—but all he could ever make out were the distant sounds of sparse traffic.

"I think we've pretty thoroughly covered our grid," Scooter said, several miles of walking later. "Cheerio hasn't found a scent trail that's interested her for more than a hundred yards or so. Unless our kid has fallen into an underground cave or stumbled onto a magic invisible castle, he's probably not here."

Probably didn't sound like enough. "You going to have her keep searching on the way back, just in case?" Lito asked.

"Sure, but she's about ready to call it a day too. Look."

Cheerio was, indeed, not zipping around quite as enthusiastically as she had been in the beginning. The bright red glow stick attached to her vest appeared to be doing slow laps all on its own, now that it was dark enough for her chocolate coat to thoroughly blend in with the dead leaves on the ground. Lito checked his watch. Barely seven. He had protein bars in his backpack, but there was probably something better back at incident command. Something warm, if they were lucky—Dave had insinuated Rick kept a portable coffeemaker in the truck.

"Team Cheerio?" Rick called a few minutes later, his voice staticky from the mediocre radio connection. "Relaying from Team Nikita—Grayson has been found! You can stop searching and head straight back in."

Scooter whooped. "Roger that." He shoved the radio back into Lito's hands and jumped around, pumping his fist in the air a few more times. "Safe and unhurt! That's awesome."

Rick hadn't said that, at least not in so many words. "How do you know he's not hurt?"

"Called him Grayson." Scooter jiggled his shoulders in a move that would have gotten him laughed off the floor in most of the clubs Lito had ever been to. "We never, ever give details of a search over the radio," he added. "You never know who might be listening in, or standing next to a family member or a reporter. If a search target is deceased, injured, or anything else other than healthy and grumpy, we say we found 'Waldo.'"

Seriously? "Not a very complex code name."

Scooter shrugged, still twisting his hips and flailing his hands in what could loosely be termed a "raise the roof" gesture. "Blame Rick. Hang on—one last boogie." He finished with a final display of jazz hands. "Okay, let's get back. I'm freezing."

The female deputy was watching Scooter's strange victory celebrations with a raised eyebrow, but nobody seemed inclined to argue with the chance to get back and get warm again. Lito was appreciating the heavy NALSAR coat Dave had presented him with at the previous practice—his one-month mark with the team—but his search kit needed better gloves. And socks. Somehow over the course of the last forty-eight hours they'd gone from seventy-degree highs to what felt like seventy below zero. Even if the real temperature was only in the high thirties, that was a good thirty degrees colder than Lito was ready to appreciate. He couldn't even put both hands in his pockets at once without dropping the flashlight.

So Grayson is safe. Team Nikita had the find. Nikita was Steve's dog, which meant Dave had been in the group that found him. Maybe that meant he'd be willing to share details on the way home. It would probably be a bit rude to ask outright—"Hey, you know that missing kid you found? How hypothermic and scared was he? Tell me all the gruesome details." Yeah, not so much.

"This is my first," Scooter was telling the blonde when Lito caught back up to them on a flatter stretch of trail. "Been doing this for three years now, but most of the time we don't find out whether we were right or not until they get divers in the water or get the ground-penetrating radar thingy out to check for human remains. Live finds are usually 'live *not*-finds,' you know?"

The deputy shrugged, not slowing her pace in the slightest despite the terrain veering sharply upward for their last climb back to Grayson's house. "We don't get many either," she answered. "Mostly meth labs and regular old bar fights out here. I like the routine."

Cheerio came back as they passed the last of the trees and climbed the final rise alongside them. Her tongue was hanging out to one side and she looked glassy but happy. Scooter took her off to his car for some treats and an enthusiastic petting once they got back to the yard, but Lito headed straight for Dave's SUV and slung his pack into the back where Dave was tying down his own bag. Dave caught it, winked, and held up his keys.

"Might as well let the engine warm up," he declared. "Start her up and I'll be done in a sec. You want some coffee? Rick's got a plug-in pot in the van. It's not café quality but it's hot. No creamer or sugar left, unfortunately. Go ahead and sit here while the car warms up—I'll grab you one."

Lito started the engine, which immediately started blasting cold air out of the vents, then slumped into the passenger seat and made a good faith effort to clomp the dirt off his hiking boots before closing his door. Tired and jittery at the same time. *Wonderful.* Coffee was probably a terrible idea, but the idea of a warm beverage—any warm beverage—was just too good to pass up. Hell, even the two-month-old protein bar was sounding less awful.

"Here." Dave climbed in from the other side and set the coffee in the cupholder between them. "You good?"

"Yeah."

"Excellent." He settled into his own seat and let out a long, peaceful sigh which ended with a bit of a giggle. "That was incredible. Kid was freezing and miserable, but not a scratch on him. Hell of a first call-out for you." He leaned his head back against the headrest and closed his eyes. "Holy shit. I'm exhausted but so keyed up right now. You hungry?"

Lito glanced over toward Rick's van, where the other team members were milling around and helping load gear into the open side doors. "Don't we have to…I don't know, debrief or something?"

"We will, but not here." Dave jabbed a thumb toward the house, where presumably Grayson and his mother were talking with the county sheriff. "In the case of a successful sector clear or a probable deceased individual, we all meet back and finish up at incident command. For a live find, though, we're just in the way. Our part is done."

"That's a little anticlimactic."

Dave grinned. "I'm too hyped up to care. Give me five minutes to tell everyone we're clear and then we can head out."

Lito sipped his coffee and let the warmth permeate his fingers while Dave checked in with the rest of the team. One by one, everyone packed up and left, until only the squad cars were left.

"Damn," Dave said, climbing back in and buckling his seatbelt. "Still can't believe it went that well. What are you hungry for?"

Chapter 6

Dave's stomach was growling too loudly to worry about being picky and Lito insisted he didn't care, so he took them home via the city of Cullman itself. It added about twenty minutes to their trip, but that was twenty more minutes of flipping radio stations and hearing Lito sing. Dave didn't want to examine too closely why that felt so appealing. Once they got cell reception again, Lito pulled up a list of the handful of restaurants that were still open at eight o'clock on a Sunday night in Cullman, Alabama.

"Chain steakhouse, barbecue, another steakhouse, burgers…isn't there anywhere to get vegetables around here?" Lito scowled at his phone. "Chinese buffet is a possibility, I guess."

"You're a vegetarian?" Dave was caught off-guard at that, although he probably shouldn't have been. Avoiding animal products in the Bible Belt was possible in theory but had to be exhausting in practice.

"Not as such, no." Lito rubbed the back of his neck in a gesture that was seriously endearing. And decidedly sexy, in Dave's hyped-up state. "Nothing that would indicate a great moral stance or anything, anyway—I just avoid red meat. My dad couldn't eat it for health reasons so we never had it growing up. I never developed the taste for it, I guess."

"Let me guess: there were about a thousand more restaurant choices in Atlanta than there are in Black Lake."

"Got it in one. Ditto when I lived near Orlando. I've got no problem with chicken or seafood, though… Yeah, the deli is closed too. Guess we might as well try the Chinese."

The restaurant was well past the main part of Cullman, right at that distance where it could only loosely be called "in town," but it did smell good and there were a smattering of cars in the parking lot. Probably church-goers who preferred the evening services. The buffet turned out to be on the smallish side, but it was otherwise was no different from any of a zillion other Americanized Chinese restaurants. They did offer cornbread and fried okra mixed in among the other options, Dave noted. That part might not have been as universal. Lito's plate was crammed with variations on "healthy-looking things in sauce," but Dave's own food choices were squarely centered on "beige and fried." After that search, he'd damn well earned the right to eat whatever he wanted.

"So the search," Lito prompted once they were both back at the table. "Scooter made it sound like actually finding Grayson was unusual."

"Let me put it this way: we do probably forty or fifty searches a year. Rick and I have been running this team for ten years. Out of all those hundreds of searches, I can count on one hand the number of times we've actually found—unhurt—the kids we were looking for."

"Seriously?" Lito made a face. "Not like in movies, then."

"Worth it when they do happen, though." Dave had never sat down to do a full mental inventory, but live finds were what fueled the team's "remember when?" stories for years to come. "It's partly because we're usually searching for adults, of course, and also because a lot of those searches are for people we're pretty sure are deceased. But mostly it's that kids don't tend to get lost in the wilderness anywhere near as often as you'd expect. The woods have spider webs and poison ivy and no place to charge an iPad—not what most kids nowadays are looking for."

"Where do they turn up, then, when they do get reported missing? Are they usually runaways?"

"That, custody issues, or they're just sneaking around behind their parents' backs like our Waldo today was." The reasons did vary, but not by much. Hell, Dave vividly remembered sitting out on the bleachers with his friends after football practice most nights, horsing around and feeling invincible. Wandering along the cut-through to the cul-de-sac two blocks from Lito's house in hopes of finding something fun to do. Funny how much two tours in the Army changed your outlook on life.

"Huh." Lito mulled that over for a few bites. "Is it okay to talk about here?" he eventually asked. "I mean, Scooter explained the whole 'Waldo' thing..."

Despite the handful of cars in the lot, the nearest diners to their table were a good ten feet away. "It's not like there's confidential information we have to hide," Dave explained, "but it's not something to go blabbing to the news about either. I'm just in the habit of calling all our search targets 'Waldo' so I won't slip up." It said something good about Lito that the guy remembered to check, though.

"What happened today, then?"

A damn good find, is what. Dave closed his eyes and felt a delicious shiver run down his spine as he remembered the moment of Nikita's jubilant alert all over again. "Grayson was tired and cold, as you'd expect, but unhurt. Nikita hit on his scent cone a ways out and followed it up a gulley to what basically looked like the kid's secret hideout. A good quarter mile from the road, tucked in under a rock overhang. Hard to see unless you already knew where it was. I got the impression he hung out there a lot—tarp, blankets, folding chair, big Tupperware bin full of Penthouse and Playboys. The usual. He did have a hell of a hangover, though, which is probably making all the aftermath a little less fun."

"Grayson was drinking?" Lito looked honestly surprised at that. "He's only in seventh grade!"

Clearly middle school in Miami was *way* different than in Alabama. Seventh grade was supposed to be for fishing, getting random wood at the stupidest of times, and drinking your first shitty beer with your friends while hiding out somewhere your parents wouldn't see. Dave had never particularly thought of his own experience as odd before.

"He definitely was this time," Dave said, "but I don't think it was a usual thing for him to drink alone." There hadn't been any accumulated beer bottles, despite a plethora of soda cans and snack debris strewn about. "Short of it was, you remember the thing his mom told you about him having a crush on a girl?"

Lito nodded. "Beth, she said."

"That's the one. He lied to his mom so he could sneak out and walk over to her house. She lives about two miles down the road—not far at all, when you're a determined thirteen-year-old. I didn't push for details, but it sounds like he asked her out and she rejected him. He decided to break into his mom's liquor cabinet and go get totally smashed in his secret clubhouse. Typical teenager drama; you know how it is."

"I didn't date until I was eighteen, so not really, but I've seen plenty of movies." Lito made a *what-can-you-do* face. "Mine was far more typical than it should have been, unfortunately."

Dave had a sneaking suspicion that this "drama" was code for "homophobia," but Lito had never actually said he was gay. There was the earring and the tight shirts and the amazing fashion sense and the bubble butt and maybe Dave was *hoping*, but the dude had a right to come out—or not—at his own pace. "Parents disapproved of who you brought home?" he asked instead. "Or—let me guess. Were you full-on goth? Refused to do your homework? I'm trying to picture you as a teenager now." He'd probably been a good-looking kid, Dave decided, skinny and smiling most of the time. And with those brown eyes…

Lito opened his mouth, then closed it again. He finally seemed to make a decision. "Didn't so much bring someone home as get caught using my cousin's fake ID to sneak into a gay club," he said in a low voice. "My family didn't take it the best."

"Well shit." *That answers that.* It made Dave feel a bit less rude for perving over the mental images of Lito that kept popping into his head as of late. Not that Lito liking men was a huge surprise, but confirmation was still good. And, he realized, something he himself had probably been remiss in not voicing earlier. Lito's skittishness suddenly made much more sense. "I'm sorry you went through that," he said aloud. "I held off on all-the-way coming out for a few years because the Army was still in the middle of Don't Ask Don't Tell, but it was an open secret for a long time. My family knew, and my non-Army friends, but I couldn't talk about it to anyone in training or when I was deployed."

That earned him a long, thoughtful look. "You know," Lito said slowly, "my gaydar has been giving me mixed signals ever since I met you and it's been driving me crazy. You didn't have that embarrassed, wary look straight guys sometimes get when they first meet me, but you didn't come off as overtly queer either."

"You're not the first to say that."

Lito snorted. "It's nice to know I'm not the only non-straight dude in Black Lake, though. Are you out to the team?"

"Oh, sure." He'd mentioned guys in passing, if not in full detail. Most of those guys had been one-night stands when he and his friend Gus met up in Tennessee to prowl their favorite nightclub together. "I'm not gonna lie to you—Black Lake isn't Atlanta. You'd probably get some strange looks if you walked through downtown holding hands with another man. Nobody on the team has a problem with me being gay, though, and it's not like any of the other squads we work with are in a position to say anything. I don't advertise my orientation, but I don't hide it either."

Dave made a point of not looking at Lito's earring. It was a tasteful little gold stud today. Absolutely nothing about Lito suggested *hide*—he probably set off gaydars for miles. Not as a hundred-percent-certain thing, more in a "damn, that guy's gotta hate correcting people all the time if he's straight" way. There was something admirable in being that comfortable with yourself. And there was definitely something good about finally having the mutually queer thing out in the open between them.

"That's…good to know," Lito said, and pushed a bit of broccoli around on his plate. "I'm assuming there isn't a 'scene' in town?"

His tone was nonchalant, like it was an idle question, but Dave had to laugh at how Lito was practically holding his breath for the answer. "Do karaoke Fridays at the VFW count?" he asked. Lito glared, which sobered him a bit. "Sorry. I know what you meant. And any 'scene' in Black Lake barely lives up to the name, especially if you're comparing it to what you're probably used to. On the rare occasions I'm looking to cut loose, I go to Nashville."

"Yeah, okay. I didn't think there would be, but I was hoping."

Dave didn't have to imagine very hard to picture Lito being totally at home in a gay club, Nashville or otherwise. He'd almost certainly wear something like that pink t-shirt he'd had on at the pet store when they first met, and he'd meticulously gel his hair so it stayed frozen in a maximally attractive swoop across his forehead. He probably owned some tighter-than-tight jeans too, and he'd have his eyes closed out on the dance floor as he ground against some other, similarly decked-out dude. Oh, and he'd totally be singing along with whatever pop diva was blasting at the time.

No, that wasn't right. In Dave's mind, the generic dance floor resolved into his regular haunt in Nashville and the "other dude" morphed a bit to look suspiciously like himself. Someone who was tall enough to get right up behind Lito and surround him as he danced, palms skimming over his chest and broader shoulders dwarfing his smaller form. Lito would lean his head back in pleasure and Dave would be able to nip at his neck and yell-whisper over the music *exactly* what he intended to do to him when he got him alone…

And that was going to get awkward pretty damn quick. "So." Dave looked down at his almost-empty plate. "Normally I'd be all for a dessert round of off-brand Jell-O and soap-flavored cookies, but I think I took more food on that first trip than I intended. I'm going to skip the encore tonight."

"Same." Lito set his fork down and nudged his plate toward the center of the table. "You want to get going? I'm not in any particular hurry—Spot is probably enjoying the chance to shed over my whole bed instead of just her usual half—but I guess it's still a ways back to Black Lake."

"Might as well." Lumpy and Woozy were almost certainly already asleep on the sofa, curled into each other and making adorable snuffling noises, but they'd be up and waiting the moment they heard the garage door. They knew the drill. "Probably an hour or so from here."

They split the bill and headed back out to the parking lot. The air had gotten noticeably colder as the evening turned into night, but there was a tiny sliver of a moon and the afternoon's clouds had blown away. Dave gave himself a moment to stare at the sky and take it all in.

"You into astronomy?" Lito asked, pausing beside him and following his gaze.

"Not the science part." Not the way his dad knew all the physics details, anyway. "It just reminds me of camping trips when I was a kid, lying in the tent with the tarp unzipped so we could watch the stars. My mom and my older brother Jack never wanted to go, so it was usually just me and Dad and my little brother Kitt. Dad knows all the constellations and all the other little random facts like which stars are how far away, which planets have which moons... Stuff like that. Kitt ate it all up, numbers and all, but I just liked the myths. He's a meteorology tech for NASA in Huntsville now."

"Huh. There was too much light pollution to see much of the night sky in Miami," Lito said, "but it's pretty. And *big*. I can see why y'all like it."

Dave looked down and caught a hint of something on Lito's face that completely knocked him for a loop. It wasn't "wonder," necessarily, but it was joyous and open and honest and Dave abruptly realized he'd do just about anything to see that same look in a different situation. One that involved both of them wearing far less clothing. Someone had to make the first move, and it might as well be him. "You know," he said slowly and with as much innuendo as he could muster, "anytime you want me to help you see stars, all you gotta do is ask."

Lito blinked at him. "You're...am I reading too much into that, or was that a come-on?"

"Depends. Which interpretation involves you having a better night? Because if you want me to take you home and pretend I never said anything, I will. If you feel like us finding somewhere with fewer lights so we can appreciate the stars from the comfort of my Jeep, though...then yeah, it was a come-on."

Lito cocked his head to one side. "Is making out in the backseat another one of those typical teenager things I somehow missed out on?"

He hadn't said yes, yet, but there was a definite interested note in Lito's voice. It was more than a little promising, and plenty to get Dave's heart pounding. "I guess I'll give you a pass"—Dave mock-sighed—"seeing as Miami probably lacks both clear skies and big SUVs. Stargazing was a staple of adolescence around here, though."

"You lose your v-card in the back seat of a boyfriend's pickup?"

Oh yeah. Definitely interested. "In an EconoLodge just after Basic, actually," Dave admitted, "but...I'll just say I spent a lot of time in high school dreaming about it." He stepped away and dared a long, thorough once-over of Lito's body. Even in the yellow-orange glow of the parking lot streetlight, the dude looked good enough to eat. "Like I said—no pressure, but you'd be fulfilling a major fantasy of mine. If you want."

Lito paused, for so long Dave was afraid he'd majorly fucked things up. Then... "I suppose I could say it's contributing to my cultural education."

* * * *

Holy fucking shit. Lito rode silently in the passenger seat and focused on trying not to hyperventilate. *Dave Schmidt really is gay, and he wants to get horizontal with me.* It felt too good to be true. And okay, the offer may have only been made because dudes who do dudes were slim pickings in Black Lake and backseat sex was apparently on Dave's bucket list, but *damn.* Lito wasn't too proud to take him up on his offer no matter the circumstances.

Dave took them through some strange network of back roads he must have known well—he didn't once consult his phone's GPS—and they ended up in an utterly dark parking lot at an overlook, out of sight from the main road. The headlights briefly illuminated a sign for a trailhead, meaning they were probably at some sort of greenway or park, but Lito didn't get a chance to actually read the name.

"Wish it weren't so cold outside," Dave muttered. "Give me one sec." He clambered through to the back—impressively agile for someone with such broad shoulders—and fiddled with something until there was a *clunk* and the back seat folded down entirely. Dave reached up to open the shade on the sunroof, then motioned Lito back to join him. There was barely enough light to make out the gesture. "Not sure I can name *all* the constellations anymore, but I can at least point out the major ones."

"Wait...you meant you actually want to tell me about the stars?" Between the flattened back seat and the huge cargo area, Dave's Jeep easily had enough room for both of them to lie down in. He'd assumed the whole astronomy thing was just a cheesy pick-up line, but apparently not.

Dave snorted. "I'll have you know I bought this Grand Cherokee *precisely* for this super-giant sunroof. I sleep back here sometimes when I go camping, and I like seeing the stars." He patted the carpeted floor beside him. "I also needed something big enough to haul Lumpy and Woozy around in. I put a sheet down when they're here so I can take it out and wash it, but I'm glad I left that at home tonight. The delightful dog smell is still pretty permanent, unfortunately—I can promise you're not going to get covered in fur and dried slobber, though."

"Yeah, thanks for that." Lito gingerly climbed through and settled himself on his back. There was still a good eighteen inches of space between his feet and the back door of the Jeep, which meant probably eight or so for Dave. The man was a damn tree. Even without the full use of his night vision, Lito could *sense* Dave's presence in the enclosed space. The air did smell a bit like Rottweiler, but—whether it was his imagination or not—it also smelled like the man next to him.

"I'll start with the easy ones," Dave said, his voice quiet and serious. "You don't get the full picture at this time of year, especially with the moon so close to full, but that bright swath across the sky just above the horizon is the Milky Way. Look out the back window there. It's not visible unless you're really out in the middle of nowhere, but in the summer it's a smear of light overhead and it's stunning. You can read all the charts and diagrams about how the universe is laid out and why galaxies are shaped different ways, and that's great, but it's always blown my mind that you can actually *see* it. We're looking sideways from the inside and you can see with your own eyes that the Milky Way really is flat. And huge."

"Makes you feel little by comparison?"

Dave's rumble of amusement was low enough Lito felt the vibration in his bones. "I've never in my life been little," he replied. "That's if you ask my mom, anyway—I was a ten-pound baby and just kept growing from there. But yeah, I think that's part of why it gets me. We're...we're *nowhere*, you know? And yet we don't even acknowledge we're insignificant. All the constellations—Orion is centered around that line of three brighter stars just there, follow where I'm pointing—all the constellations are only because the ancient Romans *literally* assumed we're the center of the universe. That our stupid little human dramas are important enough to make up all those countless stars. It does put things in perspective."

Lito was having a hard time with *perspective* at the moment. The night sky was beautiful, no question, but Dave's bicep was within nibbling distance as he pointed out the three brighter stars. Even in the near-total darkness, Lito could still tell how well-muscled the guy was. They both smelled a bit sweaty too, after the long search and all the tromping around, but Dave's deodorant was heady and slightly spicy and Lito had always had a weakness for that whole masculine scent thing. Which was outweighing the dog smell by a large margin now. "Tell me another one?"

Dave's head turned, like he was trying to make out Lito's expression in the dark. "Up there, then." He reached down and folded his hand around

Lito's, then pointed them both upward toward a clump of brighter stars in the other half of the sky. "Those four make the 'cup' part of the Big Dipper, which is also a part of Ursa Major. It's a bear in Roman mythology, but weirdly enough it's a bear in a lot of other cultures' stories too. Ursa Minor is right there next to it, including the Little Dipper. You see them?"

"Yes," Lito breathed. God, he really was acting like a teenager, wasn't he? Dave's hand was warm and bigger than his own and Lito was already getting dizzy imagining what those hands would feel like on his body.

Dave obviously noticed—instead of letting Lito's hand go, he lightly ran his palm down the outside of Lito's forearm. The barely-there touch drew goosebumps...right up until he accidentally elbowed Lito in the forehead.

"Shit! Sorry."

"It's okay."

Dave propped himself up on the offending elbow. "What I *intended* to communicate in a more suave and much less clumsy way was, are your eyes adjusting to the starlight yet? Because I can see you now, but doing something more than just looking would be even better." He ducked his head a bit. "Smacking you in the face wasn't what I meant, though, so I guess I can't see as well as I thought I could."

Lito lightly shoved at Dave's shoulder, mostly just for the excuse to touch him again. "There, we're even now." Dave didn't pull away, barely even registered Lito pushing him, so Lito gave into temptation and turned further to bury his nose against Dave's collarbone. "Same for me, though," he murmured back. "I can't see your expression, but I can at least tell where I should be kissing."

"Mmm—feel free to kiss me anywhere you like." Dave dropped down to lie on his side too, so they were face to face in the almost-dark. "Hope you'll forgive me if I accidentally get you in the face again, though."

"I'd forgive you anything right now." Lito had to grope a bit to get his hand positioned properly over the edge of Dave's jaw, but once he had his bearings it was easy to hone in on Dave's lips.

Goddamn. He thought he'd been ready, thought it would be like all the times he'd done this before with whoever he was dating or fucking at the time, but Dave managed to be simultaneously both tender and forceful. Lito had to fight to keep his brain from dissolving into mush. Not that he'd mind that, with Dave so skillfully teasing him into trying to keep up, but if he let the incredible *rightness* of the kiss drag him under he knew he'd be begging Dave for all sorts of embarrassing things soon after.

"You taste like pineapple," Dave murmured. "Now I want to kiss you after every meal so I can keep track of how you taste each time. What about the rest of you, I wonder?" He shifted sideways and downward, so he was nuzzling along Lito's jawline. "Like right...*here.*"

Lito may have groaned at the feel of Dave's tongue doing fantastic things to the tender spot right under his earlobe. "Fuck," he breathed. "I think I just forgot everything you tried to teach me about stars."

"Did you?" Dave licked again, this time accompanied by the barest hint of teeth. "I should stop, then, and tell you again."

"Shut up." It took a few tries, but Lito eventually managed to insinuate a hand under Dave's coat and t-shirt. Everything was more intense in the dark—the heat radiating off Dave's body, the way Dave's breath ghosted over the spot he'd just licked and sent shivers down Lito's spine, the press of his own cock against his zip like it thought it could get free by way of sheer optimism. The way the hair on Dave's chest caught at Lito's fingers as he slid his palm upward. *Fuck.* It was so tempting to just grab Dave's hips and slam their pelvises together so they could grind on each other, but Dave was still being maddeningly slow. Coming across as a complete idiot with no self-control would be...not good.

That resolution got infinitely harder when Dave started mirroring Lito's moves, sliding a hand under Lito's shirt and running his fingertips gently back and forth just above the waistband of his jeans. "This okay?" he asked quietly. "Because you teased me about this being a 'typical teenager thing,' but right now I honestly do feel like I'm seventeen again. I haven't had my hands on anyone else's cock in way too long and I'm dying to see what I can do with yours." He pulled back just enough to press another firm kiss to Lito's lips. "Reciprocation is highly encouraged, of course."

"Yeah, that's...oh fuck. Yeah." Lito couldn't control the reflexive buck of his hips at the thought, even as the less-reassuring implications of Dave's comment filtered through his fuzzy brain. *I'm probably just the convenient cock, then. Right place, right time. The only candidate.* It should have bothered him more than it did, but he brushed the thought aside—the rest of his brain was filled with *yes, touch, please!* and plain old anticipation. He slid his own hand down Dave's stomach (damn, he could *feel* the definition on those abs) and hesitated over his fly.

"Fuck. Yes. Do it." Dave fumbled at Lito's zipper, and a literal shiver ran through Lito's body as his cock finally got a bit of breathing room. He tried to do the same, but the angle was all wrong and Dave's muscled forearms were in the way. They ended up doing a bit of not-at-all-sexy awkward groping in the dark before Lito finally succeeded in getting Dave's jeans open. He was wearing boxers under them, the fabric silky and warm from his body heat. Dave's low groan when Lito finally pulled him out and got ahold of the hard-on underneath was just short of breathtaking.

"Like this?"

"Nngh." Dave thrust against him a few times before swearing again and sitting up so he could tug at Lito's jeans more effectively. "Like anything you want—I'm *really* not gonna complain right now. Get these down so we can reach each other."

Lito wriggled his pants down to mid-thigh, then decided *screw it* and shoved them all the way down to his ankles. The bite of the rough carpet under his hip felt grounding. Welcome. If Dave didn't care, they might as well fulfill one of Lito's fantasies too—in this case, that involved rolling them both so he was straddling Dave's hips. He braced his weight on one arm and ground down on that gorgeous body in the dark.

Dave grunted in surprise. "Toppy, are we?"

Hell yes, because turnabout is fair play. Lito stretched up to nibble at whatever parts of Dave's skin he could reach above the collar of Dave's still-sweat-scented t-shirt. "You assume because I'm little, I've got to be a bottom?"

"I…" Dave faltered at that, but quickly got his hand back on Lito's cock and resumed his exploring. "Maybe I was. Sorry—not really thinking with the right head at the moment. 'S too good."

"Good." Lito nuzzled lower and focused on Dave's left nipple through the thin cotton. "Because beyond the obvious issues like the lack of supplies, I think I'd have a problem lasting all that long inside you." He was already feeling the flutters that warned of his impending point of no return, and they'd barely done more than make out. *Fuck.* "You feel so good, you smell so good, and if you—*oh!*—if you keep doing what you're doing with your thumb right now I'm gonna have to put some effort into catching you up really, really fast." He ran his palm over the head of Dave's cock, smearing precome everywhere, then adjusted to a firmer grip and tried to match Dave stroke for stroke. The backs of their hands brushed together as they moved in tandem, speeding up the more Lito nibbled at those toned pecs, until Dave nudged him upward with a grunt and used his free hand to pull Lito down for a sloppy kiss that was more panting than anything else. Lito shifted his grip one more time and then Dave's entire body was tensing up and he was gasping into Lito's mouth. Lito stayed right where he was, easing up to let Dave ride out the aftershocks but not pulling away. Which was just as well, because Dave rallied quickly. The not-actually-a-kiss acquired a lot more technique, then Dave got his free hand on Lito's bare ass right as he did something new to the relentless rhythm on Lito's cock—he was too far gone to determine what—and suddenly he was following Dave over in a heady rush.

"Fuck." Dave held him in place for a few moments, supporting his full weight, then let Lito roll off and flop boneless on the floor beside him. "Just so you know, I think I've forgotten everything I knew about the constellations too."

Now that Lito's brain was capable of non-sex-related concepts again, he realized the faint starlight really was bright enough to see Dave's expression. A hint of it, anyway. He looked exactly as blissed-out as Lito felt. "I'd say this experience was still memorable," Lito deadpanned.

And Dave grinned. "I should hope so." He sucked in a deep breath and let it out in a long, contented sigh. "This whole day has been. Thank you."

"Ditto." Now that the fevered, frantic part of the evening was over, Lito had to lock everything away in his memory for later. No telling whether Dave would want to get off together again, but Lito had every intention of saving the experience as future spank bank material. Just the vague thought of Dave's firm pecs pressed against his stomach was going to make him hard forevermore. "Guess you can cross 'sex under the stars in the back of your Jeep' off your list, now."

Dave rolled to his side, pillowing his head on his bent arm and regarding Lito steadily. "You too," he said.

Truck sex hadn't exactly been on Lito's bucket list to start with, but he nodded anyway. "Yeah," he echoed. "Me too."

Chapter 7

*Did Spot miss you while you were gone
yesterday? I'm glad you came!*

Lito sat at his desk staring off into space for way longer than he should have after reading Dave's text. Was "came" a double entendre? Was Dave flirting, or had he totally gotten over the whole handjob thing and he was talking about the search instead? It seemed wrong to reply to such an ambiguous opener with anything suggestive—especially since he was at work—but pretending last night hadn't happened might send the wrong signal too. He finally settled on something simple.

*She enjoyed all the different smells on me,
I'm sure. We'll keep making progress and
someday we can be Team Spot together.*

Hopefully that would be subtle enough—especially since the most prominent smell in Lito's memory was the mixture of sex and sweat (and, okay, dog) while they both lay there panting after getting each other off. He really didn't want to think about what Spot concluded when he got home.

Work dragged, as it usually did on Monday mornings. He'd run out of "settling in" tasks before the weekend, his office was fully unpacked, and his inbox was empty. Time to bite the bullet and start checking out local artists. "Local" in a general sense, anyway—Black Lake was too small to house a thriving indie art scene, which meant he'd be clocking some time on the road. Dave had implied there was a scene in Nashville, however far away that was. Huntsville, maybe? His regular sources in Atlanta, if it was absolutely necessary. Usually Lito tried to find a painter in the same area the hotel in question was located, someone whose work screamed "look, this is what this town has to offer!" Having reliable last-minute backup sources was a must, though. Artists tended to be artsy, which in Lito's experience meant they flaked on deadlines a lot more often than the rest of the population. At the moment Dayspring was building a new hotel in Muscle Shoals, Alabama, renovating one near Birmingham, and was rebuilding another one down on the coast in Mobile. Muscle Shoals and Birmingham were close enough for a day trip; Mobile definitely wasn't.

> *I have faith in both of you—you're doing*
> *great so far! I've got no complaints.*

That…didn't exactly clear up the ambiguity, did it? Lito put his phone down and tried to focus on work for a few more minutes, but he finally gave in and just asked.

> *Which part of last night are you*
> *not complaining about?*
>
> *Sorry, not fishing for compliments, just still trying to figure*
> *out how much to read into the "so glad you came" thing.*

Dave's response chimed almost instantly, a rapid-fire string of texts all in a row:

> *When I wrote it I meant glad you*
> *came along on the call-out*
>
> > *But now that you mention it, I can see how*
> > *you were confused by my wording*

How's this: I'm glad you came along
to the search yesterday

> *It was just about the best possible first search*
> *experience you could have had*

I enjoyed chatting with you at dinner—
we should do that again sometime

And ON A COMPLETELY UNRELATED NOTE you should
know I jacked off in the shower this morning to the memory
> *of how you moaned when you got close to coming*

Best ever start to my day, bar none

> *I'd love to add taste to that particular memory, though*

I got to taste your mouth, but not the rest of you

> *We ought to change that.*

Was that clear enough for you? ;-)

It was. It *so* definitely was. Lito had to shift in his chair to keep his burgeoning hard-on from pressing quite so tightly against his trousers—thank God he had his own office. His sudden intake of breath and racing heart would be difficult to explain to any of his coworkers.

I'm assuming you're at work (I am too) but any
chance you'd be able to do lunch? You're at the
Dayspring Inn over near the highway, right?

> *Today I'm trimming back kudzu down at the boat ramp*
> *off Jennings Drive, so I'll only be about a mile up the*
> *road from you. It's a beautiful day for a picnic.*

No privacy for much else, unfortunately, but that's
probably for the best since I'm a city employee
and will still be officially on the clock ;-)

Lito's office had no actual windows, so he had to take Dave at his word on the weather, but the idea of a picnic lunch actually sounded really nice. So far he'd mostly been bringing a bag lunch and eating at his desk. The office did have the conference room—which Lito eventually learned was functionally more like a break room than anything else because any conferences any of them had were inevitably over the phone—but Carrie and Heather and Laura Beth tended to congregate there and gossip for their entire lunch breaks and there was no part of those conversations that Lito was even remotely interested in participating in. They were polite enough, and Laura Beth had made a point of bringing in pictures of her son's birthday celebration so Lito could see how much fun the kids had with the suggestions he'd given, but he'd never felt so much like a fish out of water. Spending some social time with Dave, even platonic, was seriously appealing.

I haven't had a picnic in ages. What time?

Whatever morning-after awkwardness he and Dave were facing, it had to be better than the alternative.

* * * *

Dave was well overdue for a break by the time Lito pulled into the boat launch area at ten after twelve. It really was a beautiful day—probably the last week of decent temperatures they'd have until the new year, thanks to Alabama's screwy up-and-down weather—but Dave had spent the last four hours hacking at the invasive kudzu vines and he felt more than a bit ripe. Sweaty and stinky weren't really ideal for a lunch date. Clearing out the underbrush around the landing had been on the to-do list for months, though, and the exercise gave him a chance to stretch after spending most of the last week in his cramped office, so plant warfare it was. He was gathering his initial debris into a pile in the corner of the parking lot when Lito pulled in.

"Hey," Dave called out by way of greeting. He waved Lito toward his work truck. "No picnic table here, but I wiped the truck bed for us. I'll join you in just a minute. What'd you bring?"

"Decided to try that sub sandwich place I keep driving past." Lito tossed him one of the bottles of water and held up two bags for Dave to pick from. "You prefer veggie or chicken salad? They both looked good so I'm fine with either. I went minimal on the toppings—but you can pick them off if you didn't like them."

"Chicken salad, then."

Dave finished piling up the cuttings and joined Lito on the tailgate of the battle-scarred work truck. They ate in silence for a while, looking out over the water. Black Lake itself wasn't all that big, but it was murky—good for fishing, bad for swimming. It was beautiful in the sunlight, though. The foliage around them was a mixture of still-green and autumn colors and the dark surface of the lake rippled gently whenever a stray puff of wind drifted across it. Dave tried to remember the last time he'd been out on the water. Just over two years ago, probably—whenever the last practice they'd used the boat had been, before Steve's ex-wife sold it. Before Jessica quit the team in a show of solidarity with her mother leaving and Steve started drinking more than he ought. Back when the team actually did things together outside of practices sometimes. Rick and Sharon used to have a big Fourth of July picnic every summer, friends and family all invited. It's how they'd recruited Scooter, once upon a time—he'd been dating someone's friend's sister and stuck around because he missed having a dog.

"Penny for your thoughts?" Lito asked. He'd already finished his sub sandwich and was now leaning back against the wall of the truck bed. "Or do I not want to know?"

It was quite possibly the first time all day Dave's thoughts *hadn't* involved sex in general and memories of the previous night in particular. "Nothing much, honestly," he said. "Was thinking about the lake and realized I haven't been out on the water since the summer before last. I miss it."

"What, boating?"

"That and fishing. Well, and running water finds with the team." God, they were all so out of practice. "We used to have a boat to use—it was Steve's—but his wife sold it two years ago. Without telling him."

"Damn."

"It was her opening shot before she served him with the divorce papers."

"*Damn.*"

"Pretty much." Dave twisted around to settle next to him, sideways in the truck bed. "Not sure whether it's been mentioned since you've been on the team or not, but Steve was actually the coroner here in Black Lake for over thirty years."

Lito made a noncommittal noise. "Nobody's said it, but I read between the lines. Got the impression he's been doing this for a while."

"The dog team's only been since he retired, but yes. He's been dealing with dead people since before they were using DNA." Dave finished off the last dregs of his water and set the bottle aside. Talking behind a teammate's back like this should have felt at least a little weird, especially since Dave couldn't remember having ever had someone to share details like this *with*, but it honestly didn't feel like gossip. The divorce wasn't something Steve had ever been particularly shy griping about, either. "The two of them were married for most of that, but she had some mental health and medical issues about a decade ago that totally changed her personality. By the time Steve got involved with the team the two of them were already pretty distant. He and his stepdaughter Jessica joined NALSAR together as a bonding thing, but his wife never approved. The divorce was a surprise, but not…well, not unexpected to anyone but Steve. Things were awkward for a long time."

"That sucks." Lito rolled up a little piece of his napkin and tossed it at the opposite side of the truck bed. "'Distant' would probably have been a good word for my parents' marriage, I think. They had nothing in common."

"By 'had,' do you mean they're divorced now? Or has one of them passed away?" Dave winced. "Sorry, didn't mean it to come out like that. I was just curious."

"It's okay. And as far as I know they're still together, but I haven't spoken with them in almost eight years now." He grimaced. "No way they'd divorce, though—the Church wouldn't allow it."

"Ah." The conversation felt like it was teetering on the edge of way too personal and was going to tip over into pissing Lito off any minute now, but Dave had no idea what to say to pull it back from the brink. "Um. Catholic, I'm guessing?"

"Yeah."

"Is that why…"

"Why I haven't kept up with them?" Lito crumpled up and threw another little ball of paper. Fidgeting. *Uncomfortable.* "It's mutual," he finally said. "I told you yesterday about how I got caught sneaking into a gay club."

Dave nodded.

"My cousin—the one who'd lent me his ID—he found out from some coworker of his who recognized me there. He went and told my parents and there was a big screaming argument about it. I'd known I wasn't into girls for a few years at that point, had half the gay stereotypes already down pat, but they'd never even considered the idea of me being gay. Mom kept saying she couldn't understand how I could be 'corrupted' so badly by the evil American media."

"They're not originally from here, I'm guessing?"

He was rewarded with a tiny flash of a smile. "We're originally from Lima," Lito answered. "Peru. My Uncle Diego runs a shipping company in Miami and he recruited his brothers—my dad and my two other uncles—to come work for him. The whole family moved here when I was two years old. My mom still doesn't speak much English."

"But they're both pretty religious?"

"That's putting it lightly."

"How did you…" Dave took a deep breath and tried to phrase himself correctly. "What happened between that and you ending up in Atlanta? And how old were you? If that's not too personal for me to ask?"

"It's fine—I was a senior in high school. I turned eighteen a few months later. A few weeks after the fight—and my parents realizing the whole gay thing wasn't just me being difficult—they essentially disowned me. Well, it was mutual, but the end result was I left. Stayed with my cousin Gabriela for the rest of the year so I could finish school, but we both knew the family would cut her off too if they found out. Day after graduation I packed a bag and bummed a ride with some friends out of town." He grimaced. "I ended up getting a job as the night clerk in a crappy little Dayspring Inn off I-4 near Orlando, mostly because they needed someone bilingual who could start right away and would work for peanuts."

"And you liked it?"

"I was good at it." Lito pinned him with a serious look. "I'm good with people, I'm a natural night owl, and I like fixing problems. Eventually I met the owners of the chain—they're an older couple from Atlanta, really sweet and *very* southern but good business sense—and I guess they liked me because I got promoted to night manager and then to the main office in Atlanta to do design and logistical management. It went from there. I've been working for Dayspring ever since."

"Damn." Dave could absolutely see it, could see an eighteen-year-old Lito pacifying grumpy tourists and being ridiculously charming while doing so. "That really does suck about your family not accepting you, but I'm glad you landed on your feet."

Lito studied him intently for several moments before saying, "You actually are, aren't you? That's…thanks."

God, it must have been lonely. "Glad you're here too, for what it's worth." *Bit of an understatement.* "I know it's probably not as exciting you're used to—"

Lito laughed out loud.

"—but I like it. You. Here." *Fuck.* He sounded embarrassingly like a middle schooler trying to ask out his first big crush. "What I mean is, thanks for meeting up for lunch with me and letting me pry a bit too much into your personal life. And I'm not just saying that because I want you and Spot on the team."

"Oh?" Lito shot him a sideways look. A sultry, sexy look. "Does that mean you want a repeat of last night? Because I wasn't sure until you texted this morning, but now you're making it sound…"

Crap. "Yes," Dave said quickly. Too quickly. "Sorry about sending that while you were at work, but I didn't want you to think…hell. Last night was good and if you'd be up for something similar in the very near future, I wouldn't be opposed. Just"—he grimaced and glanced down at his grimy *Black Lake Maintenance Department* uniform, currently covered in Alabama clay and bits of kudzu—"not now, unfortunately."

"Of course not." Lito twitched his leg where it was lying parallel to Dave's, so the toes of his shiny black shoe thunked the top of Dave's work boot. "If nothing else, my lunch break isn't *that* long." He winked. It should have looked corny but it didn't. "Not nearly long enough to get into any real trouble, anyway."

Dave couldn't help winking back. "Later, though?"

"Take me out to dinner again on Friday night and we'll see about it."

"It's a deal."

Lito really did have to get back to his office, apparently, but Dave bushwhacked invasive underbrush for the rest of the afternoon with significantly more vigor.

Chapter 8

Everyone was going to know.

Lito gave Spot a good few minutes of attention before getting out of the car the next afternoon at practice, mostly because it was an excuse to delay a bit longer. Surely Dave wouldn't have gone and announced anything (*"Hey everyone, just to let you know, that gay dude I invited to the team totally put out for me last night so we should be nice to him because he's got a cute ass"*) but that didn't mean nobody else would be perceptive.

He needn't have worried. The whole team showed up on time, for once, and the sole topic of conversation was how Steve and Nikita found Grayson White. Everybody had already heard the story, or some variation of it, but Steve cheerfully rehashed it for Lito when he joined the crowd around the picnic table.

"I couldn't believe it," Steve said for about the fifth time since Lito got within earshot. "Kid was sitting there, huddled up against the rock and wrapped up in half a dozen blankets. Didn't respond when we were calling his name, so when I first saw him I assumed the worst, but he was actually just most of the way through a bottle of his mom's rum and didn't feel like talking to anyone. Told Dave to fuck off. Nikita was prancing around—she *knew* she done good. I emptied the whole damn treat bag and chirped all big and happy at her until she finally gave me this look like 'okay, really, I know you're faking it.' Twit."

Nikita paused in her mock-wrestling with Scratch and Sniff to look up at him, a hopeful "Are you talking about me?" on her face, which made Rick laugh.

Dave was smiling too, which warmed Lito's heart in a way he didn't want to examine too closely. The man had a gorgeous little-boy smile. It should have been incongruous with his build, but somehow it fit him. He didn't do it all that often, but when he did it always felt like they were sharing a secret—or that they'd just done something naughty and their teacher was going to find out sooner or later. Lito treasured every one of those smiles he'd earned over the course of their acquaintance.

"Since we're all here and ready to go," Dave announced, "I'll make the official team debrief quick. Y'all did a fantastic job yesterday, and I'm really proud of you. Ditto for Nikita, Scratch, Cheerio, and Zeus. That was tricky terrain in the dark and everyone came prepared to give it a hundred percent. It showed too—I've gotten several comments from other rescue squads congratulating us on our find. I also got an update from the sheriff last night to let us know that Grayson is home and doing fine. The EMTs treated him for mild hypothermia and dehydration, and they monitored him at the hospital for a while just to be safe, but other than that he's in perfect health. So really well done, everyone."

There was a general round of whoops and cheers.

"I do want to remind you all to make sure you've got backups for both you and your dog—food, water, and batteries for your flashlights—and also to make sure you have a phone charger in your car just in case. We didn't end up being able to use GPS on this one anyway, but next time we might and a half-dead phone does nobody any good. That's not a criticism of anyone except me." He wrinkled his nose. "I only realized my phone was almost dead after I got home so I figured it was worth a mention. So in short—good job, y'all kick ass, and Steve and Nikita win the prize."

"Literal or metaphorical?" Lito whispered to Scooter. Scooter just winked and tilted his head toward the parking lot. Lito looked over just in time to see Sharon pull something out of her van and toss it to Rick, who then lobbed it at Steve's chest.

"You've got to be kidding me." Steve laughed, then held the object up for everyone to see. "You got her a chew toy with what, eight squeakers in it?"

"Ten. Because I know how much Nikita loves to annoy you."

Steve flipped Dave the finger, which only prompted laughter from everyone else.

"It's not an every time thing," Scooter explained in a low voice, "but Dave, Rick, and Steve all like to razz each other whenever they get the chance. And Nikita really does go nuts for squeaky toys—Steve says she can't sleep until the noisemaker is destroyed, which means he doesn't get to sleep either."

Spot had never particularly cared for noisy toys one way or the other, but Lito nodded knowledgeably anyway.

"So with that out of the way," Rick said in a louder voice, "let's run the pups who didn't get their exercise in yesterday. That's Spot, Sniff, Lumpy, Woozy, and Zeus. Y'all have a preference who goes first, or where?"

"I'd just as soon do a run on the south trail," Sharon volunteered. "I haven't had Sniff down there in ages and he's due for a good, solid, ground scent."

Steve raised his hand. "I can do that. How far do you want me to go, and how complicated do you want the trail?"

"Let's say a pattern of seven minutes walking and three sitting and we'll see how long it takes to catch up? Simulate a lost dementia patient?"

"Got it." Steve broke off from the group and started walking toward the far side of the parking lot. "I'll text you after the first ten," he called back over his shoulder.

"Dave?" Rick asked. "You want to take one of yours up the north side, or do you want to work with Lito and Spot first?"

They'd been running Spot for a good hour at almost every practice, and Lito abruptly felt a bit guilty that he hadn't realized the concentrated attention meant Dave wasn't getting to do much with his own dogs. *Some team player I'm turning out to be.* "I don't want to take up *all* your time," he said. "And Spot and I really have been, haven't we? Go ahead—your dogs are probably getting jealous of all the fun Spot's had recently."

"They'd get jealous of a ham sandwich. And then forget about it two minutes afterward." Dave scrubbed a hand through his short hair, but nodded. "Yeah, okay. Let's… Janet, you want to walk with Sharon and I'll take Scooter and Lito for a two-man find? Or would you rather hide?"

"I need the exercise." Janet sucked in her stomach and shimmied her not terribly large breasts. "Going line dancing with a guy from Scottsboro on Friday night, and it'd be nice to not be winded after two dances."

"This the insurance guy?" Sharon asked. Janet's love life was impossible to keep track of, but she had almost no TMI filter so it was hard not to overhear. Lito already knew *way* more about the problems involved with heterosexual sex after forty than he really wanted to. The insurance guy with the fabled giant cock (as told to Janet by some previous woman he'd dated and then related to the team in between practice searches) had been the flavor of the last few weeks. Luckily, Sharon and Janet ducked off to the side to chat about line dancing and hot dates and big cocks so Lito didn't have to hear the rest. For all Janet's enthusiasm about men and sex, she'd probably faint if she knew what happened on an average Friday night at any of the more entertaining gay clubs in Atlanta. (And on the heels of that thought…had Dave actually said he went clubbing in Nashville? He was probably mobbed in less than a minute, if so, because *damn*.)

"Guess I'll take Lumpy out for Scooter and Lito, then," Dave said. "If y'all are okay with that? We can do Spot and Zeus as a second round and I'll run Woozy at the end with whoever has the time to stay late."

Scooter nodded. "Let's do it."

Lito didn't have the first clue how a "two-man find" was supposed to work, other than the fact that it probably involved finding two people, but Scooter gave him an overview as they searched for a good spot. "Nobody's walking with him?" Lito asked. "I thought we were supposed to always do this in pairs."

"Eh." Scooter shrugged. "Dave's dogs are too old to go on real searches anymore—Lumpy is nearly blind in one eye, and Woozy's arthritis doesn't leave her enough stamina for the long stuff these days. He mostly just brings them to practices so they can socialize with the rest of the pack."

"They don't act their age, then," Lito said. The memory of the two Rottweilers chasing each other at top speed around the field before practice was still a vivid one, given that they did it practically every week. "Crap. I didn't push Dave into running them today, did I? I mean, Rick brought it up—"

"Dude, it's fine. Chill." Scooter stepped over a large downed tree trunk without even breaking his stride. Lito had to do a much less graceful straddle-and-hop to clear it. "He does still run practice searches every once in a while, mostly to keep himself sharp. And I'd like to see you try to bully Dave into doing something he didn't want to do. He's like twice your size."

Lito would have been more eager to argue if the damn log they were climbing over—well, that he'd climbed and Scooter had stepped over—hadn't just reinforced the point. And, okay, maybe Dave wasn't *twice* Lito's size, but he did have a good ten inches and probably eighty pounds on him and those eighty pounds were all muscle. The idea of pushing the guy around a bit had some serious appeal, though. Straddling him in the dark was one thing, but to *really* do the job right…

"None of us are really in a great position to give him pointers, other than Rick," Scooter added, oblivious. "He doesn't need anyone to shadow him and Lumpy, though, so it's really not a big deal. I've got your cell number and I know he does too—text one of us if something goes wrong. Or if it's after midnight and he hasn't found you yet."

"Oh ha ha." Lito paused next to another fallen tree, this one probably two feet across. It was propped against its neighbors at a low angle but had a huge root ball still stuck to the end. The resulting wall of dirt was big enough to easily hide either of them. "Behind this, maybe?"

Scooter shook his head. "I wanna screw with him," he said with a grin. "Keep him from getting lazy. How are you at climbing?"

Lito had absolutely zero experience climbing trees so the answer turned out to be "not very good." They did manage to get him installed about eight feet off the ground, where the top of the tree had gotten tangled up in a larger one when it fell. Eight feet looked a hell of a lot higher from a tree than it did from anywhere else. Christ, he was going to fall if he didn't keep completely still and hang on tight.

"You're fine," Scooter assured him, politely not saying anything snarky about how Lito was clutching one of the larger branches. "High finds are great—your scent comes down in a cone shape like this, see?" He delineated a vague curved line several feet away. "It makes a circle around you and drifts outward as it falls but doesn't actually go straight down. Confusing as hell for the dog, so it's the handler's responsibility to be paying attention and to look up. I think on my last one I did four or five laps of the tree before Sharon laughed out loud and I finally saw her. Really damn embarrassing, but it's a good reminder to always pay attention because your dog can't do all the work for you." He stepped back and jammed his hands in his pockets. "Anyway, you good up there?"

Lito nodded. He hadn't broken his neck yet, at least.

"I'm gonna find me a ground spot a bit further on, then. I'll text Dave when I'm ready—probably five minutes or so."

Lito maneuvered gingerly into a fork between two of the still-living tree's branches and hugged his knees to his chest. Something solid on each side helped quell the I'm-going-to-tip-over-and-crack-my-head-open feeling. He was wearing olive jeans and his favorite dark brown jacket, not the fluorescent green NALSAR team coat, so he'd be camouflaged and hopefully not too cold. And now that he was settled in his makeshift nest, all he could think about was that Dave wanted to get naked with him again.

It was really hard to decide whether that was a surprise or not. Before the call-out, Lito had been confused as hell by Dave's signals—the dude read "straight-arrow, redneck, macho Army type," but he hadn't once pulled a "no homo" even though Lito had literally been wearing a rainbow-shaped earring stud and a tight pink shirt the day they met. Maybe it had just seemed too much like wishful thinking, to imagine Dave being into dudes. Especially dudes like Lito, so much his polar opposite in so many ways. And yet.

And yet.

They'd gotten each other off while lying in the back of Dave's Jeep, watching the stars together. They'd practically cuddled afterward. How cliché could they get?

Thanks to the uneven terrain and the fact that the trees were only just—now that it was November—thinking about shedding their leaves, Lito couldn't see the source of the crashing he gradually realized he was hearing. Lumpy wasn't exactly subtle, though. Being half blind obviously didn't slow her down much. She was on her third full-speed pass across Lito's limited field of vision when Dave caught up to her. Lumpy bounced in a circle around him, paused to touch her nose to his hand, then took off at a much more sedate speed to run laps around the base of the tree. As close as she could get, at least—the downed tree plus the underbrush beyond it made for some extremely large and lumpy circles.

Lito held himself very still, trying to not even breathe loudly, but it didn't matter. Dave watched Lumpy's confusion for only about a lap and a half before looking up and catching Lito's eye.

"Nice," he said, amusement and approval clear on his face. "Give her a sec to catch on."

Lumpy did, eventually. It was fascinating to watch a fully trained dog work, aging nose or no—she was clearly adjusting her path based on Dave's body language, even while he was deliberately not "finding" Lito yet. Eventually she looked up, saw him, and screeched to a halt. She then launched herself at Dave's waist.

"Oof." Dave doubled over, avoiding what would probably have been a painful two-paw shot to the groin, but stood up again immediately. "Where is he?" he asked in a sing-song voice. "Show me!"

Lumpy ran another, tighter lap of Lito's tree, then sat and stared at Dave until he came over and reached up to touch Lito's boot.

"Good *girl!* You're such a *good girl!*" He pulled a treat from his pocket and cooed at her excitedly until she'd had enough. When she shied away from the ear scratches and started wandering off to sniff things all on her own, Dave heaved himself back to his feet and looked up at Lito critically. "I *know* you and I haven't covered high finds yet," he said with an easy hand on his hip, "but you picked a good one."

"It was Scooter's idea," Lito admitted. "And my first tree-climbing experience. City boy, remember."

"I get to be your first? Aww, that's sweet," Dave teased. "Am I wrong in guessing you may need help getting down?"

The angle of the fallen tree didn't look any more welcoming in reverse than it had on the way up. "Probably not"

"Mmm." Dave's grin turned wicked. "What do I get if I volunteer to help?"

That definitely sounded like flirting, and was much more familiar territory than climbing trees would ever be. "I may be stuck up a tree," Lito countered, "but I can still blow up your phone from here if you walk away and leave me. The signal's not *that* terrible."

Dave laughed, which drew Lumpy's attention again. "Was going to hold out for a kiss, but I guess threats work too. How's your balance?"

They ended up with Lito inching back out onto the angled trunk and dangling his feet over the edge. Dave could just about reach Lito's knees while standing on tiptoe.

"Come on, jump."

Lito eyed the drop. "I'm gonna kick you in the face with these big honkin' hiking boots you made me buy," he warned.

"I can take it." Dave adopted an exaggerated leer, spoiled by the fact that he couldn't quite keep in his laughter. "Always wanted to rescue the damsel in distress. Come on."

Damsel? "Screw you."

"Deal." Dave tugged at Lito's ankle just as Lito shifted his weight forward, which meant Lito toppled off the tree facedown instead of executing the graceful jump he'd been envisioning in his head. Dave caught him under the armpits and smoothly swung him down to the ground... and then further, so Lito was bent backwards over Dave's knee like a fainting medieval heroine. "The screwing is for after dinner on Friday, though," Dave murmured. "In the meantime a kiss would be appropriate, don't you agree?"

Their faces were only inches apart. Dave's breath smelled like peppermint. Lito didn't even bother nodding, just yanked Dave's mouth down to his own and did his best to kiss the living daylights out of him. It was going pretty well until there was suddenly a warm, wet *something* directly in his face.

"Blech! Lumpy!" Dave sputtered. He did help Lito back to his feet, though. Lumpy licked Lito again, totally unrepentant—although this time she only slobbered on his hand, which was an improvement.

"Thanks," Lito said, straightening his shirt. "Could have done without the surprise finish, though."

"Oh, I'm not finished with you. Not by a long shot." Dave's expression promised all sorts of wicked fun. "We'll have to come back to this later, though, or Scooter will come searching for us. He's not as good at it when he doesn't have Cheerio along."

Chapter 9

It was hell, having to wait for Friday so he didn't appear too eager. Dave spent the rest of the week zoning out at the most inappropriate times. There was nothing feminine about Lito, but it was still a heady feeling to be able to literally catch the guy and manhandle him a bit. Lito had been just the right combination of surprised, intrigued, and pliant to make Dave's imagination work overtime. Overtime and nighttime and most of the time when he was on the clock. Just as well he got to stay behind his desk for most of Friday and catch up on paperwork—Mike would tease him until they both retired if he noticed the hard-on straining against Dave's jeans all day.

We still on for dinner? What time and where?

Like Dave hadn't been stressing about that too. Black Lake did have some decent restaurants, even some "date" spots, but the more selfish side of Dave didn't want to share Lito with anyone for even the duration of a meal.

7:00? he wrote back. 1622 Courtland Lane.

Even if Lito wasn't already comfortable navigating his way around Black Lake—and didn't have Google street view, for some reason—Dave's house was hard to miss. Mostly because it was way out in the country and Lumpy and Woozy would probably be falling all over themselves with excitement in the fenced side yard before Lito's car even made it up the drive. They took their roles as "protector and greeter" seriously.

Dave made himself stay at work through his scheduled 4:30 and not a minute sooner, mostly to set a good example for the other guys in his department, but he was out of there at breakneck speed afterward. A quick trip to Publix for some cooking essentials and he was home and showered by 5:30. It left him plenty of time to figure out if there was anything difficult about making shrimp Alfredo. He'd never be a *great* cook, by any standard—definitely not compared to how his mother could magically transform just about anything into deliciousness—but any idiot was capable of pasta. In theory.

At 6:58, Dave had to admit his confidence had *maybe* been a bit misplaced. The fettuccine came out fine, and the sauce was from a jar so "cooking" that was merely a question of heating it up, but the shrimp were proving a bit difficult. As in, "forgot to check at the store if they were already peeled instead of still in the shells" difficult. He was halfway through massacring both the bowl of defrosted shrimp and his favorite list of Army endearments, when Lumpy and Woozy took up their chorus of "A car is here! A car is here!" from their run outside.

"Sorry," Dave said as he let Lito in. "It's taken me a bit longer to get dinner ready than I'd planned."

Lito waved his apology away. "You never told me you cooked. Or that you had such a great place. You're really way out here, aren't you? I bet your pups love all the room."

"Ten acres." Dave took Lito's jacket and ushered him toward the kitchen. "I lease the field to my neighbor who's an actual farmer, but I've got a nice stocked pond out back for fishing and nobody so close they're looking in my bedroom windows. I'm not claiming to be a cook, though." His kitchen was original to the farmhouse, dated seventies cabinets and all, and it was probably obvious he didn't spend more time in it than he had to. It was functional and not much more. "Drink? I've got water, Coke, beer, orange juice, and whatever kind of wine cooler my mother stocked me up on when she was here last."

Lito laughed. "Water's fine. And good cook or not, dinner smells delicious. Anything I can do to help?"

Dave eyed the small pile of pink shells on the kitchen island. "How do you feel about peeling shrimp?"

Between the two of them they made short work of the rest of the bowl. Dave sautéed them just long enough they wouldn't be cold anymore, then dished up two plates of thankfully not-rubbery-yet fettuccine and handed over Lito's so he could portion his own shrimp and sauce. They settled in at the little table in the breakfast nook overlooking the backyard.

"This looks fantastic," Lito said with sincerity. "I wasn't sure what to expect tonight, but—in case you're worried—I'm enjoying myself already."

He did seem thoroughly at ease, which in turn helped Dave relax a bit. "I haven't had anyone new over in ages," he admitted. "Nobody except Rick and Sharon or my family, anyway. This may shock you, but I'm not usually a big socializer. I don't *object* to large groups of people, necessarily, but that doesn't mean I seek them out."

Lito nodded, which Dave took to mean he understood. "Not everyone is," he said. "Is your family nearby?"

"Near enough. My parents are about half an hour away and my brothers ended up another hour or two beyond that, in separate directions."

"How many siblings?"

"One older brother and one younger. I'd call them my big brother and my little brother, but they're both bigger than me. Unlikely as that may be."

The conversation about his family carried them through the rest of the meal. Lito contributed a few anecdotes about his own childhood as an only kid surrounded by cousins, but reciprocal stories about his parents were noticeably absent. Dave didn't mention that he'd noticed.

"So." Lito leaned back in his seat and put his fork down with a clink on his empty plate. "Can I help with dishes, or…"

"Leave them," Dave decided. "Or rather, let's just stick our plates in the sink on our way to the den and I'll sort them out later." Suddenly his plan of *dinner, then sex* seemed to have a glaring gap in the middle. Namely the need for a smooth transition, in the sense that he didn't have one. "There's, um. I've got some movies, if you want to look?"

"Netflix and chill? Not what I expected from you." Lito grinned. "I'm in no hurry to rush home, though, so sure. Pick something you don't mind missing the end of." He winked and wandered out of the kitchen to go plop down on the sofa. "Although I'll give you a heads-up—you really don't need to wine and dine me to get me out of my pants. However much you think you've been reminiscing about this past weekend, I can guarantee you I've been doing the same thing. And I am one hundred percent looking forward to playing around some more if that's on the table. Figuratively, anyway—we'd probably have to do dishes first for that."

Dave wasn't usually one to look a gift horse in the mouth. Something about Lito's carefully easygoing tone sounded odd, though. He couldn't put his finger on it. Since he *was* hoping for sex, or at least something in that general direction, it would have been stupid to suddenly drag his feet now. Still… "I'm going to let Lumpy and Woozy in before it gets too cold outside, if that won't bother you? They've got a heated shelter in their run but usually they'd both rather sack out on the sofa in here. Or," he amended, "they'd sack out on *my* bed if I didn't close the bedroom door. They're not supposed to get up there unless I specifically invite them, but Lumpy thinks I don't notice."

"Spot does the same—I've given up trying to keep her from hogging the whole lower part of the mattress. It's just as well I'm short and don't need much leg room." Lito cocked his head to one side and shot Dave a calculating look from across the length of the den. "I guess the question is, then," he said, "would you rather we keep them off the sofa, or off the bed?"

Bed. Definitely bed. If Lito was so determined to get down to the sexy part of the evening as fast as possible, it was much better to have space to enjoy it. "Give me a sec," Dave said, and quickly went to let Lumpy and Woozy in through the garage. They snuffled around in the kitchen for a minute, no doubt picking up on all the lovely particles of Lito's scent wafting around. In the end, though, the sofa proved adequate to catch their attention. So much for the half hour he'd spent with a lint roller, trying to get all the fur off. By the time Dave got their water bowl topped up and came back to the den, the sofa was empty of anyone except dogs and Lito had migrated to the bedroom. He was sprawled out over Dave's quilt, still clothed in all except his shoes, but he looked playful. And adorable. Dave had a sudden urge to tickle him and see how he'd react. Not that he wasn't sexy as hell too—some primitive instinct Dave hadn't even realized he possessed was crowing at the sight of Lito in *his territory*—but it really would be nice if Lito were willing to stick around afterward. Maybe they could watch a movie, snuggle on the couch, throw a ball for Lumpy and Woozy, and laugh at how the pair acted like puppies who couldn't control their own limbs when a game of fetch came into play. If Lito stayed the night, they could enjoy sleepy morning sex and Dave could attempt eggs and bacon for breakfast. (Although would Lito even eat bacon? It probably counted as red meat…maybe toast, then. Or pancakes. If he was feeling brave enough to try and Lito was brave enough to eat his cooking again.)

"Didn't think I'd send your brain offline *that* easily," Lito teased, still reclining on the bed but propping himself up on one elbow. "There wasn't exactly a convenient time to mention this before, but I get tested every few months and I'm disease-free. I take PrEP just in case too. I brought condoms but couldn't find any portable-size packets of lube, so I'm hoping you've got something? Figured for my first time seeing your house it'd probably be a bit much for me to just show up at the door and be like 'Wow, like your place, I brought a bottle of wine and another of lube, what's for dinner?' And I'd just as soon avoid any bruises that would prompt awkward question from my coworkers, so if it's all the same to you—"

Fuck it. "Hey." Dave pulled his shirt off over his head and tossed it somewhere on the floor behind him. "Not that this isn't a good conversation to have—and I'm disease-free too—but there's no rush. I'm not Cinderella." He climbed onto the bed and tugged Lito toward him so they could lie face-to-face. Dude became a chatterbox when nervous, apparently. "You did say you don't have to get home quite yet, yeah?"

"True." Lito acknowledged the point with a sheepish half-shrug. "I just assumed you'd want to get me naked as soon as possible."

"Mmmm." Dave loomed over him and claimed a long, slow kiss instead. Once Lito figured out Dave wasn't just using it as a waypoint toward immediate escalation, he settled in and reciprocated. Dave tried to communicate through the kiss just how much he wanted to take his time—tease-and-retreat, occasional side trips to nuzzle at the smooth lines of Lito's jaw, soothing nips and pecks in between the deeper meeting of mouths. Lito arched and sighed into the contact.

"I think I see your point," Lito murmured once Dave pulled away enough they could look at each other at a reasonable focal distance again. "Be as thorough as you want."

"You can bet on it." Dave laid a hand on Lito's stomach and lightly caressed his abs through the fabric of his t-shirt. "What sounds good to you? I know you said you don't bottom—"

"I said I hate when guys assume," Lito corrected him. "Didn't say I can't be persuaded." He smirked up at Dave, a clear challenge in his eyes. "I may make you earn it, though."

Dave's head was immediately swamped with a wealth of possibilities. And some seriously hot mental images. He silently vowed to attempt each and every one of them, if Lito allowed. "I usually prefer to top," he admitted, "but I can be flexible too. With the right incentive."

"I can work with that." Lito waggled his eyebrows in a theatrical parody of a leer, then snaked a hand around to grab a palmful of Dave's ass.

Hell yes. Dave ground himself once against Lito's hip, the sensation nice but not nearly enough, then shifted himself downward so he could hike up Lito's shirt and put his mouth where his hand had been. The skin over his sternum was warm and smelled slightly of body wash, which meant Lito had probably taken a shower between work and coming over for dinner. Had he tossed one off while daydreaming about what they'd get up to later? Or was Lito more the kind of dude to edge himself a bit and then wait, so he'd be that much hornier when they got their hands on each other for real?

Lito propped himself up on one elbow to watch. The movement brought his abs into visible definition, which Dave realized he liked very much. Clearly Lito had some combination of good genetics, good diet, and a good workout routine going, because *damn.* Dave nibbled at a crease between the muscles and sent his best fuck-me look back up Lito's torso. Lito's brown eyes widened and Dave got the distinct impression his meaning was heard loud and clear.

"I think," Dave growled against Lito's stomach, "that you need to lose these clothes. I've decided that getting you naked as soon as possible might be on the agenda after all." He palmed Lito's hips and tugged him closer, so the definite bulge of Lito's cock was tantalizingly close to firmer contact, but ducked back down to focus some equal attention to the parts of Lito's abs he couldn't previously reach instead.

Lito's chest lifted as he sucked in a swift breath. "Not that I dislike this particular agenda," he said, "but who says *you* get to decide anything?"

There was already a hint of a waver breaking through in his voice, which ought to have been its own answer. As well as a really damn blatant call for more. "You did, when you said I can try to 'persuade' you," Dave countered. "And you like it when I manhandle you. Shirt off."

Lito peeled the t-shirt off with impressive speed considering he was still flat on his back. "I never said 'manhandle,'" he grumbled.

"You're not telling me I'm wrong."

"True." Lito bucked his hips, bringing his clothed erection into brief contact with Dave's left pec before Dave shifted far enough away the attempt would be futile. "*Fuck.* On second thought, yes. Persuade away."

"I'm persuading your jeans off next." Dave said a silent prayer (of sorts) in thanks for having such large hands and long fingers—it meant he could pop the button and unzip the fly on Lito's pants entirely one-handed. With perhaps a bit of a grope in between, which Lito didn't seem to mind one bit. He had on some Kentucky-blue briefs underneath, silky and in a mouthwatering fancy cut that only gay men who were way more fashionable than Dave was were ever able to pull off. Lito was clearly among that number because *God fucking damn.* The jeans needed to come off as quickly as possible but those briefs were definitely staying on. At least for a while.

"You're still wearing yours," Lito pointed out.

"Yeah, but you're not the one doing this." Trying not to telegraph his intentions, Dave ducked under Lito's leg and sat up. It took hardly any effort at all to arrange the scene exactly how he wanted it—Lito's shoulders on the bed and his knees hooked over Dave's delts, while the rest of his torso was suspended in the air. Even with the briefs on, he was spread open and gorgeous and he already smelled a bit like sex even though they'd hardly done anything yet. Best of all, though, the position put his balls in teasing range. It also left Dave both his hands and his mouth free.

Lito nearly yelled when Dave first sucked him through the thin fabric. He was being painfully gentle—the barest hint of suction, really. More like dampening the fabric in his mouth. Dave kept a tight hold on Lito's hips, though, restricting him from bucking, and that meant he was able to *really* settle in and play.

"Fuck. Fuckfuckfuck." Lito tightened his thighs around Dave's shoulders. "That feels so good."

Dave switched to the other side. The head of Lito's cock was peeking out from under the elastic of his waistband, now, like it was demanding its own turn. *Tough.* It was going to have to wait, because now that the blue satiny fabric was soaked through, Dave was finally able to taste *Lito* under it all and there was absolutely no hurry. He'd have been happy to spend all night like that, honestly, holding Lito's hips in the air so he couldn't squirm away and then absolutely ruining his ability to hold a coherent thought in his head. When he came—*if* Dave finally let him come from just that—it would already be one of the best damn sexual experiences in Dave's life. In Lito's too, hopefully.

They weren't restricted to just one fantasy, though, so Dave only waited until Lito was *mostly* panting before adjusting their positions once more. Still not to take off those now-semi-translucent briefs yet, just to wedge his own knees under the small of Lito's back and support most of his weight. The change meant Dave had a better angle to run his palms back up over Lito's abs. It also meant that Lito's barely clothed ass was providing much-needed friction over where Dave's own cock was still trapped in his jeans. The effect was more psychological than anything—crumpled denim was too thick to feel much through—but they both moaned anyway. Lito hooked his fingertips behind Dave's knees and hiked himself up another half-inch. It was all the leverage he had. A fat drop of precome beaded at the tip of Lito's cock and Dave was seriously tempted to say *to hell with it* and turn this whole slow dance of potential into what would have probably ended up being a fifteen-second blowjob.

"Fuck. Consider me persuaded." Lito attempted another grind against Dave's torso, with a similar lack of success. "Apparently being hoisted in the air like a blow-up doll is a kink I never knew I had."

"Royal-blue balls look good on you."

Lito let go of Dave's knee long enough to flash him the finger, but the rest of his body was still telegraphing *Yes please, now hurry the fuck up* so Dave didn't put too much stock in the gesture. He did take a mock bite out of the inside of Lito's thigh before disentangling himself enough to stand up and strip off his own jeans and boxers.

"Well-endowed looks good on you," Lito countered. His eyes stayed locked on Dave's groin even as he shed himself of his now-damp designer briefs in a few lithe movements. "Although I can't believe I've let you drag me down to the 'terrible porn innuendos' level of sex tonight. You're a terrible influence."

"I'm just getting started." Dave walked around to his bedside drawer and dug out his bottle of lube. There was no sense having to do the whole undignified sprawl across the mattress to reach it later when he was already standing anyway. "Next time I'll brace you on your elbows in an X-rated army crawl and I'm gonna eat your ass out until you can't hold yourself up anymore. For tonight, though…back or front? Preference?"

"You. In. Me." Lito sat up to dig a condom out from the pocket of his discarded jeans, then lay back with his fingers interlaced behind his head and a sexy-as-fuck smirk on his face. "I'm assuming when you get all toppy and growly like this I should sit back and enjoy the ride?"

"Something like that."

He did too. Dave tried to be extra-careful when fingering him— necessary downside to having such large hands—but Lito relaxed almost perfectly and even working up to three fingers was a matter of a few minutes at most. They were a few minutes of seriously hot foreplay, though, Lito sighing and egging him on with things like "fuck, yes, that's incredible" and "God, if just two of your fingers make me feel this full I think I might spontaneously combust before I actually get to feel your cock in me." Dave's hands were trembling a bit by the time he got the condom on his own aching dick and got himself lined up.

"Do it." Lito unlaced his fingers from behind his head—for the first time since Dave got him flat on the mattress—and reached for Dave greedily. "Manhandle away and I'll do my best to let you know how good you feel."

"If you've still got the breath to tease me like that once I get my cock in you, I'll have been doing it wrong." Dave nudged forward into Lito's slick hole with a slow glide that nearly had him seeing stars. Lito was too, if the look on his face was anything to go by. "No manhandling for this—just fucking the sass out of you until you can't remember your own name."

Lito moaned at that. "You talk big, but—"

"Lotta me is big." Dave kept easing in his initial careful thrust as far as it could go, his balls sending sparks reverberating through him when they met Lito's warm skin. "And now we're back to the cheesy porn dialogue."

"Don't care. *Move.*" Lito's fingertips dug into Dave's biceps. "I still remember my name, by the way. It's Lito. As in, Spot's human sidekick? The guy whose name you forgot at my first practice?"

Dave's *fuck you* was non-verbal but eloquent. Lito writhed, skewered and clearly loving it. Dave couldn't decide what to look at first: Lito's face, eyes closed, mouth open, head thrown back as he braced it against Dave's pillow? His cock, thick and dripping all over those impressive abs? His chest, barely there fuzz rising and falling with each desperate breath? He was the perfect picture of total submission to the way their bodies moved together, and if Dave died in that moment he'd have left a smug ghost. The vision in front of him could be his life's crowning work. Lito's hips met his own with each thrust, the rhythm dissolving as they both got too close to care.

"Touch me," Lito gasped, even as he reached down to do it himself. Dave wrapped his larger hand around Lito's smaller one and increased the pressure. "Ah, fuck, fuck, I'm—*nngh.*"

Right, scratch that. *This*, Lito coming, this was even better than Lito desperate to come. Dave held himself at bay just long enough to let Lito enjoy the aftershocks before giving in and coming his own brains out. They both ended up sweaty and limp on the mattress in several minutes of total silence.

"So despite the overused porn lines thing," Lito said eventually, "that was really damn amazing." He rolled to his side and scrubbed a lock of sweat-slicked hair out of his face. "Actually, I take that back. The terrible dirty talk was fun too."

It was, honestly. Dave couldn't remember the last time he'd been with a guy who'd made sex feel that fun. "I suppose I'll let you share the credit." *And invite you for as many repeats as you like.* "I really had intended to go for slow and romantic tonight, but 'fast and insanely hot' like that does it for me too. For future reference."

"Implying you'd be in favor of doing this again, I assume?"

Dave blinked at him, his brain still not quite back to normal speed but still aware that there was something off in Lito's tone again. "Of course," he said carefully. "Although if that's not what you were looking for, I still appreciate—"

"Shut up." Lito surged forward and landed an awkward kiss somewhere in the vicinity of Dave's lips. "I'm not blind, you idiot. You've got muscles to die for and you're sexy as fuck when you're all in command at practice and everyone jumps when you say jump. Plus when you fuck like *that*, you can top me anytime you damn well want to. The prospect of getting off with you on the regular is the one thing I think I could really learn to enjoy about living in Black Lake."

Not that that idea wasn't flattering, but…"the one thing? Like, the *only* thing?"

"You know what I mean."

"Not sure I do."

Lito groaned and let his head flop back against the pillow. "I'm a fish out of water here, is all. It was great of you to let me join NALSAR and, well, this"—he waved vaguely at their two naked bodies—"but don't pretend nobody's talking about me behind my back."

"Not in my hearing."

Lito rolled to his side and leveled him a look. "I'm a city boy," he said. "I'd literally never climbed a tree before this week. Never been 'out in nature' all that much, unless you count city parks or going to the beach. Half my friends are fabulously gay queens and our nights out are usually spent at either clubs or drag revues. Pride parades are basically my family reunions. English is technically my second language, I grew up in Little Havana in the middle of Miami where being Peruvian versus Venezuelan or Honduran or Cuban actually *means* something, and I can explain the rules to jai alai but have never actually seen a football game in person. Tell me: what out of all that is supposed to make me fit in here? Because I'm not seeing it."

Dave wished like hell he could come up with some glib answer, but he was drawing a blank. His own sporadic jaunts to the one decent gay bar in Nashville didn't entirely seem relevant to the conversation. "Give it time," he offered. *So inadequate.* "Moving to a new place is always hard—"

"Fuck." Lito scrubbed a hand over his face and let out a strangled little laugh. "Just—fuck it. I appreciate you trying to make me feel better, and I *really* didn't mean to go all whiny six-year-old on you there. I shouldn't be complaining about relocating either—the promotion came with a raise and the cost of living here is like half of what it is in Atlanta. More responsibility is a good thing, or so I'm told."

He said it, but he didn't look like he believed it. Lito wasn't the type to balk at taking charge—his sass in bed proved that much. It was obvious he could take care of himself when he needed to. Then again, Dave knew better than anyone how insidious self-doubt could be. Hell, those months right after the Army…

"I like what I do. I'm good at it," Lito declared. Like he was trying to convince himself—or convince Dave. "And there's not going to be anywhere else that will hire me for such a specialized hybrid job, especially with me having made it through high school by the skin of my teeth, so I should be glad I'm still here at all. It's just…hell, I'm so tired of trying to pretend I fit in, you know?"

Too well. Part of Dave wanted to commiserate, but it didn't sound like Lito expected him to actually answer. And yeah, plenty of people had wondered about Dave at his tiny little high school, but being on the football team had its perks. Nobody'd ever gotten in his face about it. Nobody questioned his right to be in the Army, either, even during Don't Ask Don't Tell—they'd just all tried to ignore the big gay elephant in the room and it had more or less worked. Once they were deployed to the sandbox, nobody cared.

"I'm not going to say I have an answer to all that." Hardly any of it, really. "But I can help with one part, if you want. And if you don't have already have plans for Thanksgiving."

Lito raised one eyebrow.

"I told you I'm the middle child out of three boys, right? And that we're all still in driving distance?"

"You're inviting me to a family Thanksgiving dinner?"

"Dinner plus flag football afterward." Etiquette probably dictated he should have run it by his mother before inviting Lito along to his parents' house, but fuck it. They weren't going to complain about perpetually single Dave bringing someone. "My brothers and I all played, once upon a time, and my oldest nephew is on a junior team. It's fun to go out and make idiots of ourselves once a year—especially after we've all eaten so much turkey and dressing we can't move anymore anyway. You're welcome to join in, or stand on the porch with my mother and sister-in-law and gossip about us." He wrinkled his nose. "Pretty sure that's what they do up there."

Lito smiled, but it was a bit sad. "I do appreciate the offer," he said, "but I can't just barge in on your family dinner like that."

"Yes, you can. Want me to dig out my phone and call my mom? She's southern through and through—she'll be overjoyed at the chance to feed you as many calories as you'll tolerate. She's also a much better cook than I am."

"Well in *that* case…" Lito's smile turned a lot more genuine. "Rather not have my first introduction to your parents be while I'm naked in your bed, though. Even though it's over the phone."

"Mmmm." Dave twisted around and tugged Lito's body so Lito was on top of him. "I've got a spare toothbrush in the cupboard over the sink—any chance you might want to stick around for another 'first' or two tonight? Assuming Spot won't miss you too badly?"

"I finally fixed the run outside the dog door. She can handle herself overnight." Lito stretched out to cover as much of Dave's body as possible. It still wasn't all that much. "I wasn't expecting you to ask," he murmured against Dave's Adam's apple, "but I'm not going to say no."

Chapter 10

Whatever Lito's relationship with Dave was shaping up to be, the prospect of meeting the guy's parents for a major holiday meal was more than a bit daunting. Most of Lito's Thanksgiving memories were of the entire Apaza clan at Uncle Diego and Aunt Ximena's home two blocks away from his own, crammed into the small backyard and eating all afternoon until the adults ran out of gossip. Lito's mother wasn't a bad cook by any means, but Aunt Ximena's cheese piononos were worth the holiday fanfare all by themselves. The get-together was always loud, frenetic, and all-encompassing. Especially so for the kids: the cousins ranged in age from Marco, who was four years younger than Lito, to Gabriela who had been a worldly twenty-three when he'd left home. She was the one who took him in so he could finish out his senior year. The family had all seen each other frequently at other times, of course, but big holidays were when everyone got to re-establish the pecking order. Somehow Lito doubted Dave's clan would function quite the same way.

Should I bring something? he texted.

That was the polite thing to do, wasn't it? Contribute something reminiscent of his own Thanksgiving experiences? Lito ended up spending almost an hour trying to look up a passable recipe for Aunt Ximena's aguaymanto sauce while he waited for Dave's return text. Everything he found required ingredients he wasn't likely to find in the tiny Mexican section at the local Publix. What if Dave's family subscribed to the "put meat in everything" method of cooking the rest of Alabama seemed to be so fond of? Turkey wasn't the worst thing ever, but the idea of lard and bacon in the green beans or the mashed potatoes made Lito's stomach turn.

Just bring you, Dave texted back.

Mom always cooks enough to feed an army.

> *She and Dad are thrilled to meet you, by the way. I may have laid on the "he's all alone in a new place for the holidays" a bit thick :-)*

Dave must have introduced him as a "friend," then. That was a bit better than the "here's the guy I'm screwing; hope y'all don't mind" Lito had feared. Might as well go with it. In any case, Thanksgiving dinner with the Schmidt family was likely to be the most redneck thing Lito had ever done.

* * * *

"Oh, you must be Lito! Come *in!*"

Lito found his nose abruptly smashed into Dave's mother's cleavage as she caught him up in a hug. She was five foot ten, easily. It wasn't hard to see where Dave got his build from—his parents both were twice Lito's size. Dave was doing some manly handshake-and-back-slap thing with his dad in the doorway.

"Traffic wasn't too bad, was it?" Dave's father asked. "Lito, good to meet you. Jack and Jenny are in the kitchen, the boys are throwing a ball around outside, and Kitt and Katie should be here any minute. Come on in! What'll you have? Beers and wine coolers are in the fridge; sodas in the cooler. Oh, and Connie's homemade peach tea is in the pitcher on the back porch. Dinner's in half an hour or so."

Stray guests got mile-a-minute chatter from everyone in the family, apparently—Dave's mother and both his brothers were full of conversation as well. Nobody batted an eye at Dave bringing a last minute plus-one home for Thanksgiving. Kitt and his girlfriend showed up a few minutes after Lito and Dave did, and soon the living area was full of chatter. Lito slowly teased out who was who: Jack, Dave's older brother, was a police officer in Birmingham. The younger brother, Kitt, worked for NASA in Huntsville as a meteorological technician, which Lito was surprised to learn was apparently a real thing. Jack's four boys were all built like tanks—as was everyone else in Dave's family—and probably everybody in the room other than the five-year-old could have snapped Lito in half. The cacophony was the same as Lito recognized from his own family's get-togethers. The details of a thoroughly Alabama Thanksgiving were really, really not. The conversation, in particular, ping-ponged back and forth about people Lito didn't know but remained unrelentingly civil and mostly positive. At Uncle Diego and Aunt Ximena's house, someone would have probably been off on a tirade already.

A series of beeps from the kitchen prompted the final mass migration to the table. The three women plus Dave's father all ferried in bowl after bowl of food, while the boys elbowed each other to fight for the best seats and Jack, Kitt, and Dave laughingly followed suit.

"Lito, down here!" Dave called, dodging his younger-but-larger brother's hip-check. "It's tradition—Mom always passes the tray of cookies to the left at the end of the meal, and there's only so many of each kind, so you gotta fight for your spot in line. I can't hold your seat for you much longer, tho—oof!"

Kitt held his arms up in a touchdown victory pose, despite now being squarely planted in Dave's lap. "What Dave's not saying," Kitt added, "is that the other half of the tradition is for Mom to come back in here, tell us we're acting like little monsters and setting a bad example for the kids, and assign us seats anyway." He wiggled his rump, eliciting a theatrical groan of protest from Dave. "I'm gonna take this one, though."

"Get off me, lard-butt." Dave smacked Kitt's shoulder, but he was laughing hard enough he nearly missed. "Quick, Lito! Avenge me while you can!"

"My cousin Gabriela could take all of you," Lito mumbled under his breath in Spanish. He'd never given her an excuse to pummel him—she'd always been the one to take him under her wing, for whatever reason—but her younger twin brothers were a year and a half older than Lito was and she'd learned early on to fight dirty. Some of his best holiday memories involved he and his cousins wrestling each other into submission while the adults weren't looking.

Dave's brothers and nephews all left Lito a polite berth from the roughhousing, though, so Lito skirted the tussling and planted himself in the chair next to Dave and Kitt. He then braced himself against the leg of the table and got in a precise poke under Kitt's ribs. It wasn't enough to truly count as tickling, but it worked: Kitt yelped and shifted his weight. It was enough to let Dave shove him off and elbow him out of the way.

"Well done," Dave panted, grinning in a way that made Lito's heart beat a little faster. "Don't mind them—we can be civilized enough once the womenfolk get back in here."

"We're already 'back in here,'" his mother said from the doorway, a steaming casserole in her hands. "And you boys are setting a terrible example for your nephews. Kitt, come switch places with Billy. I'm not sticking Jenny all alone at the kid end of the table."

"I wanna sit next to Uncle Dave's friend," one of the younger boys whined. "Mason said the grown-ups get the best cookies."

"Oh, for goodness' sake." Mrs. Schmidt set down the pan and started pointing out chairs. "Mason. Katie. Kitt. Cooper. Jack. Billy. Lito. Dave. Junior. Jenny. Buck, you're next to me. Is everyone clear?" She glared at the family in general and her sons in particular, the "don't fuck with me" expression *definitely* one Lito recognized from home.

A chorus of "Yes'm" echoed from everyone. Lito found himself at the head of the table, Dave on one side and the seven-year-old Billy on the other, which meant he got significantly more elbow room than most of the rest of the adults. The two youngest boys were probably too short to see anything over the incredible volume of food now covering the center of the table, but that didn't seem to stop anyone.

It wasn't exactly surprising, after Dave's glowing endorsement of his mother's culinary skills, but the food was *amazing.* Lito wasn't usually a huge fan of turkey, but this one had some sort of an orange-sage glaze that set it off perfectly. The mashed potatoes were fluffy and buttery, the dressing the perfect texture, and the green beans were deliciously crisp and made an excellent counterpoint to the gravy over everything else. No bacon in sight. Lito found himself eating more in one sitting than he'd done in a very long time.

"Do you own a dog?" Billy asked. Right while Lito's mouth was full of his third helping of the cornbread dressing. "Mom said that Uncle Dave's dogs love you."

Dave chuckled and swooped in for the save. "He does, actually. Mr. Lito and his dog Spot are on the search team with me." He shot Lito a sideways glance. "And yeah, I may have mentioned that Lumpy and Woozy both think Mr. Lito is good people."

"Are you boyfriends?"

Lito inhaled a bite of mashed potato the wrong way, sending him coughing, but before he could answer (before he could even think about how *to* answer) the five-year-old answered for him. "You can't marry Uncle Dave," the other boy stated.

"I, ah." Lito glanced at Dave for help, but Dave was clearly struggling for an answer too. *Fuck—he did say he was out to his family, didn't he?* He was definitely out to the team, and Lito thought he remembered Dave mentioning his parents being okay with it, but "my parents figured it out" is a lot different than "let's discuss gay marriage in front of the kindergartner." *Shitshitshit.* "We're just—"

"Because his name starts with an L," the boy explained. "But 'Uncle Dave' starts with a U. And also a D. They have to match."

Lightbulb moment.

Dave's poker face was terrible—the smile kept trying to break through at the corners of his mouth no matter how much he tried to nod and look thoughtful. "Like Uncle Kitt and Miss Katie?" he asked. "And your mom and dad?"

"Jenny and Jack!"

"Right. Those do start with the same letter. You're very observant." Dave inclined his head toward his parents. "What about Grandma and Grandpa, though?"

The boy nearly bounced off his chair. "They start with G! They both start with G!"

Dave's father snorted and had to cover his mouth with his napkin, breaking the awkward spell which had settled over the rest of the table. "That's true," he conceded, "but your grandma's real first name is Constance, which starts with a C. And mine is Walter, which starts with a W, or Buck, which starts with a B. Those don't match."

The kid looked crestfallen. "What letter does your name start with?" Lito asked him.

"C. It's C-O-O-P-E-R. And my second name starts with an S, but I can't spell the rest of it yet. My Ds and Bs sometimes get mixed up."

Lito flashed him a smile. "You want to know a secret? Mine starts with a C too—my real name is Carlos. But nobody calls me that."

Cooper brightened. "You can marry me, then! If you want to marry a boy. Dad says some boys marry boys and some boys marry girls and I won't find out until I have purburty."

"Puberty," Jack said gently. "But instead of embarrassing Mr. Lito, let's think of something else that starts with a C. I think Cookie Monster sang a song about them, once…"

Oddly enough, everyone was happy to immediately drop the topic in favor of bickering about cookies instead. With good reason, as it turned

out, because they were excellent. Lito claimed the last gingersnap before
Dave could snatch it and victory had never tasted sweeter.

* * * *

In Lito's family, the post-Thanksgiving-dinner activities were mostly
limited to his dad and uncles talking shop and the women doing dishes
while griping about the men. Lito and the other kids were required to help
clear the table, then were dismissed to go watch TV or to get into whatever
trouble they could find while out of the way of everyone else. Lito usually
stuck around the kitchen for two reasons: one, Aunt Ximena usually let him
take a spoon to any leftover chancaca sauce from the picarones, which was
almost entirely sugar and now made him shudder to think about eating it
straight, and two, it made him feel grown up to listen in while the adults
talked about grown-up things.

Dave's family did things a bit differently. For one thing, *everyone*
helped clean up after the meal. Dave's mother presided over the sink, but
everyone else bustled around putting away leftovers and moving the extra
chairs back to where they came from and carrying all the dishes from the
dining room to the kitchen counters. Lito found Dave standing in the guest
bathroom with the two younger boys, hoisting them up one at a time so
they could see their messy faces in the mirror and apply a damp washcloth
accordingly. The five-year-old had gravy down his front, on his left sleeve,
and in a single long smear over his right eyebrow.

"Want me to do it?" Dave asked. He knelt down, ignoring Lito loitering
in the hallway for the time being, and re-wetted the washcloth in the sink
behind him before dabbing it gently over Cooper's face. "I know you're
just going to get dirty again in a few minutes anyway, but now it won't
taste like dinner."

Cooper giggled. "You don't eat dirt, Uncle Dave."

Dave ruffled his nephew's hair and gave Lito a wink over the top of
the boy's head. "You do if you're not on my team, right? Come on—I bet
you're an even faster runner than last year."

"I can run super fast now!" Cooper jumped up and down, demonstrating
his athleticism, then turned to Lito with open curiosity on his newly-washed
face. "Are you playing football with us too, Mr. Lito? Uncle Dave would
probably let you be on his team if you ask him politely and use your words.
That means you hafta say 'please' and not make bad behavior choices."

Damn. "Dave, you were serious about the football thing?" Lito had assumed the threat of a family football game immediately after everyone stuffing themselves silly at Thanksgiving dinner had just been a joke, but apparently it wasn't. "I'm happy to watch you play—"

"You can watch from on the field with us," Dave countered. He was laughing on the inside, Lito could tell. *Bastard.* "No tackles necessary, even. Just a lot of running and masculine displays of awesomeness. Even better if you can catch, but that's not actually a requirement."

"Only the boys play," Cooper chimed in. "Mama says girls *can* play football, but she's a girl and Grandma's a girl and Miss Katie is a girl and they just watch us so if you want to play you can because you're a boy like me and Uncle Dave and Daddy and Grandpa and—"

"And me," his brother chimed in, not to be ignored.

"I think he gets it." Dave stood back up, cracking his back on the way. "Mmph. Every year I tell myself I won't eat too much, and every year I'm lying. Okay, you two, back to the kitchen and see if Grandma has anything else for you to help with." He ushered them out of the bathroom, then tugged Lito inside and abruptly pulled him into a short but scorching kiss. "Damn, been wanting to do that all afternoon. So what do you think?"

Lito had to blink a few times to reconcile the fact that Dave had just kissed him with the fact that the bathroom door was still open and theoretically any of his family members could have come walking by any second. *Definitely out, then.* "Of the kiss?" he asked.

Dave grinned. "Of all of it. You don't actually have to play flag football with us if you don't want to, but I'll warn you—if you don't, my mother will probably interrogate you instead. And possibly try to bribe you with more cookies. She's been doing an admirable job of not asking me to define my 'friendship' with you so far, but I know it's a struggle. Now that Kitt and his girlfriend have settled into something that looks to be long-term, she'll be after me next."

Lito wasn't sure how he'd define their relationship either, but he definitely didn't want to have that talk *here.* Being questioned by Dave's mom was not on his list of exciting things to do for Thanksgiving. "You did used to play football for real, right?" he asked instead.

Dave nodded, allowing the change of subject. Maybe he wasn't ready to examine their 'friendship' too closely either. "I wasn't a star player or anything, but Jack and Kitt and I were all on the football team in high school. Jack Junior—he's the oldest of the boys, in sixth grade now—started on his middle school team this fall. Dad was always more of a fan than an athlete, though, and the three younger boys just enjoy running around."

"So I wouldn't be the only idiot on the field?" Having half the players be kids made the whole thing slightly less nerve-racking…but only slightly.

"Flag football's light on rules too," Dave assured him, "so don't let that stop you. Have you really never been to a football game?"

"Only what we had to learn in gym class."

"Christ." Dave shook his head. "Tell you what: you join me out there on the field and if we win I'll show my appreciation later."

Oh, now *that* offer had promise. "So by 'show your appreciation'…"

"I mean we can make use of my Jeep having such a large cargo area again." He winked and waggled his eyebrows. "And yes, it's mostly an excuse to get my hands on you again, but I'll take what I can get. A secret back seat blowjob ought to be the capstone to any good Thanksgiving gathering, don't you think?"

Lito pretended to think it over. "I don't know," he drawled. "I might have eaten too much turkey to fit any more meat in my mouth…"

Okay, yeah, he *definitely* was going to remember the predatory look in Dave's eyes at that, even as the guy was trying so hard not to laugh. "Good thing we're going to work up an appetite, then," he countered, leaning in so he could murmur it quiet and dirty in Lito's ear. "And lucky for you, I saved some room."

* * * *

Football, Lito learned, was a lot simpler than he'd thought. On TV it seemed to involve a lot of stop and start, baffling penalties, and full-grown men throwing themselves into a giant pile at the sound of a whistle. Flag football was more about running, which happened to be something Lito was decent at.

He, Dave, and two of the boys all ended up on the same team. Dave's father declined to pick a side and chose to referee instead. The house had a large back lawn, bordered by cotton fields and a small barn on one side and a cow pasture on the other, which made a reasonable play area for a casual game. The "flags" were literally just dish towels tucked in the back waistband of everyone's pants.

"Just pull out someone's flag to tackle them," Dave explained as they waited for his brothers to finish marking the boundaries of the field. "You can only be tackled if you have the ball, and try not to squash any of my nephews. Other than that…"

"I'd just as soon nobody squash *me*."

"I reserve the right." Dave stuck his tongue out at him, prompting a chorus of giggles from the boys, and jogged over to the spot Kitt had marked as the center line. "Okay, y'all—time for you to get pummeled by Team Awesome. You ready?"

"Ready," Jack countered. "Team Best Ever is going to kick your butts."

Since there was no actual tackling and each side only had four players, there wasn't particularly a need for the big pile-up of bodies in the middle of the field. Most rounds (downs?) involved Dave's father blowing a whistle, everyone running around after everyone else, and either Dave or Jack attempting to throw the ball to someone despite all the commotion. Lito picked up that this was the quarterback's role—quarterback being a term he actually recognized—but the rest was just chaos. The boys had a bit of an advantage over the adults, actually, having not eaten their own weight in turkey and gravy before coming out to play.

"Lito!" Dave mimed, throwing the ball, then lobbed it at him for real. "Go! Just run with it!"

Running was something he could do. Lito managed to catch the football without dropping it, which was a minor miracle all on its own, and it wasn't too hard to dodge the two "Team Best Ever" nephews on his way toward the goal line. Dave let out a loud whoop.

"His first ever football game, ladies and gentlemen! And he scores the first touchdown of the game!"

It felt good. "What do I do now?"

"I'll do it!" Cooper volunteered. He took the ball from Lito, slammed it into the ground, and started jumping around with his fist in the air. "Touchdown dance! Touchdown dance! Dance with me, Mr. Lito!"

Ninety-five percent of Lito's dance repertoire would have been inappropriate in front of a five-year-old, but he gave the other five percent a good go anyway. "Like this?"

"Touchdown dance! Woo!"

"Okay, first down everybody." Jack scooped up the ball on his way past and beckoned Lito and Cooper back to the halfway point. "I see Team Best Ever has some catching up to do."

They did catch up, with two touchdowns in a row, but Dave and Junior scored the next one together and tied the game again. True to Dave's prediction, his mother and sisters-in-law came out onto the back porch to watch and cheer for both sides. By the time the game finished—called on account of dark and mosquitoes, but with Team Awesome one touchdown ahead—Lito was panting and more than a bit sweaty and feeling more alive than he had in a long time. The temporary field markers were taken down quickly and everyone bundled back inside for coffee, hot chocolate, and a second round of cookies.

"So what did you think of your first real live football experience?" Dave asked, once they were all settled in the living room and everyone had found somewhere to sit. Lito perched on the arm of the recliner Dave was sprawled in. It felt strangely intimate even though they weren't touching, but any closer would have been awkward in front of the family. They'd probably embarrass themselves, keyed up as he and Dave both were. "You make a good wide receiver—you're almost as speedy as Cooper and Mason are."

The two younger boys puffed up at the implied praise.

"Football was less painful than I expected," Lito admitted. "And there were fewer commercial breaks. Feels like it's missing something without everyone smashing into everyone else, though."

Kitt laughed. "Jack and I both played fullback in high school, which involved a lot of smashing into people. You're right—it's not the same."

"What did you play?" Lito asked Dave.

Dave's eyes sparkled. "Tight end."

The term wasn't any more familiar than "fullback," but Lito had to fight a blush anyway. Damn Dave's fine-tuned innuendo abilities. "Did that, um. Did it involve a lot of tackling, or more running instead?"

"Bit of both." Dave sat back in the chair and sipped casually at his mug of hot chocolate. "I was never all that fast, honestly—I got in a lot better shape after I joined the Army. Football did teach me how to take a fall, though. That was useful in Basic. The running was too, I guess."

"Do you still keep up with it?" Jack's wife asked. She switched the youngest boy over to her other knee so she could put her coffee down on the end table next to her. "The running, I mean. I know you do all that search team stuff—"

"Oh!" Junior perked up. "Sorry, Mom, but I meant to ask Uncle Dave something. We're having a 'health and safety day' at school, and we all get to choose which presentations we go see. Mr. S—he's my teacher—said if we know anyone who has a job to do with health or safety we could ask them to be a speaker. And I know you talk to classes about dog safety sometimes. It would be awesome if you could bring Lumpy and Woozy, and you'd be *way* less boring than the lady they always get from the hospital to talk about why smoking is bad. And I've told my friends that sometimes you get to find actual dead bodies and they think it's really cool, so can you come? Please?"

"Sweetie," his mother cautioned. "Your Uncle Dave has a regular job too. He can't necessarily drop everything to come drive two hours and bring his dogs for your friends to meet. You're leaving it a little late—"

"It's fine," Dave assured her. "We schedule school talks all the time, for whoever on the team is free. I'll see what I can do."

"There's a good chance I could come, if you need me," Lito volunteered. "You live near Birmingham, right?"

Junior nodded.

That was convenient. "I've got to get out there sometime before the end of the year anyway," Lito explained. "I've got a pretty flexible schedule for that kind of thing." It wasn't a lie, although he had yet to sit down with Vanessa and sort out any details. Acquiring an "authentic local ambiance" meant he'd be visiting all the Dayspring hotels in the state sooner or later anyway. "I don't know what NALSAR does for school talks in the first place," he added, "but I'd love to find out."

"Flexible is good." Dave didn't look up at him, but his hand twitched like he was trying very hard not to sneak a totally inappropriate grope of Lito's ass right then and there. "Yeah, Junior, definitely have your health teacher get in touch with me. Mr. Lito and I can work out more details on the way home."

The *among other things* was left unsaid.

Chapter 11

Birmingham was a good half-day drive from Black Lake. As a result, Dave wasn't entirely surprised that Lito was the only one who volunteered to come along and give a talk at Junior's school. It worked out well, actually—Lito needed to stay in the Birmingham hotel overnight, and even though Dayspring Inn & Suites was dog-friendly it would have been awkward to have Spot along on a work trip. He'd jumped at Dave's offer to dog-sit and meet up together the next morning.

Lumpy and Woozy *loved* having Spot sleep over. The three of them chased themselves silly from when Lito dropped Spot off until their dinner hit their dog bowls, then slept like rocks until five o'clock in the morning when they started tearing around again. Dave was actually kind of impressed at how they managed to keep that excitement up for the entire two-hour drive. This had to be what parents of toddlers felt like. Toddler triplets, maybe.

Lito was waiting in the parking lot of his hotel when Dave pulled up, as promised. He hopped in with a smile and two cups of coffee. Dude must have been psychic.

"You are a god among men," Dave pronounced.

Lito laughed and set them carefully in the two cupholders, which were both far enough forward the dogs couldn't investigate too closely. Spot stuck her nose between the front seats, but Lito just gave her an ear scratch and a playful noogie and then nudged her back where she belonged. "I'm lucky the manager here considered me worth impressing," he said. "The executive suite has a Keurig—everyone else gets to deal with the pot in the lobby. However stale it happens to be. The poor lady at the front desk this morning certainly hadn't had time to refresh it, not with one of *those* guests complaining at her."

"Difficult?" Dave guessed.

"That's a polite word for it." He wrinkled his nose. Dave had a hard time not leaning over and kissing it, he was so adorable, but Lito was still talking. "Used to hate them back when I was in her shoes. They stay the night, then come down in the morning to nitpick at their bill because the air conditioner was too loud or the cell phone reception wasn't good enough and they want you to give them a discount. Sometimes it's things I could have fixed if they'd told me earlier and sometimes it's totally in their heads, but they almost never give up without a twenty-minute argument. At least. We had about one a week on the overnight shift, way back when."

"Glad you're not still on the front line?"

"God yes," Lito answered immediately. "Not saying I don't still hear inane things from people at work, but at least now I'm not required to smile while I do it." He sat back in his seat and sipped his coffee in silence for a moment. "Yesterday wasn't bad, all things considered, but I'm not excited about having to introduce myself to a whole new set of people now that I'm here. At least with the Georgia locations, I'd finally gotten the managers to stop treating me like I'm on the hotel version of *Queer Eye*. I mean, I'm finally getting to see the layout of each Dayspring in person, which makes visualizing the space a lot easier, but I do miss the distance an email can give."

"I've never..." Dave shook his head. He'd always preferred getting his hands dirty versus languishing in front of a computer every day, but he thought he knew what Lito meant. "Can I say I commiserate even though I've never seen *Queer Eye*?"

That surprised a laugh out of Lito. "Clearly you've missed some required viewing."

"Is there a checklist?"

"There's a whole queer agenda, haven't you heard?" Lito let out an amused snort. "Gonna guess you've never worn heels either, even just trying them on with your drag queen friends. Or memorized Broadway musicals and belted out all the good diva parts. Or went to a gay club and got down and dirty on the dance floor."

"I think you and I have had very different life experiences." *Very, very different.* "Correct on two out of three."

Lito stilled. Dave could sense him sorting through what he'd just said. Then... "You sing?"

"Only country, and only karaoke. When Rick makes me." Dave kept his eyes on the road, but he could feel Lito's gaze on him. "I'm a pretty damn good dancer, though. In the right circumstances. Have I not mentioned that?"

"The Nashville thing?"

"On occasion."

They each drank their coffee in silence for a few minutes. It didn't take a psychic to know they were both thinking back to the previous weekend, where they'd spent most of Sunday afternoon in Lito's bed together. It hadn't been "dancing," exactly, but Dave came home feeling simultaneously more energetic and more exhausted than he'd been in a very long time. Lito was *very* flexible, as it turned out. He'd let Dave boss him into attempting some truly ambitious positions until they both couldn't take it anymore. Lito ended up riding Dave until they both collapsed and passed out for a long afternoon nap together. It had been sexy as hell and comfortably domestic and hell if he was going to be able to reconcile the two. With Lito, both descriptions fit.

"More travel now, then?" Dave finally asked.

"Yeah, probably, but who the hell knows how it will all shake out." Lito sighed and let his head thunk against the back of the seat. "In this particular hotel, they're redoing the lobby and breakfast area. I accidentally got the owners on a 'local art' kick with some of the stuff I did in Georgia, so now my big project is to revamp every Alabama Dayspring to be more local without breaking the bank. The lobby here is an odd shape, so I wanted to get a sense of the space and light levels in person."

"You have to suss out the local art scene for every town in Alabama? That's…ambitious of you."

"Shut up." Dave didn't turn his head to look, but he could tell Lito was smiling. "Janet is trying to hook me up with a friend of hers who's in some sort of Alabama painters' guild. If they've all got portfolios online, it will save me a lot of time."

"You're still going to have to visit all the hotels, though."

"Mmm-hmm."

"I didn't realize your job was so expansive."

"Neither do most other people. Including the women I work with here." He upended his paper coffee cup, draining the last few swallows, and sat up straight again. Seeming slightly more awake. "When I first moved to Atlanta, I was doing purchasing and inventory management. Then I made some executive decorating decisions because nobody else would. About a year after that, I finally persuaded Betty and Ronald—the owners—to do all the hotels in the same color scheme. Now I'm *still* doing most of the purchasing and inventory, but I get to pick most of what we get. That usually means I can spend some time with Google and at least come up with a short list of local artists, but web presence doesn't always correlate to talent."

"I can believe that." Computers weren't usually Dave's first choice for dicking around outside of work, but he'd seen enough of the internet to make that particular truism *very* clear. Which brought to mind that NALSAR needed a website too. Tracking all that web hosting nonsense down was going to be a huge headache.

"So yeah," Lito said, "more reason to travel." He twisted around so he could give the ever-patient Spot another ear scratch while he held his coffee in the other hand. "Dayspring Inn & Suites doesn't have all that many locations in Georgia too far from the Atlanta area, so in the past I've always just taken day trips before when I needed to see something. This will be new."

He didn't look enthused by the concept. More like exhausted. "I'll always be happy to let Spot bunk with my two idiots when you're gone," Dave offered. "They had fun last night. Loud I-don't-know-where-they-get-all-that-energy fun, but all three were clearly having a blast."

"Thanks."

The offer won Dave another one of those genuine little smiles.

"On a not-entirely unrelated note," Lito said, "I think I've forgotten most of what was in that 'how to not get mauled by wolves while lost in the woods' handout you gave me way back when. You're not expecting all that much teaching from me today, are you? I mean, I know the basics—"

The basics would be more than enough. "Don't worry about it," Dave assured him. "They're not going to be grading us on our presentation. Junior said it's only for the sixth and seventh grades, and the kids got a list of something like two dozen speakers to pick from. I wouldn't be surprised if we only end up with a handful who signed up to hear us."

Lito laughed. *Really* laughed. "Did your school never do these? They're universally terrible. I guarantee you, when 'dogs who find dead bodies' get stacked up against the chance to hear the school nurse lecture on healthy eating or watching a Smokey the Bear video from the seventies, the dogs are gonna win."

"Seriously?"

"Trust me."

The school wasn't at all hard to find: it was a giant brick monstrosity with a mural of the school logo painted over the entrance. Dave could have pointed it out from half a mile away. Lito got the three dogs in their vests and harnesses while Dave double-checked that everything in his box of hand-outs was how he remembered it.

"Ready?" Standing in the parking lot was a really inconvenient time to remember that he hated public speaking, but the realization usually hit right…about…*now.* Crap.

"Ready," Lito answered. He passed Lumpy and Woozy's leashes to Dave, but gave Dave's hand a quick squeeze on the way.

The nervous quiver in Dave's stomach lessened a bit.

They got about ten feet into the school before the dogs drew a giant cluster of students in the hallway. The rush cleared out quickly once the class bell rang, but they still drew more than a few curious glances as they got their VISITOR stickers from the front office and made their way toward the back door of the auditorium. Junior's teacher lit up when he saw them.

"You were by far the students' most popular choice," the man said, beaming. He was tall and thin, his hipster glasses and neatly-shaped beard not quite balancing out how much his receding hairline aged him. "We don't have a microphone hooked up for you, I'm afraid, but if there's anything else you need…"

"I don't think there is, but thanks." Dave braced himself against the wall so Lumpy could nuzzle against his thigh. "We're just doing a bit of talking and then a practical demonstration—those always get the kids' attention. And I don't mind being loud."

"Excellent." The teacher gestured for them to follow him through a cramped green room and down a short flight of stairs to the wing of the stage. The sounds of excited middle schoolers already echoed around the room as the students filed in. "It's called NALSAR, right? North Alabama Search and Rescue? You're Dave Schmidt and…"

"Lito Apaza," Lito filled in for him. "Thanks."

The teacher—Dave couldn't remember more of a name than the "Mr. S" Junior had called him—calmed the students down and gave a long-winded introduction. Junior waved enthusiastically from the second row. Dave had probably done hundreds of these educational talks over the years, to varying age groups, but actually being on a stage was unusual. A stage in a giant auditorium full of middle schoolers, whom he was expected to educate. Yeah, the venue really wasn't helping with his dislike of speaking in front of large groups. Lito flashed him a questioning look—*What's wrong?*—so Dave tried his best to focus on the dogs instead. He dropped Lumpy and Woozy's leashes and snapped his fingers, the command that said *you can wander but be ready to come back to me immediately when*

I call you. Woozy walked in a tight circle, looked up at him, and flopped herself down on his foot. The kids tittered.

Lito smiled too, though, and followed suit. He took a seat on the edge of the stage next to Woozy, dangling his legs down in the orchestra pit, so Dave sat on Woozy's other side. Eventually Mr. S conceded the fact that his students weren't listening to a word he was saying and turned the whole thing over to Dave and Lito.

This part—the actual spiel—came almost automatically by now. "Who here owns a dog?" About half the hands went up. "Who knows the correct way to pet one?" Nearly everyone. So far the students were chatty and excitable, not rude but not paying attention to the humans on stage either. Dave singled out a cocky-looking boy in the front row. "You, then—come on up and show us."

The boy strutted up onto the stage and gave Lumpy a few head pats, grinning at his buddies. Lumpy practically rolled her eyes. The gesture was exactly what Dave had expected, though, so he used the boy's mistake to explain the difference in reaction time between reaching in overhand (slower and appears more of a threat) versus underhand (easy to pull away and gives the dog plenty of chance to telegraph its intentions). Lumpy made an excellent visual aid. Lito fit himself into the talk perfectly too, helping wrangle volunteers up and down from the stage and stopping the dogs from wandering off into the audience with a subtle throat clear on the few times they looked like they might want to explore. He was surprisingly attentive to Dave's speech too, which was both flattering and a bit distracting.

"We've got time for some questions," Dave concluded, "and then Mr. Apaza and Spot will do a bit of a practical demonstration for you."

"Seriously?" Lito murmured, just loud enough for Dave to hear. "A little warning would have been nice."

"You'll do fine," Dave whispered back. "Trust your dog." Spot was behaving very well. *Incredibly* well considering it was her first time in this kind of situation. Lito running the find meant Dave could narrate. It also meant Lumpy and Woozy could continue to lie on either side of him on the stage like big black-and-brown slugs, watching the audience and letting their tongues loll out.

The students had quite a few questions, unsurprisingly, ranging from insightful to absurd. Dave tossed a few of the more obvious ones to Lito: no, their dogs weren't trained to attack people. Yes, the dogs lived with them as pets. No, they didn't get paid. The dogs didn't either. Yes, it took a long time to learn search and rescue.

"Spot and I have been doing this about three months," Lito elaborated for a girl with frizzy hair and braces who'd asked how long they'd each been on the team. "She and I probably won't get certified until sometime next year, and then learning cadaver finds takes, what, a year after that?"

Dave nodded.

"So we're newbies. Da—err, Mr. Schmidt here was the one who started the team and has been doing this a lot longer than me."

Another boy raised his hand. "What's a cadaver?"

Ha! Dave sat back and raised an eyebrow at Lito. He usually avoided that term for a reason, but sixth graders were old enough to not be traumatized by the concept. Probably. "Go on," he urged. "You're the one who brought it up…"

Lito shot him a look that promised retribution later. The students thought it was hilarious. "A cadaver is another word for a dead body," he explained. "I've only been on two or three call-outs so far—all without Spot, since she's not experienced enough—but I, personally, haven't done a cadaver search yet. NALSAR sometimes gets asked to look for people who have been missing for a long time, and when that happens our dogs need extra training because we don't always know whether the person we're looking for is alive or not. Sometimes we're pretty sure they're not. When that happens, our dogs help the police find out where they died and where their body is."

It was a calm, age-appropriate response. Way better than Dave usually did when faced with a question he wasn't expecting. *Christ, he's amazing.*

Junior was grinning like mad—his coolness quotient had probably just doubled in the last thirty seconds. The excitement in the room rose dramatically as several students started whispering to each other. The cocky boy in the front row didn't even bother raising his hand this time. "Have you ever—"

Oh, this was going to get out of control *fast.* Damn.

"Right. So." Even though it was fun and a bit hot watching Lito deal with rabidly curious sixth graders so handily, letting this particular topic of conversation continue would probably be a mistake. "Who wants to see an example of what our dogs do?"

"I've changed my mind," Lito grumbled quietly as he got Spot's attention and took her leash off. His back was temporarily to their audience, blocking them from seeing his lips move. "Running Spot on a no-warning search is preferable to giving a no-warning talk about dead people to children. Also, screw you very much for that."

"They're not going to forget this talk."

Lito glared at him, but the corners of his mouth kept twitching upward into a hint of a smile. "I'd like to elaborate on my previous statement," he whispered, "but it wouldn't be appropriate for school."

Any students who weren't already engrossed in the presentation were definitely interested now that Spot was loose. Several started trying to attract her attention, but Spot stayed cheerfully at Lito's side and ignored them all. Not that Dave blamed her—he had to crane his neck to look up at Lito, now standing a few feet away while Dave was still seated at the edge of the stage. The disparity in their relative positions sent a hot spark through his entire body. Lito looked gorgeous and confident and charismatic and Dave was extremely aware of the fact that he was currently at eye level with Lito's thighs. Lito cocked one eyebrow at him in a clear *now what?* gesture.

"Okay." Dave had to clear his throat, but climbed to his feet as well. "I'm going to need a volunteer to be 'lost' up here—you with the pink shirt. Perfect, come on up. Lito, you and Spot start out over there near the side aisle. Make sure she's not peeking."

A wave of laughter from their audience.

Dave beckoned their volunteer victim closer. "What's your name, hon?"

The stage wasn't an ideal search venue—outdoors was usually better—but Dave got the demonstration search set up fairly quickly. The girl "hid" behind a stray cardboard box toward the back of the stage. She was in view of the left half of the audience but not visible from where Lito and Spot waited. Lito had to keep turning Spot's head toward himself so she wouldn't look over her shoulder at the kids, but the students in the nearest seats found that so hilarious Dave doubted Spot would have noticed the search target anyway.

"Okay," Dave called, loud enough to be heard over the growing buzz of students whispering to each other and craning for a better view. "We've got a young woman lost in the woods back here. Her name is Lanisha. You ready?"

"What's her description?" Lito called back. They often skipped the preliminaries in practice, but this was good.

"Eleven years old, African-American, long hair in several braids. She also giggles a lot."

Laughter from the audience and the girl.

"When and where was she last seen, and what are my search parameters?"

"Last seen at school about ten seconds ago, wearing pink. Your boundaries are the edges of the stage. Go when you're ready."

Lito did an excellent job of ramping up Spot's excitement—"Ready, girl? Ready? Ready? *Go find!*"—and Spot took off like a shot. She skipped the stairs entirely, jumping straight from the floor to the stage. Several kids shouted encouragement. Her first lap took her straight across the front of the stage and down the opposite stairs to where the students were now all standing and cheering her on, but she came straight back to Lito and made her second pass further back up the stage. She was still running for the fun of it at this point. Lito angled his body perfectly, though, delineating the boundary of the search area (and the fact that the audience wasn't in it). Spot shrank her excited circles accordingly.

Dave had a sudden mental image of Lito using that same take-charge stance in a different situation. He didn't even have to talk, just *stand* there, and now Dave had the beginnings of a hard-on. *Christ.* Lumpy and Woozy both sat up to watch Spot run, but they stayed put at Dave's side.

Even after several months of practicing, Spot still overreacted when she actually found someone. This time, she *woofed* in full voice and then bounced around the girl for a good ten seconds before remembering what she was supposed to do. The rest of the students were all craning their necks to see, but it would have been hard to miss how frantically Spot's tail was wagging. She returned to Lito, sat just like they'd practiced dozens of times, then took Lito directly in and sat on the girl's feet looking immensely pleased with herself.

"Nicely done," Dave murmured when Lito and Spot rejoined him at the front of the stage and both Spot and their "victim" had been given suitable applause. "It's harder in front of an audience, I know, but you both did well."

"Not much of a challenge, search-wise," Lito murmured back. "I was expecting you'd hide her out in the audience or something. Possibly on the catwalk overhead."

Dave looked up—yes, there was a catwalk up above where the spotlights hung. "I thought you didn't like heights."

The glint in Lito's eyes turned a bit wicked, then he leaned in to speak directly in Dave's ear. "I've found I don't mind if you're there to catch me."

Dave had been vaguely turning around some tease in his head, something about enjoying the view as Lito climbed the ladder to get up there, but some things weren't appropriate to say out loud at a middle school. Including ninety percent of his current thoughts. *Well fuck.*

Instead of doing something that would get them thrown out, he motioned for the students to settle down again. "It looks like we have ten minutes left," he announced in his public speaking voice. "Those of you who would like to practice greeting and petting a dog, Mr. Apaza and I will bring Heffalump, Woozle, and Spot to the edges of the stage. Make a line, one person petting at a time, and remember to use proper hand positioning—underhand, palm up, fingers together. And always ask the owner for permission first."

There would be time for ogling, and all the rest, later. If they hadn't had the dogs along, Dave would have suggested they go back and put Lito's executive suite to use. As it was, they'd just have to wait until they got back to Black Lake. By then, he'd have had time to come up with a *challenge* Lito might like better than searching for barely hidden middle schoolers.

Chapter 12

The rest of Lito's December was a whirlwind of work, holiday preparations, and all the issues that popped up when those two things crossed. Christmas meant decorations, which meant that wonderful tightrope of secular versus religious and "holiday" versus "winter." It also meant a sharp increase in idiocy which became his problem: some teenage vandals in Ardmore trashed the hotel lobby when the overnight manager was away from the desk, a drunk man in Huntsville urinated on the breakfast buffet decorations, two boxes of seasonal items went missing in Montgomery. Lito still had his whole "local flavor" project to do, but the steady stream of stupid emergencies was an incredible time sink.

NALSAR's practices were getting shorter too, now that sunset was coming at four o'clock and temperatures dropped to what even Midwesterners would consider chilly. Spot spent less time in the backyard and more time in the house sprawled next to wherever Lito happened to be. Usually trying to look as cold and pathetic as possible, presumably in hopes he'd change the weather. She did enjoy the playdates when he brought her to Dave's house—and let her sleep in the living room with Lumpy and Woozy while Dave's bed was otherwise occupied—but the shorter days were depressing. Even though they would have been a lot more depressing alone.

Dave offered to let Lito tag along for his family Christmas get-together. Lito gave it some serious consideration. Thanksgiving dinner could be excused as "my poor platonic friend has no family nearby for the holiday," though; actually showing up again to a second Schmidt family gathering felt more *formal*. Like they were going public with their relationship. Hell, he wasn't even sure if it *was* a relationship. They fucked in the bedroom and talked about other things when outside it and other than occasional innuendo or flirting comments, the two spheres stayed almost entirely separate.

Ultimately Lito decided to spend Christmas in Atlanta with his friends-turned-family. Ian and some cousin of Chris's had taken over the lease on Lito's old apartment, and they offered crash space for him and Spot both. The new roommate turned out to be a skinny older guy named Clarence who kept evangelizing about the spiritual yoga class he taught on weekends. It sounded terrible and Lito could tell Ian was already sick of the spiel. Living out of state made Lito exempt from the hard sell, luckily.

Paul and Brandon invited everyone to their house in the suburbs for Christmas morning. Clarence declined to come along—Ian didn't look sad about that either—so Lito, Ian, and Chris all piled in Lito's car for the drive. It should have felt like old times, but something was missing. Something beyond the obvious "Jericho's still in Haiti, Geoffrey moved to San Francisco, Adam's spending the holiday in Buffalo with his family, and Tony and Enrique broke up so neither of them keep in touch anymore."

Maybe it was just that the old gang was getting older. Lito hadn't joined their group until after most of the rest of them graduated college, but Brandon and Ian and a few of the others all went back nearly a decade. *Hell, I was still in middle school back then.* Seeing the actual literal white picket fence around Brandon and Paul's house made Lito's stomach lurch.

Halfway up Paul and Brandon's walkway, Ian gasped dramatically and put his hand to his chest. "Holy shit, they've taken up *gardening.*" He said it softly enough that only Lito could hear him, but Chris did shoot them a funny look. And there was, indeed, a neat little flower bed bordering the porch. It probably looked gorgeous in the summer. "Shoot me if I ever go all Stepford like this, okay?" Ian murmured.

Fat chance of that happening. "Deal." The likelihood of Ian ever living somewhere with a white picket fence and a garden was somewhere below the chances of Lito's parents spontaneously becoming hippies. Lito would have said the same of himself, but his current house did have a fence (albeit a half-rusted chain-link dog run) so he wasn't really one to talk.

Conversation flowed comfortably, though, helped by the fact that brunch was freaking amazing. Paul was a good cook and it was clear Brandon was proud as hell of his partner. The two of them spent the whole meal playing footsie under the table where they thought no one could see. No one else could, probably, but Lito had a prime viewing angle thanks to the mirrored cabinets on the sideboard. Somehow he found himself more jealous than nauseated.

"Feels weird to not all be crammed in someone's too-small apartment," Chris commented as the meal wound down. "You two are kind of creepily domestic now, you know that?"

Brandon laughed and bent down to plant a kiss on the top of Paul's head on his way to return their empty plates to the kitchen. "Realized I'm ready for it, I guess," he answered back over his shoulder. "And I found a guy I love who makes the domesticity worth it."

Paul practically had cartoon hearts in his eyes at the declaration—then Ian made an exaggerated gagging sound, which started everyone laughing again. Lito didn't mention the footsie.

They moved into the living room for a few rounds of group games on the PlayStation. Lito, Chris, and Ian said their goodbyes after another hour or so—Brandon and Paul had plans to spend Christmas afternoon and evening with Brandon's family—but the feeling of déjà vu Lito expected at being in the same room together was strangely lacking. Wednesday night gaming online with each other just wasn't the same. Even the handshakes and back-slaps and hope-to-see-you-soons felt depressingly adult.

"I really do miss you guys," he confessed in the car on the way back. "I have made some friends in Black Lake, but they're not you."

"Awwww, that's sweet." Ian made an exaggerated kissy face. "I'm not giving up the apartment, though, so don't ask. I like your old bedroom."

"Spot's probably asleep on your bed right now, wondering why all the furniture's wrong."

"As long as she doesn't pee on it, it's fine."

"I could probably get her to pee on Clarence's, if you want her to."

Ian lit up. "God, wouldn't *that* be entertaining?"

Chris leaned forward from his spot in the back seat and smacked Ian upside the head. "That's my cousin, remember. I vouched for you. Don't be a dick."

"I didn't say yes," Ian whined. "I just said it would be funny. He's not a bad apartment-mate, he's just..."

"A bit much sometimes," Chris finished for him. "Believe me, I know."

Lito snorted. "A bit much for Ian. Never thought I'd hear that."

"Shut up. Oh!" Ian clapped loudly, which nearly startled Lito into swerving lanes. "Speaking of being a bit much—Lito, I've got a Christmas card for you. It was addressed to you as 'Carlos,' which is probably why it didn't get forwarded like everything else does, but remind me when we get back and I'll dig it out."

Who would have sent me an actual, physical Christmas card? Lito racked his brain and kept drawing a blank. "Nobody calls me Carlos. Did it say who it's from?"

"I didn't open it. The return address was Miami, though, and I assume it was someone in your family—a woman's first name, I don't remember what, but the last name was Apaza." He grimaced. "I know you and your family haven't exactly kept in touch—"

"That's an understatement—"

"—but I figured I'd mention it. If you want me to toss it out, I can do that too. Up to you."

As tempting as the offer was... "I guess I should at least look."

Lito felt significantly less merry the rest of the way back.

* * * *

Dear Lito/Carlos (whichever you're going by now), the card read:

It's been ages, but Feliz Navidad! This was the most current address I could find for you, although Google is being cagey about whether it's current. I hope you get this.

I'm guessing you don't keep up with anyone else in the family either, but if you haven't already heard: Aunt Ximena passed away right after Thanksgiving. It was a surprise stroke with no warning. Uncle Diego had been thinking about retiring, or at least cutting back how much time he spent at work, but now he's thrown himself back into it. Your dad and my dad are both trying to keep up.

Lucas and I are now out in Coral Gables, which is a bit farther from the old neighborhood but a lot closer to both our jobs. I don't know if you'd remember him—he was just a friend when you were living with me—but we moved in together about two years ago. You probably would have told me it was about damn time. He's an electrician and I finally finished that phlebotomy course I told you I was thinking about way back when. We've got a guest room in our condo, if you ever want to come visit. I miss you and your fabulous snappy comebacks.

Write back, to let me know you got this? I'm on Facebook too, so come find me there if you want to reconnect!

-Gabriela

"That bad?"

Lito was startled from the letter by Ian plonking down on the sofa next to him and offering him a bottle of Blue Moon.

"Was I right? About it being family?" Ian gestured toward the paper with his own bottle. "My mom and I aren't in touch with ours either anymore, you know. Sometimes it sucks but we both decided they're not worth the stress."

"Yeah," Lito answered weakly. "My cousin Gabriela. She's...she was the nice one."

"She the one you lived with for a while?"

"Mmmhmm." Five months, two weeks, and four days, to be exact. He'd counted them over and over. No matter how many times he counted, the numbers never went back down.

They drank their beers in silence for a while. For all that Ian was a loudmouth and a smart-ass ninety-five percent of the time, he'd always been the one who *got* Lito the most. He was also more than capable of shutting up when he sensed Lito needed it. They'd thought about hooking up, once upon a time—Ian was the one who'd first introduced Lito to their little group, actually—but it didn't take long to realize they weren't cut out to be anything more than friends. And that was fine, because friends were all Lito had for family anymore. Friends and Spot. Who was currently curled up at Ian's feet, the traitor.

"It sounds like she's doing okay," Lito volunteered after a while. "Said she has a boyfriend and a new condo. My aunt had a stroke last month and died unexpectedly. It's... I'm guessing the rest of the family's taking it hard. Aunt Ximena was kind of the matriarch."

"Were you close?"

"Yes, kind of? It's complicated." She'd liked him as much as any of his cousins, Lito supposed, and she had welcomed him into the kitchen when the rest of the boys were roughhousing and knocking each other around. Then again, she'd also been the most shocked and angry when he was outed as being gay. "It's mostly just hard to think of the family changing," he admitted. "Times like this—big holidays—we always spent together at their house. I try to tell myself I don't miss it, haven't missed it over the years, but...hell, that's a lie. Every once in a while it hits me and I mope like crazy for a few hours."

"It's okay to dream about the good parts." Ian put his empty bottle down on the corner of his desk and turned so they were mostly facing each other. "Mom cut off contact with her dad and her sisters when she was in college, right after her own mother died. I've never met them. Sometimes I wonder what they'd be like if I met them now, but I can't miss what I never knew."

"Yes you can." Maybe a happy family was a Hollywood fantasy anyway, but sometimes the longing for normal, supportive parents was overwhelming. "I spent Thanksgiving with a...good friend, I guess. He invited me along to his family get-together so I wouldn't be all by myself. His parents live way out in the country surrounded by cows and cotton fields, and they were all so *Southern*. White, Alabama Southern. He and his brothers all played football in school, and all four of his nephews like to play, and I got roped into running around with them and trying to pretend I knew what I was doing. Thanksgiving dinner was busy and noisy and everyone crammed into the house even though there weren't quite enough chairs for everyone and they were all *nice.* To each other and to me. I remember Uncle Diego and Aunt Ximena's house having lots of noise and chaos too, but there was usually also at least one major argument, too-loud music, younger cousins misbehaving, older cousins harassing the younger ones...shit. When I describe it like that it sounds awful, but it really wasn't. It's just what I *had.*"

"And you miss an idealized version of that?"

Lito had never told himself that in those words, but Ian—as usual—was spot-on. "I miss the acceptance. And having somewhere to belong. But what you said, yeah. That's basically it."

Ian nudged Lito's knee with his own. "You know we're going to be here for you no matter where you end up, right?"

"You guys being 'here' doesn't help me a lot out in Alabama. It's a long drive."

"I like road trips." Ian gave up on the whole knee-touching thing and went for a tight side-hug instead. "Hell, I would even stay *overnight* in Alabama in one of those hotels of yours if it meant I could help. On one condition."

"What's that?"

Ian pushed him away with a smile and scooted back to recline against the other end of the sofa. "You've got to tell me about this 'good friend' of yours. Is he the 'not bad looking' one who got you suddenly interested in Mother Nature?"

* * * *

Dave brought Lumpy and Woozy along to his parents' house for Christmas, like he usually did. Their property wasn't dog-proofed by any means, but Lumpy and Woozy both loved bunking down in the barn for a few days and taking in whatever interesting and new smells they could find there. Jack's boys also loved the chance to romp around the backyard at whatever speeds the dogs would tolerate. Lumpy ended up flopped on her back on the dirt floor between Billy and Junior when Dave walked into the barn Christmas afternoon. Woozy's arthritis slowed her down a bit more every year, so she'd curled up back in her bed early, but both pups wagged their tails at him as if to say *look at how well we're minding your small humans!*

"Y'all will sleep well tonight," Dave said to both the dogs and his nephews. "My two will never admit they can't keep up with you boys anymore, but they'll kill themselves trying."

"We've gotten faster," Billy pronounced proudly. "I was practicing fake-outs, and they were pretending to tackle me."

Dave didn't mention that he'd been watching through the kitchen window and had seen most of their romping firsthand.

"Thanks again, by the way," Junior announced, propping himself up to a sitting position. "For coming to my school. It wasn't as cool as getting to watch Lumpy and Woozy search for someone for real, but everyone thought it was awesome anyway."

"Did they learn anything?"

Junior grinned. "Learned that you guys search for dead bodies."

Of course that would be the part that stuck. "I usually try to avoid mentioning that particular fact."

"Yeah, but it's so cool! I want to come join your team, but Mom says—"

"The same thing I say," Dave interrupted. "When you're eighteen you're welcome to come out to practice, whether or not you have a dog. Until then—"

"You don't wanna corrupt me, I know." Junior gave Lumpy another pat on the head and pushed himself up to standing so he could go give Woozy equal petting time. "I wouldn't mind, though. I already know that you're gay, and that hasn't corrupted me yet..."

Billy sat up too. "That's because he's busy corrupting Mr. Lito."

Dave laughed before he could stop himself. He couldn't help it—Billy at nine was a little blond copy of what Jack had been like at that age, snark and all. "He's just a friend," he countered. *Lied.* "And a teammate."

Ping.

Merry Christmas! Lito's text said. *Hope you're enjoying your family time! I'm going to stay in Atlanta for a few days—got invited to a post-holiday thing at the big bosses' house, which I'm not gonna turn down—but Spot's chomping at the bit to get back out in the woods. I don't think she's a city dog anymore :-)*

"Right," Junior said, his expression making it clear he didn't believe a word of it. "It's a teammate who makes you smile like that?"

Billy nodded. "Uncle Dave, we're not blind."

Chapter 13

Ronald and Betty were in their sixties, never had kids, and lived in an absolutely *gorgeous* modern house in one of the ritzier Atlanta suburbs. Lito had been invited to their home a few times before, mostly for the company Christmas and Fourth of July get-togethers, but this was the first time since the downtown Dayspring offices closed. Betty's email had made it sound like this would be something similar…which was why it felt so odd when Lito got to their house and discovered it would just be the three of them eating dinner together.

"Not quite the same as before, I know," Betty said, picking up on Lito's confusion as she ushered him into the kitchen, "but we wanted to catch you while you're in town. How's Black Lake treating you?"

"It's different." Lito accepted the glass of ice water she handed him and made to help with setting the table, but Ronald waved him away. "I've never lived anywhere smaller than Orlando before, so it's taken some getting used to."

"Settled in at the new office?"

Lito still didn't feel particularly settled, standing out like a sore thumb in the middle of all his coworkers' gossip and feminine chatter, but that wasn't really something he could say. "Vanessa and the other women have gone out of their way to be welcoming," he answered. They were obviously making an effort. "It's been an adjustment, and tapping into the *local* local art scene for every Dayspring location in the state is gonna be a big job, but I don't mind the travel." He thought for a second. "I do like having a house to myself instead of half an apartment too. I'm renting a little two-bedroom ranch with a flowerbed I haven't killed yet and a real backyard."

Ronald snorted—Lito's not exactly green thumb had come up in conversation before, the first time they were dealing with landscaping. Planning out a new look was one thing; growing actual living herbs in the box outside his old kitchen window was something else entirely. Betty frequently lamented that she couldn't garden like she had when she was younger because they were so frequently away from Atlanta.

"You've got a dog, right?" Ronald asked. "I remember you mentioning her."

"Yeah, a two-year-old lab mix. She likes having a yard too."

"We had two, several years ago." Betty gestured toward a framed picture on the wall of two fluffy white puffballs with dark brown eyes. "Tillie and Tiny. I used to take them with me whenever I was on the road without Ron."

"I remember." *Vividly.* Lito had been an overnight desk clerk for all of about a month when his manager had whipped everyone into a frenzy because one of Dayspring's owners was going to be visiting their location overnight and checking things out personally. They were one of the few hotels around with pet-friendly rooms, so it shouldn't have been a surprise that she brought her dogs, but Lito had been taken aback by the tiny lady with giant hair and two bleached tribbles following along behind her. She'd checked into her room, put her pups to bed, then spent most of the night puttering with the antiquated computers trying to set up some new reservation system. The two of them ended up having a wonderfully frank discussion about the hospitality industry in general, Lito's ambitions in particular, and what he needed to do to get there. When the night manager up and quit with no notice six months later, Betty rubber-stamped Lito's promotion without even bothering to come interview him for the position.

"You brought them along a few times when you came to Orlando," he explained. "I was impressed at how quiet they were, even when another dog completely freaked out at them in the lobby."

"When—oh!" Betty put her hand to her mouth. "A big grumpy gray one, wasn't it? We got a complaint afterward, that's why it stuck in my mind. The owner said you weren't sufficiently apologetic that her dog suffered emotional distress while at our hotel."

That was news to Lito. "I spent forever letting her complain at me next morning—that was the first time I'd ever needed to go take a break so I wouldn't start yelling back. What's-his-name, the day manager, hid in his office the entire time, citing seniority."

"I told the woman in no uncertain terms that we only allow *well-behaved* dogs," Betty said. "And that particular manager didn't last all that long, if it's the man I'm thinking about. Balding, regrettable mustache, kind of a whiny voice? Name started with an E?"

That was…more than accurate, actually, if not exactly a flattering description. They chatted about E-something-the-ex-manager and Lito's time at the Atlanta office over the course of dinner. Which was, as usual, amazing. Betty and Ronald both loved to cook and Lito got the impression they'd been desperate for a chance to show off their culinary skills. He'd never had a vegetarian shepherd's pie before, but Ronald had somehow remembered that Lito was a vegetarian (partly right) and it was really touching that they'd perfected a new recipe just for him.

"I've got the trifles still setting," Betty announced when Lito finished thoroughly cleaning his plate. "If you don't mind waiting on dessert for a bit, though, Ron and I did want to talk shop with you. None of what we're about to discuss is public knowledge yet, so please don't tell anyone."

That sounded ominous. He should have known there'd be something like that the moment he found out the invitation to the big boss' house for dinner was a private one. "I won't," he promised.

"Well then." Ronald poked at his phone for a minute, then turned the screen and handed it to Lito. "This is the Sunshine State Motel in Miami. Or it's the original one, to be more accurate—the chain has thirteen motels total across south Florida. We've been in negotiations for the last few months with the owners, offering to buy them out."

Lito accepted the phone and swiped through the motel's listings page. Lots of two and three-star reviews. The general consensus seemed to be they were clean and cheap, but dated and ugly with mediocre customer service. "Not exactly Dayspring prices, looks like."

"Oh, we're planning to rebrand," Betty said. "The Sunshine State Motel name is a bit tarnished now—the owners haven't done more than basic maintenance in ages. Ron and I haven't come up with what we're going to call it instead, but at this point it's a 'when' more than an 'if.'"

"Which brings us to you," Ronald interjected. "I know we just asked you to take on the Alabama project a few months ago, but we're going to need someone to oversee the decor and branding for this new chain and we'd like to give it higher priority. The rates *are* going to be lower than Dayspring's, which means you'll be decorating on a budget, but the mint-and-cream makeover you talked us into was a sorely needed change and you nailed it. Customer reviews reflected that. You have good instincts and you balance the artistic requirements with the financial ones."

He'd been much less enthusiastic when Lito first proposed the new color scheme two years earlier. The praise felt wonderful. "Thanks." Lito knew he hadn't been *entirely* responsible for Dayspring Inn & Suites' ratings and revenue going up, but the more modern artwork and the noticeable lack of 1950s-era cement pineapples probably helped. Ronald had a terrible artistic aesthetic, but he and Betty both knew it and were quick to defer to Lito's eye. "This sounds like a huge job, though," he added. "If you need it done quickly I don't know if I'll be able to juggle the Alabama renovations with—"

"Oh, this would be another straight-up promotion," Betty assured him. "We're offering you a fifteen-thousand-a-year raise and we'll cover your relocation costs to Miami. I know you weren't all that keen on Black Lake initially and moving twice so close together is a pain, but this opportunity came up rather suddenly for us and you're the logical choice." She flashed him a motherly smile. "I'm not saying I play favorites, but..."

"Yes, she does." Ronald squeezed his wife's hand. "And we wouldn't offer if we didn't think you'd be an excellent fit for what we need."

Well *fuck*. Between the raise he'd already gotten when they moved him to Black Lake in the first place and another fifteen thousand, Lito would be making almost half again what he used to. "You'd want to keep me in Miami for good, then?"

"That's the other half of this." Ronald sat back in his chair. "Ideally, we'd like you to be a local presence while we sort through the staffing issues and growing pains with the new chain. Conduct interviews, help new employees receive appropriate training to meet Dayspring standards... You'd essentially be a part-time HR department for us. Betty and I will both be down there as much as we can in the beginning, of course, but we can't do everything. You're a long-time employee who knows Dayspring's culture better than anyone, and you've got a good head on your shoulders."

"It means we'll be looking to hire someone new to take on what you're currently doing in Black Lake," Betty added. "Whatever you're able to pass off. The new hire would also function as a long-distance assistant for you going forward to handle whatever tasks you think would be easiest to delegate—you know your workload better than I do. I know it's inconvenient, but you're from Miami originally, right?"

"It's...been a while. But yes, that's where I grew up." Grew up, came out, ran away—so many memories, and not all ones he particularly wanted to remember. Still, for another step up the ladder it might be worth facing his childhood demons. "I haven't been back in forever."

Betty didn't press. He'd never talked about why he left Miami with her, but she was frighteningly observant sometimes. "Think about it," she said instead. "Like we said earlier, we're still in negotiations for this, so it could be a month from now or it could be six months. We'd like to have you hit the ground running when it does go through, though. And that *is* a when. The sooner we can rebrand and get Sunshine State Motels back up and running, the better."

"We'll have one of the pet-friendly suites in the Coral Gables location available for your use until you find somewhere you like better," Ronald added. "There's no rush."

Damn. A promotion, another raise, an assistant. Plus free rent. "That's… incredibly generous."

"It's a big step," Betty said. "For you and for us. But I think we have the ability to recoup our renovation costs back quickly by offering a pet-*and*-budget-friendly hospitality experience. There's nothing like that anywhere in the area. Hopefully we'll be able to expand too, sometime in the next decade or so."

"One thing at a time," Ronald added.

"So." Betty stood and busied herself collecting their plates. "Strawberry trifle time?"

Chapter 14

Dave tried to convince himself he wasn't desperately missing Lito's company the whole week Lito was visiting friends in Atlanta. Tried and failed. The frequent sex after Dave's so-long-it-felt-like-forever dry spell was one thing—a fantastic thing—but the Lito-sized empty space in Dave's bed every morning was just as bad. Christ, when had *that* addiction appeared? Lito didn't even stay over more than two or three nights a week and already Dave was mourning his absence. Because he was a fucking romantic, apparently.

He and Lito weren't even formally "dating." Dating would be the freedom to kiss whenever the hell either of them felt like it. Not having to ask if Lito was coming over for a bit before practice so they could eat dinner together. Lito keeping more than a toothbrush and a change of clothes at Dave's house. They almost never ended up at Lito's own place, mostly because his yard wasn't big enough for three large dogs to act like idiots without bothering the neighbors, but that just made the sense of "something's missing" worse. He ended up restricting himself to texting Lito no more than twice a day so he didn't come off as desperate.

Dave spent Christmas weekend at his parents' house, then the rest of the week catching up on year-end necessities for both work and NALSAR. Donations were down substantially from when Steve and his ex were still together, back when their daughter had still been on the team. She'd been a social butterfly who knew everyone in Black Lake and half the state besides, and she'd always volunteered to take point on the begging-for-money portion of their fundraising. She was good and the team bank account had shown it. Then Steve's ex left him, his daughter left the team, and Dave was left with a list of former contacts and no idea what the hell to do with it. He ended up as the team treasurer mostly because nobody else wanted the job.

Dave didn't particularly want it, either, but at least the lack of a recent fundraiser within the last year meant the paperwork for tax time wouldn't be all that complicated. With Lito on the team—assuming he stuck around—maybe they'd have the manpower for something soon. *Was* Lito planning to stick around? Dave's brain immediately conjured up how Lito had looked at their last practice before the holiday. He'd been laughing and pretend-chasing Spot across the field after she finished her find. Spot discovered a stick that particularly needed gnawing and Dave had been literally caught in his tracks at the sight of the two of them. That night they went back to Dave's house and headed straight for the bed, not emerging until almost ten o'clock to raid the fridge together.

> *Hi honey, I'm home! You already in*
> *bed, or up for some company?*

Dave read the text twice. Then dashed to his bedroom to put on something other than his current boxers, slippers, and sweat-stained t-shirt.

> *What about company *in* bed?* he texted back. *The*
> *pups left Spot's end of the sofa open if she wants it.*

Lito showed up twenty minutes later, looking a bit rumpled from all the driving but still sexy as hell. He barely let Spot get clear of the door before he slammed it behind himself and had Dave pressed up against the wall right there in the entryway. There were probably dogs-greeting-each-other sounds coming from the living room, but Dave's mind was wholly focused on how Lito was mouthing at all the parts of his neck he could reach.

"Was thinking about you the entire way home," Lito growled. "There's a crap-ton of nothing between Atlanta and here, which makes for a lot of time to daydream."

"Mmph." Dave whole-heartedly approved of Lito being this pushy—it was usually a sign they were about to have some acrobatic and extremely satisfying sex. "You missed me, then."

"Couldn't even jerk off to fantasies of you, not with Ian and his new roommate right there. It's a small apartment and the walls aren't that thick."

God, that was even better. Lito horny and unsated for an entire week…
"What would you have fantasized about? If you could?" Lito was already
grinding against him, and it felt fantastic. "Am I dressed appropriately
for a demonstration?"

Lito sputtered through a startled laugh even as he started working
Dave's shirt open. The incredibly comfortable button-down shirt Dave had
just put on a whole fifteen minutes earlier because when he was turned on
the soft fabric felt heavenly against his skin. "Getting there," Lito said.
"*Damn*, I love this one on you. You look good in blue. Leave it there—I
just wanted it open enough I could do *this*." He pulled one side away from
Dave's chest and ducked in to catch a nipple between his teeth in a grip
just sharp enough to make Dave swallow his own tongue.

"*Damn.*" Anything else he might have wanted to say had disappeared.

"Oh, you should know by now that I'm just getting started. Gonna take
a while." Lito nipped the other one for good measure, then hooked a foot
behind Dave's left leg and tugged. It wasn't enough to *actually* throw Dave
off-balance, but he let himself fall to his knees anyway. Lito's brilliant
smile was reward enough. "There, that's more like it," he murmured.
"So damn tall—your face is at a better height now. I want to fuck your
mouth for a while."

"Yes," Dave said immediately. Lito pliant and submissive was wonderful,
but Lito toppy as hell was even better.

Lito nodded, like he hadn't expected any different, and quickly had his
own jeans unzipped and his cock out. He didn't even give enough time for
Dave to admire the sight before his fingers were splayed over Dave's skull
and were guiding his mouth to where it was needed. He wasn't cruel—he
let Dave set the initial pace—but before long Dave was pinned, the back
of his head pressed against the wall and Lito pistoning in and out of his
mouth with sharp, controlled thrusts.

"So good," Lito moaned. "*Fuck.* You look gorgeous down there with
your lips wrapped around me. Letting me fuck your mouth. You get off
on this too, I know. Maybe one of these days I'll catch you by surprise
while we're off in the woods alone and nobody can see us. I'll shove you
up against a tree and put you on your knees and make you suck me off
until I come all over your face. In your hair, your eyelashes, that sexy
beard stubble you sometimes let grow for a day or two. I'd show you how
much you turn me on just by being there with your mouth around me.
That sound good to you?"

Dave groaned his approval.

"Thought so." Lito pulled back and smirked down at him. Dave instinctively leaned closer to keep the connection before he realized Lito was just advocating a change of venue. "Come on," Lito urged. "I'm sure we're supposed to start off by asking about each other's Christmas, but mostly I just want to ride you until you can't make words anymore."

"God, yes." Dave scrambled to his feet and followed Lito to the bedroom. Lito strode in like he owned it and fuck, wasn't that a nice thought? Dave could own the house, the foyer, the kitchen, the living room…but Lito taking over his bedroom. Making it *his*. It was so different from his easygoing persona when in public. Dave's previous experience usually tended toward guys who were more on the submissive side, but Lito genuinely seemed to love both taking control and giving it up. The contrast had a growing appeal.

"On the bed," Lito commanded, Army-sharp. "Did I mention I had a *really long drive* to plan this little reunion out? Because it was. I got stuck behind a farm truck doing fifteen under on the windy two-lane road over the mountain. I've got some frustration to work out. On you."

Whatever Lito "working out" his frustrations was, Dave was in. "Do it." He sat on the mattress and reached to pull Lito down with him. Instead, Lito pushed him over backward and shoved his arms underneath his back, so Dave was lying fingertip-to-elbow with his forearms digging into his spine. The position forced him to hold his back in an arch and to thrust his chest out. His nipples were free for Lito to pinch or bite again. The brief feeling of vulnerability quickly changed to lust. Toppy Lito was creative, strict, and sexy. Hell, Lito *breathing* was sexy when Dave was this turned on.

"Atlanta's not the only stronghold of civilization," he said. Lito might have been in a bossy mood, but that didn't mean Dave couldn't sass back. "Black Lake has a theater and a Walmart, like everywhere else in America. Can't be uncivilized if you have a Walmart, right?"

Lito grinned. It was practically feral. "I don't feel particularly civilized at the moment," he growled. And swept a leg up and over Dave's hips so their cocks ground together. "Feel a bit picky tonight, actually. Keep your hands where they are—let me do all the touching tonight. You good with that?"

Hell yes. "I'm good with anything right now," Dave answered honestly. "As long as it's not 'don't come for a week.' Might have issues obeying that one, with you looking at me like that."

"Mmmm." Lito ran his fingernails lightly up and down Dave's chest, brushing the open button-down shirt to the sides. The sensation sent literal chills over the newly-exposed skin. "Trying to stave it off isn't a turn-on for you, then?"

Fuck. "It, um. Not tonight? Or at least, not for too long? I've never…" He had to swallow hard to get his voice coming out properly. Talking was great, yes, wonderful, but not when he was already trying to picture the many ways Lito could deal with his "frustrations." Later, once they'd both come at least once and could think straight again. Talk then.

"That can be remedied." Lito's fingers were working lower, now, tracing over the lines of Dave's abdominal muscles and inching toward the waistband of his jeans. "For the record, I've tried the orgasm delay thing. And loved it from both sides of the equation. We can table that for tonight, though—right now I need to get you naked." Dave started to get up, but Lito flat-out sat on top of his hips and pinned him to the mattress. "I said *I* need to get you naked, not that *you* should be doing anything. You just watch for a bit."

Watching was good too. "Might have trouble getting my shirt off, with my arms pinned like this," he pointed out.

"I meant the parts that matter." Lito scooted backward, then leaned down to press his face into where Dave's thigh met his torso. "You already smell good, though," he murmured. "I can practically taste you through your jeans, you know that? If that superb mouth-fucking hadn't gotten me hard before, this definitely would do the trick. You smell like sex already and we've barely done anything yet."

Dave couldn't help a little thrust upward. "Not for lack of trying."

Lito huffed and sat back up. "*Long* drive, remember? We've got some lost time to make up for. I suppose I could take pity on you for now, though." Nimble fingers unzipped Dave's jeans and snuck a quick fondle through his boxers, which nearly had Dave levitating off the bed. Already. "Oh God, that's good. Helpful. Hips up so I can—*there* we go. Half naked on the top and all naked on the bottom. I'm feeling overdressed."

Lito was in his usual tight t-shirt and ass-hugging jeans, white and black today, and his hair was more mussed than he ever let it get outside of the bedroom. The usually elegant swoop of bangs he carefully styled each morning was crooked and a bit limp and made him look like he'd already been fucked silly. Except tonight, Dave was the one who'd be on the taking orders side of things, however Lito had planned them. *Fuck.*

"Keep your eyes on me." Lito backed off the mattress and came around the side of the bed. "No moving, no touching. You can do all the ogling you want, though."

Right, like he would have had enough willpower to not look. "Drooling okay?"

Lito winked at him. "Guess we'll find out." He ran his palms down his front, twisting his hips as he did so, and… *Christ.* This was a striptease. Lito was going to perform a fucking striptease. Dave had to lick his suddenly dry lips. Which Lito noticed, of course. "You're going to have to imagine the music," he murmured, "because I don't really want to futz around on my phone right now. That would go against the point of all this, which is to get your cock inside me sooner rather than later. First, though…" He stripped his shirt slowly up over his head, displaying his toned abs and flat brown nipples at an agonizing pace which made futzing around on his phone look like the quicker option. When he finally got it off, he tossed it onto the bed—straight onto Dave's bare stomach. The shirt was still warm. "As it so happens," Lito said, "I've devised a cunning plan both to get your cock up my ass and to get you gibbering while I do it. I like it when you're post-verbal."

"You're doing an excellent job so far."

"Not good enough, if you're still talking in full sentences." Lito rotated a hundred and eighty degrees, hips dropping in a few teasing twerks. Dave had been ogling that bubble butt already, but now he couldn't tear his eyes away. "We've been doing this long enough by now," Lito said, "that I feel pretty confident in saying I know what you like. And you like my ass. Don't try to deny it."

"Wasn't going to." It was true, after all.

"Good." Lito gyrated back around, dancing to music only he could hear, and unzipped his jeans for the second time that evening. The front of his briefs was already a darker color—from precome or from Dave's residual saliva, it was hard to tell. "Because my ass certainly likes you. God, these jeans are too tight now. Ooh, *there* we go." He put on a good show—from multiple angles—as he got his own cock free and stepped out of his clothes so he was completely, wonderfully naked. "Next up, we're gonna need some lube. No, don't move." He shot Dave a warning glare. "I'm doing this and you're watching, got it?"

Crystal clear. "I'm leering, preferably."

"Leering works too."

Dave had stopped bothering to keep the lube anywhere except right next to the bed anymore. Between his frequent morning wood and Lito's visits, it was getting a lot of use. Lito poured himself a dollop, dumped the bottle back in its current place of pride, and turned sideways so he could get one foot up on the edge of the nightstand. The look he shot Dave over his shoulder was pure sin. "No moving," he commanded. "Don't think I won't be able to tell."

And then he let one slick finger trace gentle circles around his hole. The viewing angle was different than Dave was used to, but that just made it all the more mesmerizing. Lito teased himself with one fingertip, then two, then back to one as he finally sank it in to his first knuckle.

"Gotta get myself ready to take your thick cock," he declared. "Two fingers, you think? Or three?"

Oh, no question there. Dave groaned. "Three. Do three. Let me see."

"Leer away." Lito refreshed the lube, bent over a bit more so Dave could see better, then worked his hole so thoroughly Dave was practically drooling by the end of it. If it weren't for Lito's bossy demand that he stay still, he'd have already launched himself across the mattress and planted his lips around Lito's hole. Lito always made the most amazing noises when he was being rimmed…

"You can sit on my face if you want," Dave volunteered. "God, you look so sexy like that."

Lito twisted around to grin at him. "I will always want, but rain check on that. Right now all I want is to make sure—*ooh*, yes. You're so hard for me now, aren't you? God, I can see your dick twitching. You want this."

Dave was aching, but he kept his hips still through sheer force of will.

"Three fingers, now. Watch." Lito eased three fingers inside himself, dropping his head and hauling in a deep breath as he processed the change. His ass was gorgeous, of course, but the way the muscles in his back moved as he worked his middle three fingers in and out was pure art. Dave half-expected that if he could see Lito's face, he'd see him beaming like some renaissance Madonna.

"You're cruel," Dave grumbled. "Flaunting that sexy ass and not letting me touch you. Or lick you. I still have the taste of your cock in my mouth. *Fuck.*"

"You like me cruel," Lito countered. He did stand back up and wipe his fingers off with a tissue, though. Then reconsidered, added a bit more lube to his palm, and crawled back onto the bed so he could roll a condom onto Dave's cock and slick it up a bit.

There may have been whimpering involved.

"Don't move until I tell you," Lito commanded. He swung a leg over Dave's hips so he was kneeling over him like some sort of wrathful deity. A dead sexy one—his own cock was glistening with precome already, even though it had been several minutes since he'd fucked Dave's mouth. "Your job right now is to lie there being jealous of how I'm able to do *this*." He trailed his hand over his stomach, his chest, his peaked nipples, and finished the gesture off with a jaunty squeeze. One that had both of them sucking in a strangled breath. "I love this look on you, by the way," he said quietly. "Naked from the waist down, shirt unbuttoned so I can do my own leering. The only downside is I can't see your biceps. I have a bit of a thing for them."

"You can take my shirt off the rest of the way," Dave said. Or tried to—he didn't make it much past "You can take—" before Lito had himself lined up over Dave's cock and was sinking back down in one long, slow movement. His head was thrown back, eyes closed, and the deep groan he let out as he bottomed out at the base of Dave's erection had Dave mentally reviewing memories of cadavers to keep from coming right there and then. When Lito opened his eyes again, his gaze was disturbingly sharp. It was then followed by that slow smirk that never failed to precede a toe-curlingly good orgasm for both of them.

"Love this thick cock of yours," he murmured. "Feels so good inside me. I'm going to ride you until you can't hold yourself back anymore, then I'll *keep* riding you until you're begging me to stop and I come all over those beautifully toned pecs. I'm not going to keep you from coming, *you* are. Because you know it will hurt like a bitch if you come before me and I don't let you go."

Oh fuck. Dave gaped up at him, words not even attempting to form into coherent noises. Because damn if that that little speech just made holding back worse. Lito was like a bronze statue come to life—the nearly bare chest gleaming with the effort he was putting in, the heavy swoop of his bangs falling into his eyes, the steady up-and-down as he reduced Dave to the role of a mere willing erection. Well, that and *desperation*. Lito saw it all on his face, surely. Saw it and didn't give in.

Lito only sped up a fraction, but he did touch himself again. Pinched and rolled his nipples, splayed a hand over his belly, traced one lucky finger up and down his own cock as he took and took and *took* what he wanted. They'd had good sex before, but this time was transcendental. Dave was a hair's breadth from coming, threat or no, when Lito finally stiffened and came in four warm bursts on Dave's chest. He was in the middle of the third when Dave couldn't hold back anymore and let the cresting orgasm sweep over him.

* * * *

Lito's legs felt like they had turned to jelly, but he hauled himself off Dave anyway and stumbled to the bathroom to clean up. He brought back a damp washcloth for Dave too, who looked just as boneless. The dog noises from the living room had quieted, so presumably the three of them were all sacked out and dozing. It sounded like an excellent idea for him and Dave to emulate.

"Been looking forward to this so much," Dave mumbled, not moving even when Lito took care of the condom and cleaned him up the best he could. "Get back down here."

"One sec." Lito shoved and pulled at Dave's totally limp form until he got Dave's shirt the rest of the way off, then he pulled the covers up and over them and nestled into the man's side. The skin-to-skin contact was warm, comforting, and possibly even more wonderful than the sex had been, hard as that was to contemplate. "I missed you too," he whispered against Dave's neck.

The next thing Lito knew, daylight was streaming through the curtains and there was a wet tongue licking his bare foot. It took a moment to decouple the sensation from the dream he'd been having about how creative Dave could be in bed, but eventually it registered and he looked down to see Spot wagging her tail and nosing at the foot he'd left dangling off the edge of the mattress. She licked one final time and then, seeing he was awake, came farther up to snuffle at his face as well.

"Urgh." He jerked back on instinct. The movement startled Dave, who had been curled around him and snoring gently into his hair.

"What—oh, it's morning already. Hmmm." Dave ducked back down to give Lito a short, morning-breath-friendly kiss, then sat up and stretched. "Yeah, the bedroom door doesn't quite latch all the way, and Woozy figured out how to nudge it open a few days ago. I see Spot got elected greeter."

"You could have mentioned that," Lito said dryly. "Gave me a hell of a wake-up surprise."

"I suppose they want to go out. I'll be right back."

Spot—no stranger to this new morning routine—followed him eagerly out of the bedroom. Lito was seriously tempted to curl back up where Dave had been lying. The sheets were still warm and smelled like him and it was probably early yet, but he forced himself to sit up anyway. They hadn't gotten to the point where he was leaving clothes at Dave's house, unfortunately, which meant putting back on yesterday's travel-worn outfit. *Crap.* He did remember to bring a change of clothes along, but it was still in the car. Maybe Dave would be really, really swee…

"I put on coffee," Dave announced, coming back sans dogs. Still naked. "The pups are tearing around their run like they've never seen daylight before—even Woozy, who's usually more creaky in the mornings. I think they're showing off for Spot."

"You wouldn't do the same?"

"Show off for Spot? Mmm, no." Dave stretched casually, showing off the way his muscles moved and twisted. *Damn.* "For you, I might. Theoretically."

He was practically preening, but Lito wasn't about to call him on it and inadvertently cause him to go put on clothes. "You've got a lot to show off," Lito said instead.

"So do you." Dave looked Lito up and down, not even making a token attempt to be subtle. "Want to show off some more?"

"Not really up for a repeat so soon after last night, but—"

Dave laughed. "No, I get that. What I meant was, it's karaoke day at the VFW tonight. Come flaunt that amazing voice of yours and I'll sit there feeling like the luckiest bastard on earth while I listen."

"I don't have an amazing voice," Lito said immediately. "I'm not *terrible*, but—"

"You forget, I've heard you. In the car, every time a pop diva comes on the radio." Dave smirked. "And you *do* have a fantastic voice. Don't think I didn't notice."

"It's not *every* time," he protested.

"Yes it is."

"Only if you'll sing too."

"I'll stick to country, but you're on." Dave wandered over to his walk-in closet and pulled out a bathrobe, which he tossed to Lito. "Let me guess—you've got clean clothes in your suitcase from your trip but you left them in the car, am I right? Give me a sec to shower and get dressed and I'll go retrieve them for you."

Chapter 15

Lito left Spot with her best canine friends and went back to his own house to shower and take care of everything he'd let slide while he was in Atlanta. Dave came by to pick him up just as he was finishing.

"You're okay with eating seafood, right?" he asked once Lito was settled. "The VFW's once-a-month fish fry is tonight too. It would be worth the trip all on its own."

Lito sounded skeptical that the guys at the VFW made "the best fried catfish you'd ever taste anywhere," but Dave managed to talk him into giving it a try. It ought to be entertaining—Lito could be so expressive, and Dave was looking forward to seeing how close his O-face compared to his "God this food is good" face. He'd seen both often enough to compare the two, but never in the same evening. Hopefully tonight was going to change that.

"I'm ready to be humiliated in public," Lito announced as they pulled out of his driveway. "I doubt there's anyone with *less* military potential than me, and I'm gonna be surrounded by guys all built like you."

"That's not true. A lot of them are really old now," Dave teased. "Quite a few have walkers and canes."

"Jackass."

"You love it."

Lito laughed reluctantly. "Yeah, I do. But it does still feel weird to be going to this place I don't belong."

"Trust me," Dave assured him. "You're social, you're friendly, and you're good-looking. You'll be fine."

Lito was silent for a few minutes. Then... "I just realized this is our first time going out in *public* public together. The first we'll be around people you know, other than the team. Is this…is it a date, or am I just your totally platonic friend for the evening?"

Okay, so they were going to be a bit later than he'd planned. This conversation was starting to sound like it needed his full attention, though. Dave pulled into the closest parking lot and turned the engine off, the better to talk face-to-face. "What brings this about?"

"Oh, you know." Lito gave a seriously unconvincing shrug. "I'm not exactly subtle about my orientation. It would be pointless to try to pass for straight—I'd never come across as all that masculine even if I tried. Plus that's really not me. *I'm* used to the stares and the comments and the micro-aggressions, but I'm guessing you're probably not. So if you want me to play the part of your totally straight 'friend' who just happens to look and sound a bit 'gentle-if-you-know-what-I-mean,' tell me ahead of time. It takes me some time to get all the way into the right mindset and I don't want to embarrass you."

Dave was surging forward to kiss the idiot before he even realized he was doing it. When he pulled back, Lito was smiling but still had a wary look in his eyes. "I told you I'm not in the closet," Dave said.

"Not to the team, but I didn't want to presume—"

"Not to *anyone*." God, it was important to get this right between them. For Lito to understand that they *did* have this in common. "I don't go around volunteering information about my sex life, but I'm not trying to hide anything either. Some of the other vets know I'm gay and some don't, but that's just because it's never come up."

"Have you ever brought a date with you to something like this, though?"

It had been ages since Dave had last gone on an actual "date"—including, he realized, ever having gone on a real one with Lito—so it wasn't an easy question to answer. "I don't think so," he said slowly. "But that's more about my lack of dating anyone than about trying to stay in some metaphorical closet."

The wary look in Lito's eyes gave way to a sad one. "Is that by choice, or the lack of local options?"

"Bit of both, I suppose." There were occasional token efforts to have some sort of inclusive social justice event, but "lesbian/gay" was usually lumped in as an afterthought behind the black/white thing, the "there are other minorities too!" thing, calls for awareness of various disabilities or diseases… Black Lake wasn't going to be hosting a Pride parade anytime soon. "There are other gay men in town, I'm sure you've found out by now, but not enough of us to really have a community."

Lito sighed. "I'd hoped I was missing something, but I guess not. That sucks."

There's always Nashville. Maybe he could take Lito up there sometime, show him off a bit. Spend the night grinding on each other until finally holing up in their hotel room and fucking like rabbits for the rest of the weekend. The idea had definite appeal, but he didn't want to jinx it.

Lito looked out the window and stayed silent for the rest of the drive.

The small parking lot was half full when Dave pulled in, suggesting they were going to have a decent turn-out. Fish fry nights always brought more people to karaoke, although not all of them stayed for the singing. If the first two or three karaoke hopefuls were all terrible the hall would clear back out to its usual dozen or so regulars pretty darn quickly.

Dave did note the absence of Rick and Sharon's van. Since he only decided to go out tonight after he woke up and enjoyed some lazy morning sex with Lito, though, he and Rick hadn't discussed going together this time. While Dave knew most all the vets and many of their spouses by sight and about half by name, it would have been nice to have at least one other actual friend there besides Lito.

Lito was oddly subdued as they made their way past the bar and into the main hall. The designer side of him must have been cringing, Dave realized—the VFW was practically a memorial to the mediocre-est the sixties had to offer. Renovating had never been a priority and the old-timers liked what felt familiar, so wood-paneled walls and vinyl floors it was. The bar itself was a thing of tacky beauty, a giant block of oak paneling with beer signs all over the side. It also had Janine, one of the few female Vietnam vets Dave had ever met, behind it. She gave them a nod and a smile as they passed.

"What do you think?" Dave asked Lito quietly.

Lito snorted. "About like I expected," he murmured back. "Although it feels like the flags should all have forty-eight stars instead of fifty, with the time warp y'all have going on in here."

"You'd do better?"

Lito gave him a look that said *you damn well know it* loud and clear.

The main hall was just as bad, Dave realized as they made their way in. It looked like every summer camp dining room ever, including the uncomfortable folding chairs and the rows of rectangular tables. It also smelled *heavenly*. If heaven had fried catfish, at least. Dave steered Lito to the end of the short line of people with Styrofoam plates and plastic forks, waiting for the next batch to come out of the fryer.

"Dave! Good to see you!" A bald man whose name Dave could never remember came up and gave him a hearty clap on the back. "Been a while since we've seen you at a karaoke night, but I'm glad you're here! And you've brought a friend?"

He was clearly expecting an introduction, but it was about to be hella awkward when it ended up entirely one-sided. Dave could have told Lito about the guy's two kids, his Harley, the fact that the only beverage he'd drink was Diet Coke and he got hell for it regularly…but not his name.

Lito, as usual, was perceptive. He took in Dave's expression at a glance and clearly just understood. Instead of waiting for Dave to do the formal so-and-so here's so-and-so thing, he offered a handshake and a bright smile.

"I'm Lito Apaza," he said brightly. "Nice to meet you."

"You too—I'm Jake Finnegan. You here for the karaoke, the fish fry, or both?"

Lito shot a sideways glance up at Dave's face. "Both, apparently. I'm told I've been deprived of experiencing the best fried catfish I'd ever taste. And I'm curious to hear whether Dave can sing."

Jake—Dave *knew* that, had reminded himself of the guy's name a hundred times in the past—laughed and faux-slugged Dave on the arm. "You're in for a surprise, then," he teased. "You wouldn't expect a big guy like him to have such an impressive falsetto, but he's a killer at karaoke death matches. Speaking of which." He turned to Dave. "Chad is here tonight too—you up for a rematch from last time? We haven't all been to the same karaoke night in ages."

"I'm probably going to wish I hadn't asked," said Lito, "but what on earth is a karaoke death match?"

Jake grinned. "One person sings, but the previous person picks their song. Anything in the book. The goal is to make less of an ass of yourself than the other guys. You want in? There's not a formal *winner*, per se, but often it ends with us buying the winner's beers."

Lito bit his lip, making a show of thinking it over, but then he nodded and returned Jake's smile. "You're on."

Oh, this was going to be a slaughter. The other guys would never know what hit them when Lito really opened up at the mic. And some deep, primal part of Dave was already crowing at being able to show off *his* partner. He wasn't particularly looking forward to trying to ham up "Damn, I Feel Like a Woman" in front of Lito, or whatever else Jake and Chad were going to throw at him tonight, but any potential embarrassment was going to be *so* worth it.

* * * *

Lito and Dave got a table all to themselves, on the far side of the room from where everyone else was socializing. Lito had assumed Dave would want to chat with his friends, but Dave just shook his head and winked in response to Lito's questioning look.

It was all made clear once they actually started eating—Lito barely stopped himself from moaning aloud at the first bite of his dinner. Dave was watching his face intently, waiting for his reaction—God only knows what he saw, but if it made him smile like that it had to have been near pornographic. The catfish really was *amazing*, though. Fresh and hot from the deep-fryer, just the right amount of crispy, salted and spiced perfectly. He wanted to attack the rest of his plate, to wolf down the home fries and the onion rings as well, but eating those would have meant he wasn't eating the fish.

"Told you," Dave teased. "I wanted to keep that reaction all for myself." He took a much more leisurely bite of own and closed his eyes in pleasure. "*Damn.* I've tried to do these at home sometimes, when I've caught something worth eating, but it never comes out the way they do it here."

"I forgot you fish."

"Do you?"

"Seriously?" Lito pointedly looked down at himself—burnt-sienna corduroy pants, a navy button-down, and his favorite silver Salvatore Ferragamo sneakers with a lighter gray around the eyelets—and raised an eyebrow. "City boy, remember? No, I don't fish."

"Could try sometime." Dave raised one eyebrow back, then winked. "I've got the pond out back—you've seen it. Has a little dock and everything. Granted, if I'm out there Lumpy and Woozy like to splash around and scare away any fish, but occasionally I leave them in their run and head out to have a beer and maybe catch some dinner. It's…calming, I guess. Quiet. I'd love to take you out there once it gets warmer."

Lito could picture that. Dave was shirtless in his imagination, for some reason, but Lito had no trouble envisioning him relaxing in the sun in just his jeans and work boots, fishing pole loosely resting in one hand and a cold drink in the other. Which might possibly lead to the two of them naked, lazily frotting against each other on the dock with nobody but the dogs to see or hear it. Dave having to help him put the worm on the hook and throw out the fishing line and rewarding him with little kisses and touches whenever he does something right. Watching the sunset with Dave's arm around him and Dave's body heat as the evening cooled back down.

Damn. That got really domestic, really fast. Lito cleared his throat and quickly tried one of the fries. Good, but not as amazing as the fish. "That would be fun," he said evenly. Surrounded by Dave's friends in the middle of the VFW was not the best place to get a hard-on, and definitely not if he was going to have to stand up in front of everyone and sing. "Tell me about your military service? Or is it something you don't talk about?"

Dave kept it light, but Lito still got a pretty decent picture of Dave's life in the Army. Intense work stateside with his assigned dog, a six-month-old German Shepherd named Ranger. Then to one of the larger US bases in Afghanistan, where they underwent more intense training. Then to somewhere—Dave didn't say where, but Lito got the impression he wasn't supposed to tell—and he and Ranger did sweeps for IEDs.

"How long did you work together?" Lito asked.

"Four years." Dave flashed him a sad half-smile. "Rick and I met in Basic, then bumped into each other again over in the sandbox. Got to be good friends in the last six months or so—we were talking about re-enlisting together, actually."

"What happened?"

Dave's shoulders drooped, even though he was still talking in the same factual tone as when they'd first walked in. "IED, unsurprisingly," he said. "On a totally routine patrol through what should have been already-cleared territory. Ranger alerted on it and I was trying to narrow down where in the area it was when it went off."

"Damn."

"Pretty much." Dave looked away, down toward what must have been a particularly interesting square of tile on the floor. "Ranger was between me and the IED, so he took the brunt of it. Bled out in less than a minute. He"—he took a shaky breath—"he kept his eyes on me the whole time he was dying. Not accusing, just...*fuck.*"

"Dave, I'm sorry." Lito wanted to grab his hand over the table and give it a squeeze, but he settled for trapping Dave's foot between his own and squeezing that instead. "You don't have to tell me, and I shouldn't have asked." He looked up at the dozen or so people already in the room—none of them close enough to hear the conversation, thank God. "I definitely shouldn't have asked you about it here."

"No, it's okay." Dave sat up straighter, pulled his shoulders back. "It was ten years ago; I'm over Ranger by now." He didn't look it, but Lito wasn't about to call him out. "It was that same explosion that sent Rick to the VA, though," he continued. "They were able to save most of his legs but not his feet. He's not a good candidate for prosthetics either, hence the wheelchair."

"He's alluded to something like that in the past, but I figured he's probably got rude people asking him all the time about it and I didn't want to be one of them." It was obvious Rick was otherwise healthy, except for the chair thing, so Lito had assumed some sort of accident. "Did you come back at the same time?"

"I got to shuffle paperwork for the last few months until my four-year enlistment ended. Rick was in rehab and therapy for a lot longer than that. When he did get out, though, he didn't really have anywhere to go. No family he was close to, no friends stateside who would be waiting on him, no girlfriend. I came back here to be nearer to my parents because why not, so I talked him into coming too."

"And then he met Sharon in Black Lake," Lito surmised.

Dave's lips quirked up in his first true smile since they'd sat down. "When she and her ex split, she got the kennel in the divorce. The whole small business thing had been his big thing, but he was terrible with money so Sharon was already doing most of the managing anyway. The kennel was a lot smaller back then and they really only did baths and boarding. Then she and Rick started dating and he was able to start up some obedience classes, one-on-one work for dogs with behavioral problems, things like that. They extended the kennel a few years back and now have space for two dozen dogs. Plus Scratch and Sniff, of course. They've got the run of the place."

God, it was good to be back on a less fraught topic. "Do they get to play mascot?" Lito asked. "You know, advertise how well dogs can behave?"

Dave snorted. "Scratch spends most of his days sacked out next to wherever Sharon is. Sniff hangs out in the office and lets them know whenever a car comes up the driveway."

A blast of feedback from the speakers interrupted their conversation. The DJ fixed it almost immediately, but everyone at the bar seemed to have taken it as a "we're starting" signal—the tables filled up quickly. Jake plopped down next to Dave and another burly man slid into the chair beside Lito.

This one Dave did remember. "Chad, Lito. Lito, my friend Chad."

Lito and Chad exchanged nods.

"So," Jake said, leaning in to talk over the short test clips of karaoke songs the DJ was playing. He plopped a thick black binder onto the table between their two plates. "Who's up first? You're still gonna let my boy here drag you into our musical death match, Lito?"

He really had nothing to lose, except his dignity. And possibly his hearing, if Dave turned out to be a horrible singer. "It won't be the first time Dave's talked me into doing something dangerous or stupid," Lito said. "That's pretty much how I joined NALSAR."

Jake laughed. "Dave's up first, then. Here—you pick out something for him. Doesn't matter what it is, or if he knows it. Close your eyes and point, if you want to. If the song is by a chick, even better."

Lito scanned a few random pages of the list. It had obviously been well-used—there were grease spots here and there on the paper, and some of the songs were circled or underlined. They were alphabetical by artist, which would have been more helpful if he knew half of who these singers were. Lady Gaga, he knew. Teegarden & Van Winkle, not so much. He could feel Dave watching him as he browsed.

"This is my chance to hear you impress me," Lito murmured, turning his head so only Dave could see his lips moving. Probably couldn't hear him over the terrible acoustics of the room, but that was okay. His eye caught on a one-hit wonder country hit he vaguely remembered hearing when he was a teenager. "This one," he said louder. "'Saturday Mornin' Drinkin'" by Rodger Williams. Nineteen eighty-four. You know it?"

"Think so," Dave drawled. "Reckon I can summon up some good ol' redneck singin' for ya."

God, the country twang was practically *dripping* from him. The accent shouldn't have been sexy, but it was. Even more so than Dave's regular Southern disregard for proper vowels.

Jake and Chad were both already grinning. Dave shook his head at them, but he was smiling too. He took out one of the loose slips of paper from the front pocket of the binder, wrote his name and the song number on them, and walked them over to the DJ. Someone had gotten there first, a gray-bearded man with some impressive ink on his arms, but Dave secured the second slot. He wiggled an eyebrow at Lito on his way back to the table.

The guy who went first wasn't all that terrible, Lito decided. He sang an over-the-top patriotic but well-known tune. Several of the audience members joined him on the choruses—part and parcel of being ex-military, probably. *God, I'd be a crap soldier, wouldn't I?* Nothing like being five foot five and a hundred and thirty pounds soaking wet and then sitting next to three brawny Army types who could all bench-press him twice over to put everything in perspective. Hell, even the old guy on stage could probably take him apart in a fight.

Dave bounded up to the stage next, with a cocky little smirk and a general wave to the rest of the room. He glanced over at the DJ and nodded. Damn, he was sexy.

I'm left sittin' here thinkin'

'Bout you, 'bout me, 'bout how it could be

But it's just me and my beeeeer

And I'm Saturday mornin' drinkin'

Yeah, so round that up to *really fucking sexy.* Dave obviously knew the chorus a lot better than the verses, but he sang the whole song with a confidence Lito couldn't help but respond to. Neither could the rest of the room, apparently—Dave exited the stage accompanied by substantially louder applause than the first guy had gotten. He flashed Lito a private little smug smile as he sat back down. *Guess my ogling wasn't exactly subtle.*

"That one was a softball," Jake complained, but there wasn't any actual malice in his tone. "Let me guess—you want Chad to go next?"

"Eenie meenie miny moe." Dave pointed to Jake, Chad, and Lito in turn, but immediately swung his finger back to pointing at Jake. "Let's see what you can do with some Madonna, tough guy."

The answer, as it turned out, was "parade around on stage and try to vogue, not even remotely succeeding." Lito wasn't a music snob by any stretch of the imagination—anything except NPR would do—but seeing Jake butcher the Queen of Pop was both painful and humorous. There were a few more singers, of varying quality, then Chad did a passable rendition of "Billie Jean." He had a mediocre voice and none of the theatricality of the original, but he had a good range and he got almost as much applause as Dave did. He sauntered back to their table and slapped an already-filled-out paper slip in front of Lito. "You're up, kid."

Lito looked down at it—and had to stifle a laugh. "Ana Maria? Really?" The Puerto Rican twenty-year-old was currently on all the top forty stations after winning some sort of reality TV contest, but she'd had a decent following before that in Atlanta's Hispanic community. That included Lito, who could have sung "All My Sistas (Mi Gente)" with his eyes closed.

Dave reached over the table and slugged Chad none-too-gently on the arm. "Jackass. *You've* never managed to get all the way through that one. Lito, you don't have to—someone pulls that 'Sistas' song out every time we do this, and every time it's a train wreck. Everyone knows the chorus and then has to resort to making funny faces during the rap parts."

Chad grinned. "Think of it as a trial by fire, then. Although maybe you'll manage rapping in Spanish better than we do."

Oh, for fuck's sake. The comment had to be because he was a brown-skinned Latino. The guy wasn't being malicious about it, but it didn't take a huge mental leap to figure out why he assumed Lito would be bilingual. And okay, he *was*, but that wasn't something Chad would have been able to tell just by looking at him. Lito knew damn well he didn't have a telltale accent. Maybe "American," but that was it. In the grand scheme of things it was no big deal, but it made him suddenly conscious of how he was the only non-white person there. Dave had introduced him to an African-American woman earlier, but she wasn't in the room so she must have left already. Like Lito needed one more reminder of how much he didn't fit in.

Now wasn't the time to get all pissy about assumptions, though, especially since Chad probably hadn't meant anything by it. "I think I can manage," Lito said. "As long as your expectations aren't too high."

"I dunno—can you do that hip thing like she does?" Chad raised his hands and shimmied in his chair, to Jake's loud laughter. "I mean, no homo, but that shit is *hot.*"

"Hey." Dave had scooted his chair over, close enough he could lean in and speak quietly into Lito's ear. "Chad's a nice guy, but you may have noticed he's kind of an ass. Want me to say something to him later? Or to pick you a different song? I know you do speak Spanish because I've heard you grumble under your breath when you don't think anyone's listening, but that doesn't mean you should have to perform for anyone."

Lito took a deep breath and tried to let the irritation drain out of him. "I'll be fine," he murmured back. Hell, he'd jumped into this with both feet—might as well ride it out. Plus it was kind of sweet that Dave was paying attention to him that closely. "I happen to know the song pretty well, so it wasn't as bad a choice as it could have been."

Dave snorted softly. "If Jake makes me sing 'I Feel Like a Woman' one more time I'm gonna go all-out Barry White on him. See if I can do the whole thing an octave lower. I probably can't, but I'll try."

Oh, that sounded hilarious. "I'd pay to hear that."

"Private performance later, maybe." Dave winked at him and nudged Lito's leg with his knee. "Once we're recovered from our all-fried dinner."

Neither of the other guys seemed to notice, or care, that Dave and Lito were sitting so close together. Lito took the chance to surreptitiously nudge Dave back. "I think you'd be just as sexy no matter what you sang," he murmured.

Dave let out a smug little contented *hmmm*. "Ditto."

Lito's turn came up three songs later. Despite the modest size of the room and the "stage" being what looked like a shipping pallet with some carpeting tacked over it at one end of the room, it really did feel like stepping into the spotlight. The one flood lamp in the room, anyway. The DJ looked to him for confirmation and started the song.

All my sistas, all my sistas

We gonna dance tonight

Lito didn't actually need to watch the little TV screen scrolling the lyrics, so he was free to look around the room from his new, slightly taller vantage point. Nineteen people, including the DJ and the guy now shutting down the fryer. One middle-aged woman and the rest men of varying ages. There were two up near the front who looked close to Lito's own twenty-five, all the way up to a white-haired man with osteoporosis and a walker in the very back who could well have been a World War Two veteran.

Let's rock this club, mi gente

Show 'em how we do it when we really wanna move it

Lito hadn't particularly been intending to dance, but the hip motions and the modified salsa steps were entirely involuntary. He'd probably watched the music video too many times. There were a few "woo!"s from around the room, so Lito let himself close his eyes and move with the music. Even the rapid-fire rap section in the middle of the song deserved some acknowledgment with more than just words. He looked at Dave just once, but once was enough—Dave was sitting up in his chair, back perfectly straight, and practically panting. In the best of ways. *All the more reason to show off a bit*. Yes, Lito could carry a tune, but more than that he knew how to *dance*. This wasn't really the place for club moves, but salsa was more about the feeling and the motion of the music than the overt sexiness of club dancing anyway. The end of the song came sooner than he'd have liked. He was greeted with a standing ovation and more than a few cheers and whistles when he stepped down from the stage.

"Damn," Jake breathed, shaking his head. "That was amazing. I vote for Lito having won tonight, by a landslide."

"Oh, definitely." The heat in Dave's eyes was pure promise: *I'm going to fuck you through the mattress.* It was one of Lito's favorite looks. He managed to summon a pleased smile to his face, but inside he was already begging Dave for more. Of everything. Dave was welcome to absolutely fucking take him apart as soon as they got home and Lito was going to be right there every step of the way. *Fuck.*

"That was way better than when any of us have tried it," Chad chimed in. "I've never seen a straight dude dance like that."

"Still haven't," Lito said, the comeback slipping out before his brain caught up. *Dave did say he was out, didn't he?* If not, it was probably too late now. Lito deliberately didn't look over to see Dave's expression.

Jake laughed again, mostly at Chad. The pause in conversation got less and less subtle the longer Chad took to finally make the connection.

"You're—oh. *Oh.* Is that, like, a gay thing? Being able to dance like a hot chick? Sorry, I didn't...you are saying you're gay, right? LGBT? Queer-something? I don't know what the term for it is now. I swear it keeps changing."

"Gay, fuckhead," Dave interjected. "And no, dance skills aren't automatic. There are plenty of us with two left feet."

Chad's eyes went wide. "Shit. I totally forgot that you're—I mean, you don't talk about it, really. Sex with dudes who—yeah, I'll shut up now."

"Who what?" Dave arched one eyebrow. Lito immediately recognized it as his *oh-shit-your-ass-is-in-trouble* face. Woozy actually laid down and rolled over to show her belly whenever Dave pulled out that look on her. "Dudes who suck cock? Dudes who get off with other dudes? Dudes who do it in some nasty bathroom in the back of a gay bar? Which *dudes* did you mean, exactly?"

Shit. This was going to get out of control quickly, and it was one hundred percent *not* the kind of scene Lito wanted to be making. "It's okay," he said quietly in Dave's direction. "He wasn't being intentionally rude and he already apologized. Just let it go."

"It's not okay, though," Dave snapped back. Loudly enough some of the guys at the nearest tables to them were turning to see what the problem was. "Why is it that whenever anyone mentions the word 'gay' everyone immediately starts thinking of sex? Like that's the only thing worth noting in a relationship between two men? Just for once—for fucking *once*—I'd like to be able to introduce my partner without everyone immediately wondering which one of us likes to top and which likes to bottom. Lito is a lot more than his dick. Or his skin color, or his hip-swivel dance whatsit, or what we do in bed. So show some fucking *respect* already."

Partner? Part of Lito's brain was listening to the rest of Dave's outburst, but a much larger section was stuck on that one word. *Partner*. He'd been thinking of Dave as a boyfriend, if anything—something nebulous, maybe, since they'd never actually defined their relationship with a formal talk and negotiation of terms, but generally a boyfriend-ish idea. They spent a lot of time together, not just in bed. He'd had Thanksgiving at Dave's house. So yeah, maybe they weren't just fuckbuddies anymore, but *partner* sounded a hell of a lot more formal. And permanent.

"I'm sorry," Chad said again, his hands up in that patronizing defensive gesture Lito always hated. The "calm down, it was just a joke" one. Not that Chad had been trying to joke, but…

"The correct response," Dave retorted, "would have been 'Wow, Lito, you're a great dancer and you also have a really good voice. Thanks for being willing to jump into this juvenile karaoke game with us even though you don't know anyone else here. Oh, and I'm sorry about assuming that you're fluent in Spanish based on how you look. I didn't intend for my song selection to come off as racist."

"Dude," Jake interjected, "he said he was sorry. Can we put this past us and listen now? They're waiting on us to finish talking before they start the next song."

It was true, Lito realized. The DJ and the middle-aged dude on the stage were both silently watching Dave rail at Chad with no subtlety or volume control whatsoever. "Dave, it's fine," Lito reiterated. He let his palm rest on Dave's lower thigh—not an attempt at being sexy, just trying to calm him down. "This kind of thing happens *all the time* and I'm used to it by now. At least this time your friend was right—I do happen to love Ana Maria and I have pretty much memorized all her songs. Including the Spanish parts. Can we not make a scene over it?" Obviously this was a hang-up for Dave, but right now Lito just wanted to let someone else be the center of attention. Anyone else. Without having to be caught up in everyone staring at them.

Dave closed his eyes and covered Lito's hand with his own. Then he lifted them up high enough for everyone to see and placed a deliberate kiss on the center of Lito's palm. "You're right," he said. "Let's go home."

Chapter 16

Lito was uncharacteristically quiet on the drive back to Dave's house. Dave put the radio on the pop station, something Lito would usually at least hum along with, but tonight there was no reaction. Lito had insisted everything was *fine*, though, so Dave kept his own mouth shut and drove in silence. They'd developed a routine over the last several months: Dave parked the car, Lito put out some fresh water for the dogs, Lumpy and Woozy did their little happy dance while Spot bounced in place and whined at Lito, then Dave opened the lid to the dog food bin and all three dogs went to stand in front of their respective bowls while blatantly ignoring everything else. Woozy was a little stiffer than normal for the first few minutes, which meant she'd probably been on the bottom of a snoozing puppy pile and her arthritis was acting up, but otherwise everything else should have felt reassuringly normal. It didn't.

"Hey," Dave prompted. "You want to curl up and watch some Netflix with me? Or we could go out for a walk around the pond—I've got some extra gloves and a toboggan somewhere, and Spot would probably love to come with."

Lito shook his head. "Sorry, I'm just…thinking. Probably going to be an early night for me."

"Does that mean you're headed back to your place?" Dave wrapped an arm around Lito and tugged, drawing him closer until they were within kissing distance. "Can I maybe convince you to stay?" Lito met his lips without any hesitation, so Dave lengthened the little peck into something deeper but still gentle. "I'm told I can be very persuasive when I try," he murmured. "Let me make you feel good and we can fall asleep whenever we're ready."

The soft huff of Lito's laughter wafted warm against Dave's jaw. "Ever the bossy one."

"Among my other talents." Lito truly did look like tired. Drawn-out and exhausted, really. Maybe "bossy" really was the right word—at that moment, all Dave wanted to do was bundle him into bed despite whatever objections he might have and do whatever it took to get him smiling again. Granted, some methods *were* more fun than others… "Come on," he said, and swept Lito off his feet and into a bridal carry.

That earned him a surprised giggle. If it hadn't put Lito at risk of being dropped, Dave would have stopped right then and there for a kiss. "You going to carry me over the threshold of the bedroom like some fairy tale virgin?" Lito teased. "Because you might be in for a surprise once you get me naked and discover what I've got instead of a vajayjay. I'm a bit past the deflowering stage too."

"Mmmm. Guess I'll have to inspect you more thoroughly once we get there." Dave shouldered the bedroom door closed behind them—better to keep three curious dogs from wandering in and spoiling the mood—and lay Lito down sideways on the bed. "Lie back and let me do this tonight, okay?"

"If you want." Lito tucked his hands behind his head and closed his eyes, holding himself perfectly still. *Gorgeous.* Trusting and compliant and Dave wanted to keep him like that forever.

God, he really did want *forever.* The thought wasn't as startling as it should have been. It wasn't until Lito murmured something and shifted a bit that Dave realized he was just standing there and staring. He quickly toed off his own shoes and socks, then unlaced Lito's sneakers and eased them off his feet. *Little* feet, compared to his own. Actual massage was a lot more difficult than it looked, he knew from past attempts, but he managed a decent foot rub as he peeled off Lito's socks.

Lito wiggled his toes in thanks. "That feels nice," he said quietly.

It was tempting to retort with some sort of terrible innuendo, the kind they'd bickered with and laughed about so often already, but this didn't feel like the time for it. Dave climbed up Lito's body instead and nosed the hem of his shirt up to bare his lean abs for closer attention. They were flat and smooth, with only a sprinkling of dark hair until it condensed down to a tempting treasure trail. Dave tugged the shirt higher, getting it out of the way, then took his time kissing and nuzzling every square inch of skin he could reach.

Lito slid his fingers through Dave's hair—the fact that he could do that at all reminded Dave he was probably due for a trim—and let out a little contented hum.

When there was no more skin to taste, Dave tugged Lito up to a sitting position long enough to get him out of his t-shirt and then shucked his own shirt as quickly as possible. Jeans could stay on for now. Slow and sappy was nice, but Lito's nipples were *begging* to be teased. Not too rough—just enough to make him do that little hip-shimmy again. Dave crawled onto the bed and hovered over him just high enough to not touch.

"Tell me what you want."

Lito shrugged, still flat on his back. "Not picky."

The apathy sounded...off, somehow. Dave sat up so he could see Lito's face at a better angle. "Would you rather we just curl up in bed together and skip the sex tonight?"

"It's fine. Either way would be fine."

Yeah, that was *so* not encouraging. Dave was all for partners trading off who was controlling the scene and who was lying back to just enjoy it, but sex was not supposed to be merely *fine*. "We don't have to do this," he said, shuffling even farther away so there was no chance of them touching unless Lito instigated it. "You're not sounding all that enthused right now."

Lito frowned at him. "I'm not saying no..."

"You're sure as hell not saying 'yes,' either." Dave stood and retrieved their shirts from where they had ended up on the floor. "Here—this is starting to feel like we ought to be dressed."

Lito pulled on his own shirt too, and sat up to lean against the headboard. It put them at opposite ends of the bed.

He didn't seem to be starting the conversation anytime soon, which left Dave blindly guessing. "Are you not feeling well? Need me to get you something?"

"I'm fine."

"You're not fine. This feels very far from fine." Dave pointedly eyed the expanse of mattress between them. "I'm not complaining if you don't want sex tonight, I just want you to tell me what the issue is. I can't fix it if I don't know."

"You don't have to fix it!" Lito snapped. "I'm a big boy; I've gotten this far on my own. I don't need you as my knight in shining armor riding in to *fix* everything. I just..." He stared resolutely at the door and sighed.

"This isn't about sex." That was pretty damn obvious. "You're mad at me, and you're refusing to tell me why."

Lito snorted. "*Brilliant* deduction, Sherlock."

"You going to make me guess?"

"You didn't see it before—you're sure as hell not going to see it now."

"See *what?*" He was being infuriating, and a large part of Dave wanted to stomp out of the room and go sulk on the dock out back until Lito got over the whatever-it-was and came out to coax him back inside. The feeling was childish and it was way too cold out, so he didn't give into it, but the temptation was there. "Something about our date tonight?"

Lito raised one eyebrow at him. Waiting. *Damn it.*

"You didn't like the food? You hated my singing? The décor and ambiance were terrible? *What?*"

"Fine," Lito spat. "I'll spell it out for you. That crowd tonight? That was your world. Not mine. You easily pass for straight—muscular white dude, ex-Army, joking with your friends but never talking about yourself. How the hell can what's-his-name have forgotten you're gay? Because you're hiding it. You *can* hide it. Look at me!" He spread his arms wide. "The only Latino guy around. Half your size. Queer and *proud of it.* You're so far removed from the daily 'what it's like to be gay' experience that you went all white knight on me when your asshat friend said something even a little bit homophobic. Dave, that is my *life.* And you just don't get it."

Oh, fuck that. "That's a load of bullshit," Dave countered. "You don't think I got shit about liking dudes when I was in the Army? Don't Ask Don't Tell was hell for me. Anyone I told could have turned me in and gotten me kicked out—I had to hide that side of me every damn day from everyone but my absolute closest friends."

"But you *could* hide it." Lito crossed his arms and glared. "I got disowned for it, thank you very much. I worked my ass off in a stupid front-desk job for ages where I had to deal with hotel guests smiling uncomfortably at me and then saying vile, homophobic shit behind my back. Sometimes to my face too. I had to stand there and pretend it didn't bother me, because that was my fucking *job.* You don't deal with a tenth of the shit I do, because everyone assumes you're straight. I don't have that luxury."

"Everyone I care about knows!"

"Yeah, but that's it, isn't it?" Lito groaned. "You think you're out of the closet, but it's only to the people you know won't spit in your face for it. Something I have literally had happen to me, by the way. Your buddy at karaoke said one vaguely homophobic thing—*one*—and you went off at him on this big indignant speech. If I did that every time someone said something to me, I'd spend every day being hoarse by noon. I'm never going to fit in here, Dave. Ever."

"Maybe you should leave, then, if we're all so backwards."

"I'm tempted." Lito smiled grimly. "Ronald and Betty offered me a promotion at Christmas, actually. Move to Miami and help them get a new chain of motels started. I'd get paid more, there'd be an actual scene, and I wouldn't stick out like a sore thumb for daring to be Latino. There's no volunteer search and rescue team down there, but I think I can live without it."

Fuck. Dave knew Lito was speaking out of frustration, but if that's what he really felt about Black Lake… "Take it, then," he said. "Get away from us rednecks and go be somewhere you fit in. Lord knows Black Lake isn't going to change anytime soon."

"It's really not, is it?"

For a moment he looked a bit sad, like he hoped Dave would convince him to stay. That would have been cruel, though. Dave may have been a selfish bastard, but trying to keep someone like Lito in a tiny nothing town in the middle of nowhere wouldn't be good for either of them. Some part of him—the part that wasn't defensive and angry and snapping—still wanted Lito to be happy at the expense of everything else. *That's not going to happen here.*

Lito nodded at Dave's continued silence. Like that was exactly what he'd expected. "Right, then," he said quietly. "Thanks for introducing me and Spot to all the search team stuff—it was fun while it lasted. If I don't see you again before I leave, say bye to the team for me and have a nice life."

Chapter 17

Betty was overjoyed to hear that Lito was willing to make the move. "We're still not sure how soon we'll get all the paperwork done," she told him when he called to officially accept the new job, "but it's looking like it'll be somewhere between six and eight weeks if all goes well. Will that give you enough time to finish up the things you already have on your plate?"

"Yeah, probably." Everything immediate, anyway. The whole long-term "network and source from Alabama artists" thing wasn't something he could do from Miami, so presumably that responsibility would be passed on to his hypothetical future assistant. "I've got the sketches for the Birmingham renovation done and passed onto the contractor, which was my current big project. Shouldn't be hard to fast-track the other purchase requests I already have, either. I assume the 'find local art' initiative will pass on to whoever else replaces me here?"

Networking was going to be a longer-term goal anyway.

She laughed softly. "There *is* no one else like you, Lito, but I'm glad to hear it. We'll be in touch as soon as we know."

The weeks passed. Lito waited to hear back. He found it was surprisingly easy to pack back up; he'd never owned that much *stuff* anyway. Other than acquiring some cheap furniture right after the move from Atlanta with the vague intent to replace it with something better later, he really hadn't settled into his rental house as much as he'd thought he would. Probably it had something to do with how he and Dave almost always ended up at Dave's place…

No. He wasn't going to let himself go down that road again. The last few weeks had sucked enough even without actively thinking about Dave. Spot was as eager as always for their now-twice-daily run, but sometimes she had a confused look in her eyes that made him think she missed Lumpy and Woozy and the rest of the dogs on the team. She was probably wondering what was taking him so long to get her back to practice. Lito sank down on the couch and gave her a thorough petting in apology.

Just as well he and Spot hadn't put down roots, really. Not counting time spent with the NALSAR team and various members of the north Alabama oil painters' association, he hadn't exactly delved into the Black Lake social scene. The company he'd rented the house through had been willing to retroactively adjust their agreement to be a six-month lease and then monthly after that—as long as he gave thirty days' notice he was in the clear. Nothing he did at work directly impacted his coworkers' jobs, even, so moving out of the Black Lake office probably wouldn't involve anything more complicated than physically packing up his stuff. Vanessa might put together one of her team lunches as a goodbye, maybe. She didn't usually need much of a reason.

Deciding what to say to Gabriela took a lot more work. What could he tell the cousin who had saved him from being on the streets, but whom he hadn't bothered contacting for years? She'd mentioned her boyfriend's name was Lucas in her Christmas card. Lito had a vague memory of a rumpled-looking guy with glasses and a bit of a gut coming with Gabriela to a family get-together or two, once upon a time—that was probably him. Hopefully he'd grown up some.

Lito finally settled on sending an actual letter back: Sorry, been gone from the area for a long time, it'd be great to see you and Lucas again, the offer of the guest room is really generous, thanks. Probably going to be apartment-hunting in Miami again soon and it might take a while. Oh, and Spot would be coming along, is that a problem? The day after he sent it, he second-guessed himself and went hunting for her on Facebook anyway. She looked gorgeous in her picture, a soft smile on her face and the wind whipping her long hair around as she posed on an overlook somewhere. Lucas didn't look at all familiar—if it was the same guy as Lito remembered, he must have gotten contacts and lost a lot of hair—but the parts of Gabriela's page he could see were refreshingly free of any extreme political opinions or glurgy religious memes. His own were pretty blatantly rainbow-themed, but then she already knew that about him. He sent the friend request. She accepted it almost immediately.

Got your letter! she messaged him a few days later.
Yes, we'd love to have you stay with us! Spot too.

*Our condo isn't dog-proofed, since we've never had
a dog or kids, but I'm not worried about it. You and
Spot are both welcome to stay as long as you like—
just let me know when you're planning to come!*

Perfect. That was going to be perfect.

* * * *

"You're late, dude." Scooter beckoned Dave over to the picnic table
with a jerk of his head. "I swear, you haven't been yourself lately. Have
you been sick?"

Not sick, just…drained. "I'm fine," Dave said. Rick gave him an 'I don't
believe you but I'm not gonna call you on it now' look, but he continued
on through the team meeting agenda as if Dave's belated arrival was a
totally normal thing instead of something that had almost never happened
prior to Lito leaving. Lumpy and Woozy sniffed the rest of their pack like
they'd been gone for months instead of just a week.

"Okay, anyone have any specific practice requests tonight?" Rick asked
everyone. Dave had been late enough to miss the entire business meeting,
apparently. *Crap.*

No one did, so Rick sent the rest of the team out all at once to run each
dog on multi-body finds. He kept Dave back on the pretext of going over
some NALSAR tax paperwork. Dave kept his butt on the bench until
everyone else had sorted out who was hiding and who was finding and
who was observing, but sitting still was more difficult than it should have
been. He was up and lavishing attention on Woozy before the rest of the
team had even cleared the tree line.

Rick let him pretend for a few minutes, just idly watching him while
he put off the inevitable. He snapped his fingers, then, and Woozy ran to
sit by his side. *The traitor.*

"You're not sick," Rick declared. "I've seen you power through much
worse than this without even acknowledging something was wrong. Your
dogs appear to be in their usual good spirits too. You totally blew off
practice last week, though, and now you're half an hour late. Anything
you want to talk about?"

God, he *so* didn't want to talk. About anything, but especially not about
Lito. "It's been busy at work, I guess. Spring coming means more to do." It
wasn't a complete lie—he really had been spending more time in his tiny

office. And doing more solo projects, so he didn't have to deal with anyone asking him what was up. And...*dammit, I guess I really have been hiding.*

Rick wasn't buying it either. "This wouldn't happen to have anything to do with Lito not coming to the last few practices, would it?" He arched an eyebrow at Dave, a look which was somewhat spoiled by Woozy trying to crawl into his lap to get more attention. She backed off at Dave's sharp cough.

"I haven't talked to him in a while, so I wouldn't know." Christ, that sounded sullen even to his own ears.

Rick didn't *literally* roll his eyes, but the implication was there. "Correct me if I'm wrong," he said, "but aren't the two of you dating? You never made a formal announcement to the team—not that you should have to—but I damn well know I didn't imagine all those fuck-me looks you two have been giving each other. Spot has calmed down around you too, like she's seeing a lot of you outside practice. Or maybe you're seeing a lot of her. Although maybe if you and Lito aren't talking..."

Fuck. "It's not like that." Rick had been his best friend for more than decade, which meant he knew exactly the right buttons to push to get Dave to spill his guts whether he wanted to or not. Might as well surrender to the inevitable. "We were seeing each other, I think, but he ended it."

"You think." Rick snorted. "Seems like the kind of thing you'd notice."

"You know what I mean."

"Do I? I would have thought you meant that you and Lito were besotted with each other, totally head-over-heels, and you didn't care who knew it. That maybe you two carpooling to and from practice together more often than not meant you were spending a lot of time in each other's company. I recognize that look you get when you think he's not watching you—I still get like that over Sharon sometimes. Like you can't believe you're so lucky and you're terrified you're going to fuck everything up."

Too late. Dave shook his head. "We never talked about 'where is our relationship going' or any of that crap—I just *like* him. Like being around him. And I thought he felt the same about me, but I guess not. I'm too protective and too country redneck for him."

"Since when?"

"Since he got a promotion and is moving back to Miami, where he grew up."

There were several seconds of silence from Rick. Scratch and Sniff both came over to see what was wrong with their human, but Woozy was loath to relinquish her spot. "Is he already gone?" Rick finally asked.

Dave honestly wasn't sure. "It sounded like it was going to be soon, but I don't know if he's started the new job yet," he admitted. "Miami is better for him anyway, though."

"How so?"

Because he can meet someone more like himself. "Did you know he'd never actually been in the woods before joining the team?"

Rick *hmm*ed. "I didn't, but I'm not surprised."

"He gave this a fair go, but I can't begrudge him the chance to start over somewhere else. Somewhere life is more the pace he's used to from Atlanta. Where there isn't quite such a high concentration of homophobes."

"Oh, that's not true." Rick grimaced. "You can begrudge the hell out of him for it. Being silently not okay for long periods of time is one of your more developed skills. That being said..." He tossed the clipboard with the budget printout on it to Dave, who only caught it out of reflex. "Let's get these team expenses sorted and then you can come over for a beer later tonight. Sharon's got beef stew in the crock pot and she always makes enough to feed ten people anyway."

Dave would have rather gone home and moped some more, but Rick was right—he did need to get out of the house and get over himself. "As long as we don't have to talk feelings all night," he said, "I'm in."

Chapter 18

Rick didn't mention Lito at all that night. Or for the whole next month. He must have said something to the other team members too—usually they'd all be gabbing about news like Lito getting a promotion and moving away, but there was a pointed absence of idle chatter whenever Dave was in earshot. They worked harder when they weren't distracted with gossip, though, so it was probably for the best anyway.

The one bright spot in Dave's April was that his old Army buddy Gus came to visit. They'd met during his first tour and kept in touch after that, even after Dave and Rick came back to the States and dropped off the Army's radar. Gus was two years older than Dave, an equal-opportunity, varsity-level flirt, and the best damn airplane mechanic Dave had ever met. Also the cockiest.

"I can't believe how long it's been since I last drove all the way down here," Gus said, emerging from Dave's junk-room-turned-guest-bedroom. He was dressed but barefoot and his hair was still damp from the shower. "You sure you want to take the day off just to shoot the shit with me? I'm getting old, dude. Not as many wacky adventures to talk about anymore."

"You and me both." Even if they ended up saying nothing to each other all day—which had happened more than once—it would be nice to just sit by the pond and watch Lumpy and Woozy snuffle around the yard together. Fish a bit, maybe. "I've been putting in a lot of overtime in the last couple of weeks. It's fine."

They shared a leisurely breakfast—Gus had gotten in too late the previous night for them to eat a proper dinner—and did do some idle catching up. Dave was just deciding whether to bother with the handful of dishes or leave them for later when he got the call from the Black Lake police department. Gus silently took over rinsing their plates while Dave answered the phone. Fifty-seven-year-old man with early onset dementia, lived alone, son says he went missing sometime since the previous evening. Could be hypothermic and in need of his medications if he wandered off during the night, or could be totally fine and merely lost if he disappeared more recently. Even more fun: his house was on a cul-de-sac that backed up against Black Lake's biggest cemetery. That was a lot of acreage to cover. *Shit.*

"NALSAR thing?" Gus asked after Dave had hung up.

"Call-out." The police had already done a drive-by around the other neighborhoods in the area, but the cemetery dated back to the 1800s and had a lot more trees than it had paved roads. "Looks like I would have been calling out from work today after all."

Gus turned off the water and leaned up against the counter. "You know, for all you and Rick have talked about what y'all are doing, I've never gotten to see you in action. Is this something I could tag along for?"

"Yeah, I don't see why not." It was going to be a decent search to watch, honestly—the weather was partly sunny, comfortably warm as long as you had a jacket along, and incident command would probably be Rick, Dave, and *maybe* a handful of police officers. All of whom he'd worked with before, so no departmental posturing issues there. "Search gear is in the front hall closet if you want to go. I'm gonna go get changed into sturdier boots and my team shirt; you go ahead and dig through the loose stuff in the gray bin and see what you can find. Pretty sure I have duplicates of all the important things, especially for a daytime search in easy terrain like this one."

"Oh come on," Gus teased. "This was your chance to talk up how big and dangerous search and rescue is. You tell me it's easy, I'm gonna think you've gone soft after all."

"I have gone soft. Can't scale a cliff with an eighty-pound pack the way I used to." Dave flipped him a casual finger and headed for his bedroom. "The only hard part of this call-out is going to be searching in a cemetery, honestly."

"Seriously?"

"You'll see."

Cemetery searches meant the cross-trained dogs were going to have a bitch of a time focusing on live scent. Especially in cases like this, when the police didn't know for sure the search target hadn't passed away from exposure over the course of the night—it had been pretty damn cold when Gus had pulled into the driveway a bit before midnight. Dave mentally sorted through his available team members. Scooter and Cheerio hadn't gotten all that far into cadaver training yet, so Cheerio would probably be okay, but Nikita and Zeus were going to have problems. Lumpy would have been perfect—her live and deceased signals were unusually specific—but her nose really was too old to be reliable in a situation like this. Scratch, maybe…

Lito. Dammit. The team couldn't show up with one and a half dogs. Everything in him rebelled against making the call, but Dave forced himself to dial Lito's number. It rang long enough he assumed he was going to have to leave a voicemail, but Lito finally picked up.

"Something wrong?" he asked by way of a greeting.

God, hearing his voice was harder than Dave had expected, even with that healthy dose of annoyance in it he'd been expecting. *I miss you* was out of the question, though. "Hey."

"Hi." There was a shuffling of something on Lito's end of the line. "You're usually at work this time of the morning—why the call? I'm headed out on Friday, so I'm kind of busy getting everything packed…"

"Sorry to interrupt, then." *Fuck. Friday.* That was only three days away. It meant Lito was still in Black Lake, though. "I know you've quit the team, but the thing is, we've got a call-out. Could really use you and Spot."

Lito didn't laugh in his face and hang up. Dave chose to take that as a good sign. "Why us?" Lito asked. "Spot's not certified and she's probably never going to be."

There weren't any volunteer K9 search-and-rescue units in Miami-Dade County. Lito had said that, but during the middle of the night a few weeks earlier when Dave couldn't sleep, he'd looked it up himself. Not that it was any of his business whether Lito liked it enough to continue or not.

"It's a dementia patient," he explained instead. "Sixty-two years old, living alone. His son reported him missing this morning when he came by to bring breakfast and his father's front door was open. Thought it was a burglary at first, but his dad's hat and cane were gone and apparently our guy won't leave the house without them. We're treating this as a live find search unless we get some reason to do otherwise."

"Okay…and?"

And it's going to be a pain in the ass. Shouldn't say that, though. "His house is just a block away from the Shady Garden cemetery. I guess you'd have no reason to have been there before, but it's almost eighty acres. Did I ever tell you about the first time the team got a call-out like this? None of us had as much experience with this type of search yet, so here Steve and Sharon and Rick and I go, looking for this seven-year-old who ran away from home up in Meridianville. Steve's dog—his last one, before

Nikita—anyway, his dog gave a great alert right at the start. Then she ran to the nearest gravestone and started trying to dig."

"Well shit."

"Exactly. We've worked more on cross-training since then, to help the dogs focus on just live or just cadaver scent, but Lumpy and Woozy are the only ones currently on the team who we can be a hundred percent sure won't go dig up someone's grandma—and they're both too old for this. Cheerio and Spot are the only two dogs who haven't been through cadaver training yet. The team could really, really use you if you can come."

"Does the team agree?" Lito asked. "Or is this going to be awkward for everyone?"

"We'll be fine. I'll be fine." *I just have to be distant and polite and you'll be leaving Black Lake in a few days anyway.* It was going to suck, dealing with everyone watching them for clues for future gossip, but they were both adults. They could do this.

"I guess I'm free," Lito told him. "Where should I meet you?"

* * * *

Lito was second-guessing himself the whole drive over. Spot was mostly just excited to be wearing her search vest and riding in the car again. He'd been expecting a big, busy scene when he got to the cemetery, but incident command was maybe half a dozen people milling around Rick and Sharon's van.

"Thanks for coming," Rick said, rolling himself back a little ways away from where Dave and Sharon and a police officer were talking so he didn't have to shout. "Dave said you're packing for your big move, so hopefully this won't take *too* long. Shady Grove is old enough for the trees in the historic parts to make line of sight difficult but it's all pretty flat and there's no water to worry about. You and Spot doing okay?"

"Yeah, we're fine." Lito glanced back over at his car, where Spot was happily sticking her head out the passenger side window and sniffing the breeze. "Sorry I never officially told you guys I was leaving, but—"

"Don't worry about it." Rick cocked his head to one side, studying him. "I should ask, though: do you want me to pair you with Dave, or would you rather he be on Team Cheerio for this one?"

"I, um." *Damn it.* Rick was being super-casual about the whole thing, which meant he and Dave had probably been talking. Hopefully Dave hadn't painted him as a complete jackass. Or maybe...*hell.* A second possibility occurred—maybe Dave didn't care anywhere near as much as Lito did. Maybe Rick was being casual because Dave had totally shrugged off his maybe-probably relationship with Lito and hadn't felt there was anything to talk about. Maybe Lito was the only one left feeling like shit. "I'm okay with either," he lied.

Rick put Dave with Scooter and Cheerio and one of the police officers. Sharon and the other officer took Scratch in the opposite direction, toward the part of the cemetery which was more landscaping and memorial plaques than actual graves. Lito was left with Rick, Spot, and a tall man in a well-worn t-shirt whom he'd never met before.

"Gus," the man said, offering a handshake. "I'm actually stationed up in Clarksville—Tennessee—but I come down to visit these idiots every once in a while."

"Gus was over with Dave and me in Afghanistan," Rick explained. "Not our unit, but we ended up at the same base for a while. He's a total jackass and has a twelve-year-old's sense of humor, but despite those two lovely qualities I suspect you guys would get along just fine. We're short bodies, obviously, so would y'all be okay on your own together? Cell reception all through here is good, so call me if you find Waldo or if Spot alerts somewhere inaccessible. We can get the EMTs out to you quickly if they're needed but there was a three-car pileup on the highway this morning so they didn't have the manpower to keep an ambulance here waiting."

Christ, no pressure or anything. They must really have been desperate for another dog. "Y'all will cover my area again if we still can't find him, right?" Lito asked. "It's been more than a month since Spot last got to do this and she might not even alert on the right scent anyway." Gus looked confused. "Spot and I are still pretty new to this," he explained. "And moving to Miami next week, so we haven't been around much."

"Ah. This is my first," Gus explained. "I'm not gonna be much help, but at least I can follow you around and tell you embarrassing stories about Rick and Dave."

Rick aimed a swat at him with his clipboard, which Gus dodged easily. "Don't you dare."

"Not within earshot of *you*, of course," Gus retorted. "Your name's Lito, right? Nice to meet you. Let's do this thing."

Spot's search area started about two hundred yards in, covering the newer portion of the cemetery. It was generally flat and only studded with gravestones, monuments, and a few trees. Sharon and Scratch had taken the bulk of the wooded areas, thank God. At least on the flat Lito had a decent chance of finding the search target visually even if Spot didn't give a clear alert.

It was a good day for a walk, though. Rick had ribbed Gus about his sense of humor, but Lito found himself enjoying the company a lot more than he'd expected. Gus was a good storyteller and he did have a huge collection of funny anecdotes to pull from. Even the ones about Dave didn't hit too close to home for comfort. If Gus noticed Lito tensing up the first few times Dave's name was mentioned, he didn't show it.

One thing Rick had failed to warn Lito about was the fact that Gus was a ridiculous flirt. Truth be told, it was a bit flattering. A tiny bit. Score one for Lito's earring and fashion sense setting off the guy's gaydar, presumably—even if he flirted with everyone exactly the same way, it was good for Lito's ego.

"So what's up with Dave, anyway?" Gus asked, capping off a long story about Rick and a care package gone wrong. The question caught Lito by surprise. "He's mentioned you exactly zero times, which is usually a sign he doesn't want me to ride his ass about something. Or someone. Any idea why he's been in such a shitty mood lately?"

Lito couldn't tell whether that was supposed to be a hint that Gus knew about him and Dave or not, but he sure as hell wasn't going to be the one to bring it up. "I haven't talked to him in a few weeks, actually. I wouldn't know."

"Huh." Gus's gaze kept tracking Spot as she ranged ahead of them, but it felt like an examination anyway. "I only bring it up because Dave has been a serious homebody ever since this fall. I assumed it was because he had someone new in his life and didn't want to jinx it. That was a gossipy question to start with, I guess—Dave won't tell me what the hell is going on and Rick just keeps telling me to go ask Dave. Never mind."

Okay, yeah, definitely some hinting there. "Was there ever a time he *wasn't* a homebody?" Lito asked.

Gus laughed, startling Spot into looking back at them instead of scenting like she was supposed to be. "Sorry," he said. "Didn't mean to distract your dog. It's just…there's a place in Nashville where he and I go sometimes. Used to go, I guess—he's blown me off the last couple of times I've asked him to come up. If you weren't about to move, I'd invite you to come join me. Assuming you lean that way too, obviously."

"You mean a gay club?" Dave had mentioned trips to Nashville with "a friend" before, but never in any detail. "Dave claimed he could dance, but I half expected him to mean square dancing or something."

"Oh, that means you do!" Gus winked, one of those I'm-only-teasing-unless-you-want-it-to-be-serious flirty things he seemed to constantly drop in his wake. "He's gay; I'm pan. My wife and I take a weekend off every once in a while to go have some fun—she stays over with her girlfriend and I go down to Nashville with Dave and see who we can find. And yeah, Dave's always been an introvert, but he's never had any trouble picking up some damn fine eye candy. He can be charming and a damn good flirt when he wants to." He flashed Lito a toothy grin. "Not as good as I am, of course, but it works for him."

Oh, hell. Dave in clubbing clothes... Lito nearly tripped over his own feet at that mental image. Even with what little Dave had mentioned about his Nashville trips, Lito had never made the full connection. He would have pegged Dave as more at home in a country-western bar than a club. Especially the kind of club you went to for no-strings-attached sex. Now that the thought was in his mind, though, it was all too easy to imagine Dave in a mesh tank top that showed off how built he was. Maybe with a pair of jeans slung low on his hips and that intense fuck-me he got in his eye sometimes... *Hell.* Lito knew *exactly* how good a flirt Dave could be.

"I did discover that there isn't much of a scene around here," he admitted aloud. "Or, you know, anything at all. Black Lake feels kind of claustrophobic sometimes, like it really is its own little world."

"Oh, I know it. Dave has complained about that before. Although it's all a load of shit, isn't it? He wouldn't want to be anywhere else."

Lito hummed a non-committal little acknowledgment. It must have given away more than he intended, because Gus gave him a long sideways look.

"You know..." He turned his head upward toward the sky and drew in a deep breath. "There are some benefits of living out in the boonies. Fresh air, for one."

"Except during pollen season? That's what everyone keeps telling me."

Gus huffed out a soft laugh. "Except for that. The more important one, though, is you don't have to be 'on' all the time. People meet you, react to your baggage however they're going to react, and then they move on. Clarksville is bigger than Black Lake and a helluva lot bigger than the godforsaken town I grew up in, but sometimes I miss everyone having already formed their opinions of me. Fort Campbell is a busy base—it's hard to make long-term friendships because everyone gets moved around so often. Sometimes I do envy Rick and Dave for having put down roots."

Roots. Just what Lito needed. If he could just figure out where the hell he belonged, he'd probably be a lot happier.

All in all, he and Gus had about an hour to walk and chat before the group text came through:

> *Waldo found by police patrol in front of the*
> *public library. Come on back to IC for debrief.*

"Guess we should get back," Gus said. "It was fun walking with you, though." He waggled his eyebrows and made an exaggerated pouty face. "Look me up if you're ever in Tennessee?"

"You gonna give me your number?" God, he *so* didn't need one more thing to remind him of Dave after he got to his new job and started trying to move on, but Gus was funny and cheerful and Lito could see himself swapping snarky texts with the guy.

> *Call me when you get sick of those Florida*
> *boys,* Gus texted him. *Clarksville, Tennessee,*
> *nearest real airport (and real fun) is Nashville.*
> *I'd make the drive for you. -Gus*

"Aww, that's sweet." Lito texted him a quick *thanks* back. The chances of him calling a near-stranger for a long-distance booty call were slim, but Lord only knew how pathetic his social life in Miami was going to be. Probably just runs with Spot and video games with the guys for a long time.

Christ. I'm already ancient at twenty-five.

Rick filled them in once they had all gathered back at incident command: their wandering dementia patient was found sitting on the steps of the public library and singing to himself. It wasn't even the police patrols who found him—a friend from church recognized him and didn't have the son's number so she called the non-emergency police line instead.

"Small town," Scooter said, nodding sagely. "Funny how that happens, isn't it?"

Lito could feel Dave's gaze on him, but he didn't look up.

Chapter 19

Gabriela acknowledged Lito's entrance with a nod of her head and a little smile, then went back to stirring whatever she had in the saucepan on the stove. It smelled vaguely Italian—spaghetti sauce, maybe. "How was your first day at the new job? Sorry I wasn't up to see you off this morning—my late shift ran even later than normal last night and I didn't get to bed until almost one o'clock. Grab a drink and tell me about it?"

He did, settling at the small kitchen table with a glass of iced tea. "I'm not settled in yet, but it went fine." Spot looked up at him from her pillow in the corner, huffed, and put her head back down. Sitting still was nice. "Betty and Ronald are here for the next two weeks," he added, "but since it's a brand-new office we spent most of the day unboxing computers and putting together furniture."

"How big is it? I thought HR was basically just you."

"It is. There's only four rooms—an actual office, an office-slash-storage-space for Betty and Ronald to use when they're in town, a front reception area, and a fourth that they're probably going to turn into a small conference room. Longer-term, it's probably just going to be HR and a regional manager in there."

"Whom you haven't hired yet, right?"

"Exactly." It would probably be another week—at least—before Betty and Ronald would be ready to start sorting through applications, but they'd put the hiring notice up online that morning and already had a few applications. "Renovating all thirteen motels at the same time would be ridiculously expensive, so Betty's decided they're going to start working on the first two here in Miami right away and the others can continue to run under the Sunshine State Motel name until those are finished. That gives me less than a month to put together a redesign plan for the entire chain. No pressure or anything."

Gabriela laughed. "I've got faith in you, chico."

"I'm not eighteen any more, cocha."

"I noticed that." She turned the burner off, shifted the pan to an already-cool one, and came to join him at the table. "I also noticed that when you mentioned the long-term plan, you said 'HR.' You didn't say 'me.' And even though most of your stuff is sitting in your free hotel room, you and Spot are over here more often than not. Which is fine—I'm not complaining—but it certainly looks like you might be feeling lonely. Are you having second thoughts?"

"Yes. No. Maybe." Lito sighed. "I committed to this, so I can't back out now, but maybe in a few months once the initial hiring is finished... I don't know."

"You miss your friends in Alabama?"

More than he'd ever thought possible. Gus had been right, during that last search—Black Lake was good for putting down roots. Miami, not so much. It was true he saw a lot more diversity, in skin color but also in personal style. So many people—and it all felt forced, somehow. Like all those people had made their conscious choice about "this is what I want everyone to think when they see me" and then had to spend all their time upholding that image.

It had never been like that with the NALSAR team. There hadn't been any sidelong looks, no whispering as soon as he turned away. No awkward questions from anyone fishing for gossip about his exciting gay sex life. Just people, and dogs, and Dave.

"You've grown up so much," Gabriela said softly, "and it throws me off sometimes. I honestly wasn't expecting to hear back from you after Christmas—I was thinking of you when I was sending out cards so I figured I might as well reach out. I've thought about you a lot, actually."

Probably because he'd run off like an idiot and cut off all communication. "I'm sorry, I should have—"

"No, I wasn't trying to guilt you." She put her hand over his. It was the same thing Aunt Ximena used to do, and the sense memory hit Lito in the gut like a sucker punch. "What I'm saying is, you're an adult now, and that keeps catching me by surprise. I think it catches you by surprise sometimes too. You're not the same mouthy teen who ran off to start a new life, and you're not the same twenty-year-old who presumably had a wonderful time with the big-city scene. Am I right?"

More than right—dead on target was more like it. "...Yes."

"So now you're starting a new phase of your adulthood, one you'll probably stay in for a while, and you get to choose what it will be. Live on the move, don't try to plan ahead, and take your adventures as they come? Enjoy being young and good-looking in the Miami and spend your days working and your nights out partying? Start looking for someone you want to settle down with?" She got a soft, warm look in her eyes. "Lucas and I opted for starting something together, close enough to see both our families but far enough away we could carve out our own lives. You have the chance to do that too, if you want, but it's not required. None of it is." She squeezed his hand one more time, then got back up and went to stir the spaghetti sauce.

* * * *

"Lito!" Rick sounded surprised, but his tone made it clear he was trying to pretend Lito calling him was a totally normal thing. They'd never done more than text before, and that was always in the context of NALSAR group announcements. After a lot of putting it off, though, Lito decided this conversation was worth the actual call. "How's Miami?" Rick added.

"Hot, mostly." Suffocating would have been more accurate. From both the humidity and the pace of the city. "Look, I know this is a bit out of the blue, but it's, um. It's looking like I may get the option to come back to Black Lake in a few months instead of having to be here on-site."

"Oh."

"Yeah."

There was the sound of a door closing, then the background noise on Rick's end quieted considerably. "That was surprise," Rick said. "I didn't mean 'oh' like we wouldn't welcome you back on the team. It's been quiet here without you."

"How is everyone doing?"

"How is Dave doing, you mean?"

Fuck. "Yeah," Lito admitted. "Before I left, I didn't mean to... I'll just say things were awkward."

"You want the truth?"

"I...yes? I don't know whether I'm hoping he's happier than ever or that he's missing me."

Rick made a commiserating sound. "The truth is, he hasn't mentioned you once since you left."

Fuck. Lito hadn't realized how much he'd been hoping—

"He also hasn't gone out to have fun in ages," Rick continued. "Not to go visit Gus and not even for a beer with me."

Gus had mentioned it in one of his occasional flirty texts, just in passing: *"Dave's standing me up again this weekend—sure you don't want to come visit the Music City?"* He and Lito exchanged gripes once every couple of days. And, now that Lito thought about it, he hadn't exactly been painting the town red himself. "Oh," Lito said.

"He's taking on extra hours at work to finish projects that don't have to be done for months. He's doubled down on recruiting for the team too— without you there, we're always one sick handler away from not being able to fully cover call-outs. He's drawn up a whole fundraising campaign to find the team a boat and trailer so we can do water searches again. The dogs are doing better than ever because he's pushing everyone harder, but to be honest…something has to give. And soon."

"Fuck."

"I'll let you draw your own conclusions."

The conclusions were obvious. The solution, though… Lito looked down at the paper where he'd sketched out his idea. It could be modified. They had time. "So back to the thing I mentioned earlier—I'm maybe going to be able to come back around mid-May. And I was thinking of something that might be good for the team…"

Chapter 20

Dave hopped out of Gus's pickup and closed the door behind him with a hollow thud. Gus had been strangely excited the whole drive, but now he was grinning like a loon.

"Are you plotting to blindfold me or something?" Dave asked. "You've got me worried now."

"Nope." Gus swept a deep bow and gestured dramatically toward the park. "This is your big surprise—from here on out is up to you."

There were a handful of tents up and probably several hundred people milling around the large greenspace. People and dogs. *Lots* of dogs. Something about that sounded familiar, possibly in a memo from work… The name suddenly popped up in his mind. "Dog Days," he said aloud. "Mike is on clean-up duty after this finishes up tonight."

Gus laughed. "I assumed you'd have been all over this, but Rick said you haven't been paying attention to outreach stuff recently. I guess he was right." He pointed toward one of the tents on the near side of the field. "Recognize those goofballs?"

Rick cheered at him once he and Gus came within hearing range. Sharon, Scooter, Janet, and Steve whooped and clapped as well. "'Bout time you idiots got here," Rick called out. "The fun started an hour ago!"

"You decided to do a booth at a community fair and wanted to surprise me with it?" Not that he wasn't surprised, but it didn't seem like the kind of thing Gus would have been so excited about. Or something the rest of the team would have done without him—usually most of the scheduling was Dave's job. "I should have brought Lumpy and Woozy."

"Not today," Gus said. "And your team didn't just set up a booth at some fair. This whole thing is a fundraiser for NALSAR. Gonna buy you a boat."

Dave's brain ground to a halt.

"Well," Sharon said, "it's split between raising money for the team and for the Second Chance animal shelter. They've got about thirty of their adoptable dogs here today—two found new homes already, or so I've been told. Everyone gets to vote for them winning various prizes—scruffiest, biggest, most interesting mixed breed, stuff like that. It's supposed to raise interest in some of the less cute ones."

"Ah." Dave belatedly realized his mouth was hanging open, so he closed it. "How'd you guys keep this a secret from me? It must have taken ages to plan."

"That's the other half of the surprise." Gus planted a hand on each of Dave's shoulders and turned him ninety degrees. "Walk in that direction until you figure it out."

The suggestion didn't really help much, but the entire team was watching him with anticipatory looks on their faces so Dave started walking. Now that he was taking the time to actually look, the festival layout made more sense—several tents around the perimeter, some with corporate logos on them and some without, probably giving out swag and brochures. A large roped-off area in the center of the field with a little stage on it. Demonstrations of some kind, perhaps? Two food trucks in the opposite parking lot were doing decent business, judging by how many people were walking around with ice cream and popcorn. And the last tent at the end of the line, backed up against the trees and the side of the maintenance building, was—

Damn.

Lito dropped the towels he was holding and trotted toward Dave, stopping right in front of him. He was shirtless. And wet.

"Hey," he said quietly.

Dave couldn't get his throat to work, so he just stood there stupidly.

"Want to come meet my friends?" Lito asked. There was a hesitation in his voice, a nervousness which snapped Dave out of his shock.

"Your…"

Lito reached for Dave's hand but drew back at the last second. *Fuck it*—Dave covered the remaining distance and enveloped Lito's hand in his own. *He's back and he's not mad at me.* Everything else was a bit slower to come into focus. Lito's smile when Dave responded, though, was all Dave really needed. He tugged him toward the final tent in the row. "This is my Atlanta crew. Everyone, this is Dave."

The group of similarly wet, shirtless guys waved.

"Dog-wash station," Lito explained. Needlessly, because after Dave finally managed to tear his eyes away from Lito's naked chest, the hoses and the kiddie pools and the huge pile of ratty towels were kind of a dead giveaway. Oh, and the smell of wet dog.

He was standing and staring again. "Hi," Dave managed.

Lito's posture relaxed a bit, and he started pointing down the line. "The guy on the end is Ian, who let me and Spot crash with him at Christmas. Chris is the blindingly pale one with the red hair who pretty much had to bathe in sunscreen before coming out here. Then the tall-dark-and-handsome guy is Jericho, and the idiot on the end there is Adam."

"Hey," Adam protested. The African-American guy next to him—who really was Dave's height, if not taller—elbowed him with a smirk.

"It's not the whole clan," the first guy said, stepping forward to shake Dave's hand, "but we're the ones who had the weekend free. Lito asked if any of us would come do this surprise thing for you and we all jumped at the chance. I had to meet the guy Lito couldn't stop talking about all week at Christmas."

"Hey," groused Lito. "That's...okay, that *is* accurate. But y'all kept asking about him, so that's not all my fault."

"Not me," Jericho said. His voice held a hint of an accent Dave couldn't place.

Lito acknowledged that too. "Jericho just got back from Haiti, what? Last week Thursday?"

The guy nodded.

"Right. So this is a welcome-home party for him too. Or welcome-to-the-States, at least." He stuck his tongue out at the dude. "Lord knows where your ugly bod is going to end up once you actually get hired somewhere."

Jericho struck a muscle-man pose. He didn't particularly have a lot of muscle—his was more of a tall, skinny, and wiry build—but he started making silly faces while he did it and he drew a few laughs from other people passing by.

Lito seemed to suddenly notice their spectators too, because he waved Jericho back to the soapy kiddie pool he'd been standing next to and directed a lady with a boxer over to him. "You guys okay if I take a minute with Dave?" he asked.

The red-haired one made kissing noises. The guy next to him splashed him with the hose. Jericho waved Dave and Lito away. Lito retrieved his shirt, ran a hand through his damp hair, and fell into step at Dave's side.

"So, um." He steered them toward the tents on the opposite side of the greenspace, which looked like they provided shade for an assortment of folding tables. "I owed you an apology and I figured this might be a way to show you I meant it."

"Half-naked but for a good cause?"

Lito shot him a wary look, but his posture relaxed when he saw Dave was teasing. "I'll admit that wasn't totally accidental, but no. I meant back here, with the team and with you and with everyone else in Black Lake wandering around. I said some things I shouldn't have, and I'm sorry."

"They weren't entirely…" Dave sighed. "You're not the first to call me a redneck, you know. And I *do* avoid bringing up my orientation sometimes. I hadn't really thought about it, but you were right."

"I never said 'redneck,' but I was still being a dick." Lito grabbed his hand and pulled them both to a stop. "You are who you are and you can't change that, just like I can't. It's not your fault that you're all built and masculine and handsome and everyone assumes that means you're straight."

"I did overreact to Chad, though," Dave said. "You said I was acting all protective white knight and I was. That stuff he said caught me by surprise—I really don't hear all that many things I can't just brush off, and those bothered me more than usual because they were about you. I can…I can try to tone it back in the future." *Please let there be a future.*

"Funny you should mention that." Lito rubbed his thumb over Dave's knuckles. "As it so happens, I talked Dayspring's owners into letting me move back here if I want to. Anytime in the next six months. They haven't been able to find anyone capable of taking over the stuff I dealt with while I was here, and now that things are up and running they don't really need me for day-to-day decisions down in Miami, so…yeah. Right now the plan is for my previous supervisor here to take over what I was doing down there. She's scarily efficient and she'd be fantastic at it. Then I could do a mix of telecommuting and local stuff."

Dave nearly forgot to breathe.

"I'm saying I want to give this another try, twit." Lito brought their joined hands up to press a kiss on the backs of Dave's fingers. "If you're willing to give me another chance." He wrinkled his nose. "Well, me and Spot. We're a package deal."

"Yes." God, yes. "As soon as you want, however you want. If you—I'll understand if you want to take this slow, but Lumpy and Woozy really do sleep better when Spot is there, and my house is big enough—"

Lito's eyes lit up. "Really?"

"Really. On one condition."

The wary look immediately came back to Lito's expression. "What?"

"Cover for me with your friends? There's no *way* I'm going to remember everyone's names, and I don't want to put my foot in my mouth."

Lito yanked him down into a kiss. "I could put something else in your mouth instead," he murmured in Dave's ear, "but that will probably have to wait. There are kids around, and I need you here to judge the dog talent contest at two o'clock."

Hell yes. "Tonight?"

"Tonight is a welcome-home shindig at the hotel for Jericho, but I think they'd be okay with me bringing a plus one. And they'll understand when we leave early."

"We."

Lito grinned at him. "I'm diving back into your world—this is your chance to get a taste of mine."

It sounded wonderful.

Chapter 21

"So you were in Haiti for *three years?*" Dave asked, for the second time that evening. He hadn't been lying about being shit with names—Lito remembered that very well from their first meeting—but he seemed to be soaking up everyone's stories and anecdotes just fine. Especially the ones about Lito when he first fell in with their group back in Atlanta.

Jericho nodded and slung back the rest of his rum and Coke. "I was planning to just do one, but I liked it there. It was excellent hands-on experience and I was actually helping."

Dave shook his head. He was pleasantly warm, nestled against Lito's side on the hotel suite sofa, and acting more than a little tipsy. Hell, Lito was feeling a little floaty too and he hadn't drunk more than half a beer. "I'm still stuck on how you could live in one of the most backward, homophobic countries in the world for *three whole years* and not go batshit insane," Dave said. Also for the second time.

Ian shrugged.

"I want to get back to talking about how wonderful Lito is."

Adam laughed. "So that's how it is, is it. I'd say get a room, but—"

"But I already got you *all* rooms," Lito finished for him. "And you're lucky I did, because y'all are too drunk to drive anywhere. Definitely not all the way back to Atlanta."

"Not me," Gus chimed in. He was sprawled on the area rug in front of the pull-out couch, feet tangled with Ian's. "I just came down here to tell Dave that he's being a dumbfuck who needed to get his head out of his ass and grovel until you came back already. The fact that y'all had a whole *thing* planned made it a lot easier."

"Lito's been an idiot too," Chris chimed in. "Speaking of which, *get yourselves a room already!* I'm sick of all the sexual tension in here."

Dave wriggled his ass backward against Lito's hip and looked thoroughly smug.

"I'm not," Gus said, eyes never leaving Ian. Who also seemed to be more than happy to be playing public footsie. "I'm in favor of Dave getting laid, though. Y'all won't believe how grumpy he's been lately."

Jericho snorted. "Lito doesn't get grumpy," he said. "Just melancholy."

"Melancholy?" Adam threw a pillow at him. "What the fuck, dude? You wouldn't even know, you and your saving-the-world shit."

Dave was apparently done with mere snuggling, which Lito found out when Dave twisted himself around in his seat and started kissing every part of Lito he could reach instead. Lito's mind went blank.

"Just go get it over with," Gus said, grinning. "Dave, I'll get the rest of my stuff from your house tomorrow. I'm sure I can find somewhere else to crash tonight."

Ian licked his lips.

"Every single one of you is ridiculous," Lito said, and stood up. It took some tugging to get Dave to follow suit. "*We* are going to go back to Dave's house. We'll have fantastic make-up sex and plan out the rest of our lives together in a soppy and thoroughly nauseating manner. Then we'll have more sex in the morning and talk about how soon Spot and I can move in. *Y'all* can all crash in here or split up to your own rooms, either way. This was a slow weekend and the hotel's only half full, so it's not like they're going to waste otherwise. Gus, I'll warn you—Ian snores. I'll text y'all when I'm good and ready tomorrow and not one minute before. Goodnight!"

Dave buried his face in Lito's hair for several seconds before being willing to move. "Love you," he murmured.

Lito twirled around to give him a quick but thorough kiss. "I love you too," he whispered in Dave's ear. "And the sooner I get us back to your house, the sooner we can both prove it."

Dave grabbed his hand and practically towed him out the door.

Worth Waiting For

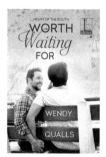

If you enjoyed *Worth Searching For,*
be sure not to miss the first book in Wendy Qualls's Heart of the South series,

A small town in the Deep South isn't where most gay men would choose to go looking for love. But open hearts will find a way . . .

Growing up in the Bible Belt, Paul Dunham learned from a young age to hide his sexuality. Now he's teaching psychology at a conservative college in Georgia—and still hiding who he really is. If Paul hopes to get tenure, he needs to keep his desires on the down-low. But when an old college crush shows up on campus—looking more gorgeous than ever—Paul's long-suppressed urges are just too big for one little closet to hold . . .

Brandon Mercer has come a long way since his freshman year fumblings with Paul. Now he's confident, accomplished, proudly out—and the sexiest IT consultant Paul's ever seen. When Brandon asks Paul to grab some coffee and catch up, it leads to a steamy reunion that puts their first night of passion to shame. But when Paul's longtime crush turns into a full-time romance, he receives an anonymous email threatening to expose their secret to the world. If Paul stays with Brandon, his teaching career is over. Yet if he caves under pressure, he risks losing the one true love he's been waiting for . . .

A Lyrical Shine e-book on sale now.

Chapter 1

The chair of the psychology department was a mean, small man with a bad toupee and a permanent air of smugness pervading his office. His summons always evoked a feeling of impending trouble, but Paul stepped inside and closed the door anyway.

Doctor Kirsner looked up briefly, then went back to his typing. Paul waited in awkward silence for a full minute before his department head finally sat back in his chair and nodded for Paul to take the seat opposite.

"There have been some complaints about you," Dr. Kirsner announced.

"Sorry?"

He slid a stapled sheaf of papers across his desk toward Paul. "Employee code of conduct—you may remember signing it when you were first hired. I gather it's been giving you trouble recently."

Paul took the papers and flipped through, his mind whirring. Saint Benedict's wasn't officially a Christian college any longer, but it did hold its staff to a fairly archaic standard of behavior. Still, he'd done everything expected—*more* than anyone could reasonably expect—to ensure he never put a toe out of line. Tenure was so close he could taste it, and a major violation of the code of conduct would have been the easiest way for this new department head to knock him out of the running.

"I don't know what I could have done wrong," he said aloud.

Dr. Kirsner seemed to expect the denial, and leaned in for the kill. "Kissing," he hissed. "In front of students, no less."

"I'm sure that's not against the rules, and I wouldn't be dumb enough to do it in front of students if it were." *Plus I haven't kissed anyone in ages.*

"Ah. So your girlfriend didn't kiss you goodbye this morning in the parking lot, right outside my window?" Dr. Kirsner gestured to the quad outside. "You arrived at campus together well before classes started. She had an overnight bag. It doesn't take a lot of imagination to figure out what the two of you had been doing without the benefit of marriage." He tapped the code of conduct. "Which *I'm* sure *is* against the rules."

Oh. Paul heaved an internal sigh of relief that it was something he could explain. "She's not my girlfriend, and it wasn't really a kiss."

"Girlfriend, one-night stand, lady of the evening, it doesn't matter. The 'no immoral sexual conduct' clause covers having a partner stay at your place of residence overnight."

For all you know, we could have been having a tea party and playing videogames. Paul took a deep breath and counted to three before releasing it. "What you—and any student up that early—saw was *my sister* giving me two friendly kisses on the cheek as I said goodbye. She's been in France for the last two years and the kiss on both cheeks is a French thing she's picked up—there's nothing sexual about it. And surely whoever's complaining also noticed that she and I have the same color hair, same eyes, nearly the same facial structure, and a similar build. *Not* a girlfriend."

Dr. Kirsner's self-satisfied smirk froze on his face for a long moment, then slowly dissolved into a poor attempt at neutrality. "Sister?"

"*Twin* sister." Paul shrugged and tried not to grin too blatantly at seeing his overbearing department head at a loss for words. "We're not identical, obviously, but when we're together most people pick up on the family resemblance. I don't get to see her much anymore, so she stopped by after her flight got in—it's a long drive to my parents' house from Atlanta and I'm on the way. We took my car last night so I gave her a ride back to campus this morning to pick up her rental from the visitors' lot."

Paul was treated to the delightful sight of Dr. Kirsner trying very hard to fake a relieved smile and failing miserably. It was no secret the man wasn't fond of him. Paul refused to allow his private life to become cannon fodder in the departmental pissing match for dominance the way everyone else did and Dr. Kirsner could never quite wrap his head around why. The truth—Paul was clinging to the lingering security of being firmly in the closet—would have been the *coup de gras* for what would have been a short but promising academic career at St. Ben's. Much better to keep his mouth shut and let everyone think he was shy.

"Was that all, Dr. Kirsner?" Paul returned the department chair's fake smile with a much more genuine one of his own. "Because if so, I should really go prepare for class."

* * * *

The air still had a bit of a bite to it, but the sunshine felt wonderful and it was a beautiful Georgia spring day. Paul was more than ready to escape Dr. Kirsner's office and get outside for a while. The "prepare for class" line had been a bit of an exaggeration—his first lecture on Thursdays wasn't until eleven, which meant he technically didn't have to be on campus yet—but Danielle had been in a hurry to get home so Paul had planned to spend the morning in his office. Not that he'd accumulated all that much paperwork to do, with spring break so recently out of the way and no major assignments currently looming on the horizon, but sometimes it was nice to at least *feel* professional.

The quad was starting to awaken too, some students stumbling blearily into the campus coffee shop and others wandering between early classes. Someone was bravely attempting a game of Frisbee shirtless, despite the temperature. Paul tried not to look, but it was hard not to notice that whoever-it-was had a lot to show off. He settled himself onto the low stone wall outside the psychology building and pulled out his phone, angling the screen to compensate for the bright glare.

"Paul Dunham?"

Paul looked up. A striking dark-haired man in khakis and a smart jacket stood before him. "Hi?"

The man grinned and held out his hand. "Been a while, so you may not remember me, but I sure as hell remember you. Brandon Mercer—we were hallmates freshman year."

Paul shook the offered hand on autopilot. It couldn't be, after all this time. *Brandon Mercer. Holy crap!* "Of course I remember," he said, his voice breaking a bit. "You were pretty memorable."

"So were you." Brandon took a seat on the wall next to him and cocked his head. "You teach here now?"

Paul smiled and shrugged, careful to seem casual. "Psychology. Finally got on the tenure track last year, so hopefully I'll be sticking around for a while. What have you been up to?"

"IT consultant," Brandon said. "Mostly security issues and such."

"I should have guessed from the beard." Paul nodded toward Brandon's neatly groomed chin. "Your look screams 'computers.'"

Brandon laughed; the humor lighting up his eyes. "I'd say you were exaggerating, but you're right—in this field, it's practically a uniform."

It looked good on him. *Very* good. Brandon had been handsome enough ten years ago, when they were both eighteen-year-olds on the tail end of puberty, but the beard sculpted his face a bit and brought out the angle of his jaw. Which in turn matched the very nice angles making up the rest of him. *Handsome* was now a grossly inadequate word.

"What brings you back here, then?" Paul asked, managing to keep his thoughts from coming through in his voice. "I assumed you were off to make your mark on the bigger world."

"I'm based out of Atlanta now, but St. Ben's wanted someone on-site to take a look at something and I thought it would be interesting to see what's changed around here." Brandon raised his head and looked out over the quad, a small smile on his face. He was much less subtle about ogling the shirtless Frisbee player. "Not a lot, I'm guessing."

That was truer than Paul wanted to admit. "I like it better from this side of the desk, at least."

"Oh, I bet." Brandon fixed him with a knowing smirk and one delicately raised eyebrow. "Should I even ask?"

"Um." Paul could feel his face heat from the insinuation behind the otherwise innocent question. *Not really the time or place to talk about my personal life, especially after Dr. Kirsner's attempt to ream me out this morning—*

And Brandon seemed to get it. "Coffee," he announced. "You and me. Not here. Well, if you've got time, that is? I'm parked just around the corner. It'd be nice to catch up."

Paul swallowed and nodded. "That…sounds good. Thanks."

* * * *

The coffee shop was an independent little hole-in-the-wall, one Paul had heard of but never been inside. Its primary benefit seemed to be its distance from campus; the coffee certainly wasn't anything to write home about. Paul and Brandon got a corner table in the nearly empty dining area and sat in silence for a little while. It felt oddly normal. And didn't at all explain the butterflies in Paul's stomach.

"So," Brandon started. "You finished up your degree at St. Ben's, then stuck with psychology?"

"Yeah." It had been the only field that interested him, even back then. "It's a pretty campus and it has a good cognitive program. Once I finished undergrad I went ahead and applied for the graduate program—it's close enough to my hometown to see my parents sometimes, and I didn't really want to go farther away."

Brandon nodded. "And St. Ben's doesn't have a problem with you being gay?"

Paul couldn't suppress his flinch, even though he knew nobody was listening. "I, um…"

Brandon's eyes widened. "You're still in the closet? *Seriously?"*

Like I have a choice. "Coming out isn't really something I can do right now," he admitted.

Brandon took a long sip of his coffee and didn't say anything, but the silence was just as eloquent as words. Finally he put his cup down and sighed. "I don't regret leaving, you know."

"I know."

"I didn't… I mean, I assumed my parents would freak out. When I came home that summer and told them I was gay. But they were fine with it. My mom gave me a hug and my dad and my brothers clapped me on the back and the next morning there were brochures for Emory and Georgia Tech sitting outside my room. Mom even called to get all my transcripts and paperwork from St. Ben's, so I'd have everything ready to transfer whenever I wanted to. And I lucked out. Georgia Tech doesn't usually take transfer students that late, but my dad's got a friend who works in admissions there and somehow they managed to pull some strings." Brandon flashed Paul a crooked smile. "It was the best thing to ever happen to me."

And it left me behind. Paul tried to smile back, but it probably came out more as a grimace. One year, then *nothing.* One year of longing looks and the uncomfortable awareness that this attraction wouldn't go away. One fabulous night when fate happened to put them both in the right place at the right time to admit to each other it was mutual. Paul had been forced to confront the fact that yes, he really *was* gay. And then finals were over and they both went home, and Brandon had never come back.

"How did you…" Brandon seemed to be picking his words carefully. "How was it for you? Staying?"

"It wasn't anything, really." *Confusing and frustrating, but that was nothing new.* "I just went back to not doing that. Nobody thought anything of it. Plenty of students here don't really date."

"So did you ever…" He trailed off and waved vaguely.

Paul stared down at the polished wood of the table with more focus than was probably warranted. There was a slight wave to the grain under the varnish. "Once," he admitted quietly. "Sort of. When I was in grad school there was a guy, and we kind of clicked. We got an apartment together eventually, to save on rent. It went from there."

"You said 'sort of,'" Brandon pointed out. Paul didn't look up, but he could *hear* his amusement. "How's that work?"

God, this is awkward. How can I possibly describe Christopher? "He was—is—kind of a lot to take in," Paul finally explained. "Friendly guy, but abrasive too. We never made it official or anything, but I never said no either. He made it clear he was interested in me after we had been living together for a while. We tried that for a bit, but I just couldn't. At least, not with him. It ended badly."

"You dumped him?"

"I guess so." Paul let out a long breath. "I didn't want to…to do everything he wanted to. We got in an argument and he wouldn't let it go. I finally moved out about a year and a half ago, when I realized nothing was going to change. Got my own place. He stayed at St. Ben's until this past September—not my department, but I still had to see him sometimes and it was always awkward. Honestly I was kind of relieved when he quit; the new IT lady is much easier to work with."

"And all this time, you stayed in the closet."

I did, and it sucks. "Pretty much." The words came out more evenly than he expected. "I had to, though—I can't leave St. Ben's. I have another year or two until my tenure review. And even though they don't require a statement of faith from their faculty anymore, having an openly gay professor isn't something the administration could easily overlook."

"I see." Brandon leaned back in his chair and studied Paul for a long moment, his face inscrutable. "So you're not claiming you're straight now? Dating women?"

Not really. He wasn't in denial, didn't argue with the label, just—being gay was inconvenient. Paul made a vaguely negative noise.

"You're missing out, you know."

He winced. Yes, he knew. The whole darn world seemed to be conspiring to tell him exactly how much he was missing out on. That kind of life wasn't compatible with working at St. Ben's, though. Speaking of which… Paul checked his watch and stood. "Look, I hate to cut this short—"

"Don't suppose you'd want to do dinner sometime?"

Paul snapped out of his self-pity party and only barely prevented himself from gaping at Brandon. "Like, dinner-dinner? Or date-dinner?"

"Either." Brandon smirked. "Don't you feel like we got separated too soon, back then? I agonized for ages over whether to call you once we went home for the summer, and even now I'm not sure why I didn't." He leaned forward in his chair, his long fingers practically caressing his little paper cup of coffee, as if he was about to impart a secret. "I truly would love to hear what you've been up to and all," he confessed, "but I'd also love to… well. I've got some time—I have no idea how long it will take me to tease out these glitches in St. Ben's servers, but it will probably be at least a week or two. I assumed I'd spend it skulking around my hotel room and feeling stupid sitting all by myself in restaurants, but spending some of that time with you would be infinitely more appealing." His tone—and the glint in his eyes—made it clear *exactly* what he was offering. "Dinner-dinner would be perfectly fine, of course, but I'd love it to be more than that."

He leaned in farther, close enough Paul could smell the coffee and a hint of toothpaste on his breath, and ran one gentle forefinger over the vein in the back of Paul's hand as Paul clenched his cup. "I get that you'd rather keep your private life private, but I'm not exactly a coworker," he murmured. "And after you were so absolutely breathtaking freshman year, I couldn't stop thinking about it for ages. Kept wishing we'd had the chance to do more. And if you've decided to never do anything like that again—in that case, I'd say it was a real shame. Because I've picked up a few tricks over the years too, and I'm a pretty damn good teacher."

Oh God. Paul berated himself for each and every time he lay awake at night, fingers tracing over the outline of his cock, remembering back to how Brandon's confident hands had felt on him. They say you never forget your first time. Well, whoever "they" were, they *seriously* understated the situation. "You will obsessively replay the encounter over and over" would have been more accurate. And it would be so easy to lapse back into that memory, to give in and take Brandon up on his offer and try to recreate that one golden middle-of-the-night experience, but then where would he be? Alone again afterward, furious with himself and twice as miserable as before. A heroin junkie relapsing after staying clean for the last year and a half. *(Almost a year and three-quarters,* a voice inside his head pointed out.) Even if the physical sensations left him darn near rapturous, it wouldn't be enough to counterbalance the negatives.

He must have been quiet too long, because Brandon sat back again and made a big show of finishing his coffee. "Sorry," Brandon finally said. "I guess I forget what it was like, before. I didn't mean to make you uncomfortable."

"It's fine." Paul forced a smile. "And I'm flattered, really, I just… It's a no. I'm sorry."

Brandon nodded, a hint of disappointment on his face. "I understand. Come on; we should both probably get back to campus."

Meet the Author

Wendy Qualls was a small town librarian until she finished reading everything her library had to offer. At that point she put her expensive and totally unrelated college degree to use by writing smutty romance novels and wasting time on the internet. She lives in Northern Alabama with her husband, two daughters, two dogs, and a seasonally fluctuating swarm of unwanted ladybugs. She's a member of both the Romance Writers of America and way too many online writers' forums. Wendy can be found at www.wendyqualls.com and on Twitter as @wendyqualls.

CPSIA information can be obtained
at www.ICGtesting.com
Printed in the USA
LVHW030309310821
696470LV00004B/746